"Breathless tension coats Raphael and Susan's interactions with a right-on-the-edge-of-passion thrill....I am eerily hooked....It's a thought-provoking read that, like Mary Shelley's *Frankenstein*, may cause readers to question their definition of a monster."

—*USA Today*

"By the end of the book, I realized that I had entered a series that was far more epic in scope than I'd anticipated, with the unfolding of the beginning of a classic good versus evil battle unto the end. I came to the end wondering how I'm going to be able to wait for the second installment! The writing is action-packed, the characters are intriguing, and the plot is exciting and superbly crafted."

—ChristianFictionAddiction.blogspot.com

"*Kiss of Night* is good supernatural Christian fiction, a genre that's relatively new to me but one that I absolutely love. Along with the idea that no one is beyond redemption, the story effortlessly weaves in themes of sacrifice, love and prayer that flows well and is never preachy....I will definitely be reading upcoming books in this series."

—*Truly Bookish*

"*Kiss of Night* ends with the reader hanging on a precipice and desperately grasping for the sequel. I can't wait to sink my teeth into the next one...."

—*The Overweight Bookshelf*

KISS OF
Revenge

THE KISS TRILOGY BY DEBBIE VIGUIÉ

Kiss of Night

Kiss of Death

Kiss of Revenge

Kiss of Life (ebook short story)

Available from FaithWords wherever books are sold.

KISS OF
Revenge

A Novel

DEBBIE VIGUIÉ

NEW YORK • BOSTON • NASHVILLE

The author is represented by Alive, Communications, Inc., 7680 Goddard Street, Suite 200, Colorado Springs, Colorado 80920, www.alivecommunications.com.

FaithWords
Hachette Book Group
237 Park Avenue
New York, NY 10017

www.faithwords.com

Printed in the United States of America

OPM

First Edition: October 2013

10 9 8 7 6 5 4 3 2 1

FaithWords is a division of Hachette Book Group, Inc.
The FaithWords name and logo are trademarks of Hachette Book Group, Inc.

The Hachette Speakers Bureau provides a wide range of authors for speaking events. To find out more, go to www.hachettespeakersbureau.com or call (866) 376-6591.

The publisher is not responsible for websites (or their content) that are not owned by the publisher.

ATTENTION CORPORATIONS AND ORGANIZATIONS:

Most Hachette Book Group books are available at quantity discounts with bulk purchase for educational, business, or sales promotional use. For information, please call or write:

**Special Markets Department, Hachette Book Group
237 Park Avenue, New York, NY 10017
Telephone: 1-800-222-6747 Fax: 1-800-477-5925**

ACKNOWLEDGMENTS

I need to thank first and foremost my amazing editor, Christina Boys, whose humor, passion, and dedication have made this whole project a joy to work on. I couldn't ask for a better editor. Thank you to Kevin Roddy at UC Davis, who makes medieval studies the most exciting classes on campus. Thank you to all the fans of the series who have gone on this journey with me. To my husband, Scott, thank you for all your support and encouragement. Thank you to my parents, Rick and Barbara Reynolds, who have read every version of this story over the last twenty years. Thank you to Chrissy Current for always believing in this story and reminding me of that frequently!

To Beth Jusino, who fought on my behalf to make this series happen.

Kiss of
Revenge

PROLOGUE

Gabriel, Count of Avignon, stood in the shadows of the mosque, watching carefully the carnage that was unfolding before him. The young knight had entered the mosque a few minutes before and had been battling his way toward the front ever since.

Gabriel had been shadowing the knight, Jean, for days as he tracked down the rumors of a holy treasure. It served his purpose to let the knight be the one to find it and dispose of him later.

Gabriel reached out with his mind, touched the mind of the knight. Jean truly believed himself on a holy quest; the fire of his faith burned bright in his heart and soul in a way that it did for few others.

As he slaughtered a foe in front of him, another was sneaking up behind him, ready to behead him. Gabriel couldn't allow that to happen just yet.

Turn! Gabriel commanded silently, implanting the thought so intently in Jean's mind that he knew the crusader would probably swear he'd heard someone speak out loud. Perhaps later he would attribute the word that saved his life to God. If he lived to think on it at all.

Jean moved just in time to plunge his sword through the abdomen of his would-be killer. As the last man died, Jean dropped the body to the floor. He then turned back, approached the altar, and fell to his knees in reverence.

Beneath Jean's knees rivulets of blood coursed and pooled over the stones. Behind him lay the bodies of half a dozen who had stood between him and what he had long sought. Tears streaked down his face and he wiped at them with a bloody hand. He laid down his sword and grasped a silver cross that hung around his neck.

Gabriel studied the cross. It looked like one that would belong to a woman; a token from the woman he loved, no doubt.

Upon the altar there was a small box made of wood, ornately carved and decorated with a few small, glittering jewels. It was beautiful, the creation of some skilled craftsman for a wealthy patron. It was enough to turn any man's head, but Gabriel knew that Jean didn't care about the box, only about what he prayed was inside it.

Gabriel could feel the hunger growing in him as the smell of blood filled the air. He would feed soon, but for now he watched the knight curiously. Centuries of practice had allowed him to control his instincts and urges in a way no mortal man could ever dream of. Jean had killed the men whose bodies littered the mosque's cold stone floor without hesitation. He was not the most skilled warrior, but he had an intensity of purpose, a driving focus, that sustained him in battle. Yet the same hands that had taken life with such determination trembled when he lifted the box from the altar. The box covered the palm of Jean's left hand and as he opened the lid with his right he closed his eyes.

Gabriel risked moving closer then. He wanted to see if the rumors that had led them both there were true. What he saw inside the box surprised even him. He could feel Jean's fear, his hesitation. He knew the young knight was desperately hoping he was right and that his long journey had been worth it.

Open your eyes, Gabriel urged, and watched as Jean did. The surprise on his face mirrored what Gabriel felt. Was still feeling. After a few moments Jean recovered sufficiently to shut the lid and rise to his feet. He tucked the box inside his tunic and picked up his sword. Gabriel moved forward, and Jean spun around, eyes probing the shadows. Gabriel stepped farther into them and even though Jean stared right at him he did not see him.

"I am for God, and I will protect with my life that which He has led me here to find," the knight said, challenging the darkness with a statement that was half threat, half prayer. Gabriel allowed it to go unanswered and watched as Jean left the mosque. Gabriel stepped carefully around the bodies, not wishing to leave any evidence of his presence by so much as a boot print. He moved to the altar where the box had stood and touched it hesitantly.

He closed his eyes and could swear he could feel some sort of warmth emanating from the place where it had been. Whatever doubts he had harbored vanished in a moment.

"So many have searched for so long and it was found by a simple knight," Gabriel mused out loud. It was God's sense of humor, that was what Paul would say. What even

Paul could not have anticipated, though, was that there were two relics instead of one.

He turned and glided through the entrance of the church. Night cloaked him as he followed Jean, who left the city far behind before making camp for the night. When the young man finally fell asleep Gabriel considered taking the relics from him. It would have been a simple thing to retrieve the box without waking him, simpler still to retrieve after killing him. Instead he decided to wait. Paul would have said it was mercy that motivated him. There was something else, though. Something about the knight gave him pause. At any rate he knew where the relics were. He could afford to wait.

CHAPTER ONE

*For the preaching of the cross is to them
that perish foolishness; but unto us which are
saved it is the power of God.*

—I Corinthians 1:18

The cross. It's all about the cross, David Trent thought as he sat numbly at the kitchen table in a house on the outskirts of Prague. He watched the two vampires in the living room pace back and forth like caged animals. There had to be somewhere they hadn't searched yet, but none of them had thought of where. Susan Lambert sat silently on the couch, her arms wrapped around herself. If it hadn't been for the tears still streaking down her face she might have looked like she was asleep.

David was not crying. He was sitting, staring into space, reliving the whole thing over and over. There was nothing he could have done to stop it, he realized. He couldn't have reached Wendy's side any faster when the vampire had grabbed her outside the cathedral hours before.

I should have protected her. Her and the cross necklace she was wearing. There had to be a reason that the other vampires wanted it so badly. Was it just because it seemed to be even more effective against vampires than average crosses? All David knew about the cross was that it had belonged to an ancestor of Wendy and Susan's named Jean who had fought during the Second Crusade. Their grandmother, who had died recently and insisted her funeral be here in Prague, had left it to Susan. She had also left a letter hinting that the cross contained a great secret but gave no clue as to what the secret was. If Susan had been wearing the cross instead of Wendy, would the vampire have taken her instead?

David wondered if this was what going insane felt like. Just days ago he'd arrived in Prague for work. If he hadn't met Wendy and Susan he'd be sitting at a desk, tapping on a keyboard right now. He'd be blissfully unaware that vampires even existed, let alone that they were at war and one of them, Richelieu, was building a formidable army of them. But he didn't regret meeting Wendy. His only regret was that he couldn't do anything now to help her.

They knew the vampire with long blond hair who had taken Wendy worked for Pierre, her grandmother's lawyer. Susan had had several dealings with him regarding aspects of their grandmother's estate, but they'd had no idea until a few hours ago that he was a vampire. Not only that, it seemed his connection to their family went all the way back to when he was human. Eight hundred years ago, Pierre had been a magistrate in the Inquisition in France and had condemned his young wife, Carissa, to a fate worse than death. They had read about him in Carissa's journal, never expecting he was still alive, let alone so close. They had also read about how it was Gabriel who had saved Carissa's life. Susan had seen a portrait of Carissa and swore that Wendy looked just like her.

Is that why Pierre had her kidnapped? David thought. *Or did he want the cross?*

"At least Richelieu didn't get his hands on the sudarium," Susan said suddenly, making them all jump.

David glanced at the document tube clutched in his right hand. Inside it was a relic, the Sudarium of Oviedo, a burial cloth that was purported to be stained with the blood of Christ. Yes, they had fought Richelieu and saved the cloth, but they had lost Wendy in the process.

He felt a lump form in his throat. He had come to care for Wendy deeply in the short amount of time they'd known each other. "There has to be some way we can find her," he ground out.

"There's nothing more we can do tonight. The sun will be rising soon," Gabriel said, his voice eerily calm.

David glared over at the two vampires. "You should have told us, warned us that Carissa's husband was a vampire and here in Prague. How were we supposed to know who Pierre was?"

Gabriel gave no sign of the earlier distress he'd expressed over hearing Pierre's name. "We did not know he was in Prague," he said simply.

"I feel like there are secrets you're both keeping from me," Susan said, anger flashing across her face.

Neither vampire responded to that. Instead there was silence for several minutes before Gabriel turned back to her. "We can do nothing now. We must wait for night. The sun is rising."

Raphael, the other vampire, was heading for the staircase, swaying slightly on his feet. David glanced out the kitchen window and could just see past the one curtain that it was, indeed, getting light outside.

"I suggest we all get some sleep," Gabriel said, moving to follow Raphael upstairs.

Susan had reverted to staring vacantly, and he doubted she'd be getting any sleep for a while. She was in shock and he wished there was something he could do for her, but he didn't even know what he could do to help himself.

"We'll find her, you know," he said, his voice sounding hoarse as he choked back his own emotion.

Susan nodded, and he was grateful that she didn't ask the question that wouldn't leave him alone. *When we find her will it be too late?*

David forced himself to pry his fingers loose from the tube as he stood up. His body was battered. His fractured ribs were still incredibly painful and the fight with Richelieu had done more damage. He was exhausted and he needed to sleep, but how could he shut his eyes even for a second when Wendy was somewhere out there in the clutches of a monster?

EUROPE, PRESENT DAY

Wendy woke slowly, her mind muddled. She couldn't remember where she was and when she was finally able to open her eyes and sit up she realized that was because she truly had no idea where she was. Overhead fluorescent lights gleamed down, illuminating the room.

She looked slowly around her. She was lying on top of a bed that was in a corner of what appeared to be an unbelievably large studio apartment. Across the room was a massive, antique rolltop desk and some other worktables. In the center of the room was a kind of sitting area with a couch, a table, and some chairs. A covered silver platter on the table caught her eye.

She stood slowly, continuing to look around. There were no windows anywhere. What appeared to be a short passageway past the office area led to a staircase. At the top there was a medieval-looking door with iron fittings. She ran up the stairs and tried the door, but it was locked. Moreover, it was so massive and solid that there was no way she could batter it down. There was a small rectangle at about eye height that looked like it could be opened, but not from her side.

She ground her teeth in frustration and turned to survey the rest of the room. There was art on the walls, some of it rare and valuable looking. There were curio cabinets displaying all sorts of knickknacks. She had missed seeing a small kitchenette earlier and after walking back downstairs she headed over to it. There was a refrigerator, a microwave, and a sink. She opened the refrigerator and stared at row after row of bags of blood like you'd find in a blood bank.

She slammed the refrigerator shut and spun around. What was this place? A luxurious dungeon? A panic room for vampires?

The possibilities were frightening. Her stomach growled and she realized she had no way of even telling what time of day it was, let alone what day.

How long had she been here?

She remembered running outside the church, holding on to the tube with the cloth in it, when a man had grabbed her and thrown her into a car. After that she didn't remember much. Had she been drugged?

But by who, and why would they bring her here?

She thought of Susan and David and prayed that they

were okay. They would have to be sick with worry over her. She wondered what had happened to them. Had they escaped Richelieu's men and retrieved the sudarium?

She knew Gabriel and Raphael were worried Richelieu had been trying to find a holy relic that had the blood of Christ on it so that he might ingest it. Blood was life, and power, and spirit, and when a vampire took the blood of another, he made that other person part of himself. They were afraid what would happen if a vampire tried to make the blood of Christ part of himself.

She pressed shaking hands to her temples. It was all too much to take in.

Can't panic, just have to breathe and think.

Her stomach rumbled again.

And eat.

Her eyes turned back to the table and the silver platter on it. She walked over hesitantly and put a hand on the lid. It was warm. She couldn't help but think that when she lifted it she'd find something terrible, like a severed head or a human heart.

She took a deep breath and yanked off the lid.

Steak, mashed potatoes, and roasted vegetables. They were hot, too, with steam coming off them. It all smelled delicious.

She sat down on the chair. The food was for her. There was no other explanation. The question was, why? It didn't make sense for it to be poisoned. It would have been simple enough to kill her if that was her abductor's plan.

She picked up a fork that was sitting beside the plate and pushed it into the mashed potatoes. She gave it an experimental nibble and then wrinkled her nose when she realized that it was laced with garlic.

And now she was even more confused. Was it a test to see if she was a vampire? There were better ways to go about that. Or was it meant to reassure her that she wasn't about to get eaten by a vampire since garlic repelled them painfully?

Either way she was too hungry to question. She prayed over the food, hoping God would protect her from whatever ill might come of it. Then she dug in and ate.

She was hungrier than she had thought and a few minutes later she had cleaned the plate, including the steamed carrots, which she normally despised and which had also been laced with some sort of garlic powder.

When she was done she grabbed some water from the sink and then got back to exploring her prison. The more she saw, the more she was convinced it had to be a shelter of some sort and not a dungeon. There were too many items of a personal nature and the artwork alone was clearly too valuable to use to decorate anything other than a private residence.

So, a vampire must live there or use it as a sort of backup place. The question was, which one? She hardly thought it was Richelieu. It didn't seem his style. Plus he'd been ready to kill her inside that cathedral. The only thing that had stopped him was—

Her hand flew up to her throat and she was relieved to feel Susan's cross still there. She searched the apartment for anything she could use to try to batter down the door but had no luck. Next she sat down at the desk and began looking at the collection of papers she found there, hoping to discover a clue to the identity of her captor.

Finally she found a letter addressed to Pierre de Chauvere. She believed that was the attorney in Prague

Susan had been in contact with. He had been at the cathedral to see the sudarium and he had remarked that she looked just like Carissa.

"Pierre, what is it you want with me?" she said softly as she looked through the rest of the desk.

There were literally dozens of cubbyholes in the desk, and it took time to go through them all. There were a lot of boring-looking legal documents, some of them seemingly quite old.

And then she started yanking out drawers, dumping their contents. She hoped one of them had a false bottom. The third drawer granted her wish when she saw a piece of paper wedged into a crack toward the back. She retrieved a paperclip from the middle drawer, inserted it between the back of the drawer and the bottom, and yanked.

The wood came up, and inside she found several very old parchment papers with fine, tiny handwriting on them. She felt excitement mounting within her.

It was the same kind of parchment they had found stuck into Carissa's diary. Gabriel had given the diary to Susan to read and they had eagerly devoured the story of their many-times great-aunt and all the tragedies that had befallen her.

She picked up the pages and sat on the bed, leaning her back against the wall. She studied the writing more closely and realized that, like Carissa's diary, these pages were in French.

Wendy had studied the language in college and now she scanned the ancient papers eagerly, hoping for a sign of what they could be. Finally she saw the name Jean, Marquis de Bryas, and her heart nearly stopped. That was Carissa's father, the one who had given her the cross that had been handed down for generations that Wendy herself was now wearing.

She put the pages down on the bed and examined the room again. There truly was no way she could see to escape this place. Frustration filled her. There was nothing to do now but wait for her captor to make himself known or for the cavalry to come riding in to her rescue.

She said another quick prayer for all of them, that they were all safe and might be swiftly reunited.

The pages called to her and she could feel curiosity burning brightly inside her. Maybe they would reveal to her what the secret of the cross was.

When had their lives gotten so fantastical? There were hints, whispers in the back of her mind that they had always been so. Susan and Wendy's grandmother had been gifted, called upon by God to leave her home at all times of day and night to go and pray for friends and strangers alike. It had always fascinated and frightened Wendy, that amount of faith.

There had also been the recent revelation that her grandmother knew of the existence of vampires and had even known Raphael. Wendy was still dying to know how all that had come about. But like so many other people in their family, her grandmother seemed to have taken her secrets with her to the grave. It was incredibly frustrating, but it also made sense. Who would have believed her? Wendy herself had only listened halfheartedly when her grandmother would talk about the magic and mystery of her hometown. She'd always put it up to a mixture of nostalgia and overactive imagination.

Right there and then Wendy vowed that if she survived this and someday ever had kids she'd tell them all the important stuff before it was too late. *God forgives every-thing. I'll always love you. Vampires are real, watch out for them.*

She was going to have to make a list at this rate so that she didn't forget anything. She got up and circled one last time. This time she focused on looking for anything she could use as a weapon. There wasn't so much as a flashlight. Unless she threatened to bash someone over the head with a priceless work of art she didn't see an escape plan that was remotely viable.

Which meant there was nothing to do now but wait. Resolutely she picked up the pages and began to read.

There are days when I hardly believe myself what has transpired in the last two years. How I dearly long to tell Marie about all of it, but I dare not. This secret is too great, too burdensome, and I would not risk her life with it. Still, if I should die the secret will be lost. So, however loathe I am to do so, I must make a record of what transpired in the Holy Land and upon my return home from there as well. For I fear that strange things are happening and I worry about the meaning of it all.

The Templars are pressing me sharply to join their ranks and I fear their wrath if I continue to refuse. I do not know why they are so keenly inter-ested in me in this manner. I fear it is because they guess at the truth, but how could they? From what lips would they have learned of it? For all who knew what I carried away from that mosque should have been silenced.

And then there is him. I saw him again at the

party that the king held. He spared my life, saved it, but he still terrifies me like no other could. Is it only a matter of time before he comes for me in the night? And if he spares Marie, what then shall she think?

No, I must leave an account and I will seal it away so that none should find it unless I am dead.

This then is how I, Jean, found a great and terrible treasure....

CHAPTER TWO

And as they came out, they found a man of
Cyrene, Simon by name: him they compelled
to bear his cross.

—Matthew 27:32

Jerusalem itself was under the control of crusaders, but Jean could not trust them with something so precious as what was hidden inside the small box in his tunic. They would squabble over it just like the soldiers who had cast lots for Christ's clothes. In his heart he knew that what he carried was a symbol of love and sacrifice, but he also knew that men's hearts were corrupt and many would kill to get their hands on it.

Once outside the city walls he kept a sharp eye out for the sentries that circled the city. He did not need to be challenged on his way. He saw one riding in the distance and he touched his heels to his mount's flanks and his horse soon outdistanced any possible pursuit.

Well clear of the city, Jean pulled his mount to a trot. As he rode he thought about the treasure he carried with him. There were two relics. He could present one to King Louis VII and the other to Pope Eugene III. Putting one piece in the hands of the king would be easy, but the pope would be a different matter. Jean wasn't about to entrust the relic to a bishop. It had to go directly to the pope, but how?

He was coming up on one of the camps of the German king and he took pains to avoid it. The crusade had made the kings allies, but like all political alliances, it was a fragile one. Jean had no doubts that if the German king or his nobles suspected that Jean carried anything of value, they would not hesitate to kill him for it, allies or no.

He urged his horse on, searching the landscape for a safe place to make camp. A small stand of trees caught his attention and he made for them.

As he ate some smoked meat and stale bread from his saddlebags he contemplated the stars overhead. He always felt small and awed by their presence. During his time in the Holy Land he had taken to staring up at the sky more often than he used to, wondering if Christ Himself had watched those same stars.

His hand slipped to the box and stroked it for a moment, reassuring himself that it was real and that its contents were safe. The best choice, he had realized, was to give both relics to King Louis and allow the king to present one of them to the pope. Something about that seemed very right to him. The relic belonged in the hands of the church and was as fit a gift as a king could give.

He slept fitfully, starting at every sound, and was up before dawn. He had a four-day ride still ahead of him before he would reach Damascus. He was on the road by the time the sun came up and he reveled in its warmth and marveled at its power to chase the shadows away, both the real ones and the ones in his mind. The Holy Land was not as he had imagined it would be. There was so much death, so much destruction, and it saddened him.

At midday he stopped to give his horse a rest and to stretch his legs. As he walked he couldn't help but wonder who else had walked on the same earth he did. Jesus? The apostle Paul? He touched the box again and was warmed by its presence.

Later in the day, he could see a caravan of soldiers in the distance, heading toward Damascus. The battle there should have just begun and Jean was curious how his brothers were faring. He started to move his horse to join the caravan since it was the best and safest way to travel but stopped short at the last moment.

Until he had surrendered his prize he couldn't trust anyone. So, he continued on, alone, riding until the sun had almost set. As he made camp he noted that his horse seemed restless, constantly gazing off into the dark and starting every time Jean moved. "I don't blame you; I'm not going to relax until we see the king, either," Jean told the horse, speaking in slow, soothing tones. "But then, God willing, it's back to France for us. What do you say?"

The horse looked at him, ears pricked forward, beginning to calm down. The sun had gone down and the darkness pressed in around them. He knew of the large striped dogs with humped backs that skulked about at night and the giant spotted cats that blended into the dappled shadows. Both hunted in the night and though they usually stayed away from large camps of soldiers, a lone tethered horse was an easy meal to them.

"I used to hate the dark," he confessed to the horse. The sound of his voice seemed to comfort the animal. "It seems I always have. My grandfather used to tell me terrible stories about witches and demons and monsters of all types. I would wake up screaming after hearing one of Grandfather's stories. My father said they were nothing, that there were no monsters. He used to say, 'If you can't see it, it isn't there.' I didn't believe him, though. Just because you can't see something doesn't mean it doesn't exist. I asked him once what he believed about God since he couldn't see Him. He whipped me so hard I could feel it for a week."

The horse nickered softly, and Jean couldn't help but smile. "I'm guessing you know what it's like to get a good whipping, too. Somehow I doubt yours have anything to do with matters of faith."

Somewhere in the darkness an animal screamed and Jean lunged to his feet, sword in hand. If the predator killed his horse or even injured one of its legs, Jean would be as good as dead. He cursed himself for having stared at the fire instead of letting his eyes adjust to the dark. He might as well have been blinded. Whatever was out there wasn't, though. Whatever was out there could see perfectly fine.

Whatever is out there can see me.

Suddenly there was a crash in the nearby brush. He swung in that direction, sword raised and ready to strike. "I am for God," he announced when nothing made an appearance. "What I carry I take to my king for the glory of God. I shall protect it with my life and curse you with my death."

Only silence greeted him. The hair on the back of his neck rose and he spun around. There, standing several feet away, was a man concealed in a cloak. Jean blinked and he was gone.

He took a ragged breath. He didn't know what had happened, but he sensed the withdrawal of whoever or whatever it was that had been watching him. Still he stood, alert, looking around warily.

When his horse fell asleep and began to snore, Jean lowered his sword and found that he was shaking uncontrollably. He sat down and stretched his hands to the fire, but it was not the cold of the night that seemed to be affecting him. It was something far grimmer that had invaded his mind, brushing icy tendrils of fear and doubt across his soul. He began to pray, the words little more than a jumble as they tumbled from his lips.

It was not humanly possible to reach Damascus without sleeping along the way. Still, he wished he could keep moving at night and sleep during the daytime. Whatever it was seemed to hunt him only from the shadows and he had no desire to lay down, as helpless as a sheep, and be slaughtered in his bed. The moon was dark, though, and it made the road impassable at night. He had to continue on, riding during the day, sleeping at night.

He stopped praying and took a deep breath, trying to calm his senses. Then he listened. There were only the normal sounds of the night to be heard. He no longer felt as if he were being watched. Was that a bit of trickery or the truth? He didn't know, but he had to trust in God.

For the next two days he rode unchallenged and slept undisturbed. He almost wondered if his mind had been playing games with him, if he had really seen a figure made up of shadows. As he drew closer to Damascus, though, he turned his mind to a more pressing problem.

He worried for the safety of the relics that he carried. He meant for the king to give one to the pope, but what if he didn't? What if he decided to keep both for himself?

On the final day of his journey he made his decision. He stopped his horse for a short rest and took out the box.

He hesitated, praying that he was making the right choice. Then slowly, carefully, he opened the box, using a clean bit of cloth picked up one of the relics, careful not to touch it. He wrapped it up gently and then concealed it inside his tunic. He closed the box, sealing the remaining relic safely inside.

If he was wrong it would be a simple enough matter to explain to the king. He could say he had hidden one along the way, so as not to risk losing both on the journey if he should be attacked.

On the other hand, if he was right, it was far better that the king never know of the existence of the second one.

Finished, he let his horse rest a few more minutes before he remounted. "We're going to eat well and rest well tonight," he promised the animal.

PRAGUE, PRESENT DAY

Gabriel awoke suddenly and lay for a second as the sleep paralysis lifted from him. He could hear footsteps heading upstairs. A shadow darkened the doorway: Susan looking in on the three vampires before she continued to the bedroom. That was good. She needed the sleep.

He turned his head and glanced at Paul. His sire was still lying, immobile, his body turned the color of ash. The burns he had sustained when they tried to attack Richelieu's stronghold were killing him, but they were doing so slowly. He wished he knew of some way to call the vampire monk back. Gabriel sat up and turned to look at Raphael. The younger vampire had a snarl twisting his lips and something about him at that moment reminded Gabriel of the first time he'd laid eyes on him.

THE HOLY LAND, 1148 AD

For four days Gabriel followed just out of sight of the knight Jean as he headed for Damascus. When they finally arrived outside the city the knight headed straight for the encampment of the French king.

Gabriel skirted the battlefield. The sweet, ironlike smell of burning wood mixed with blood filled the air. It was all around him, and Gabriel began to tremble. To the crusaders the Holy Land was being made holier by the blood being spilled upon it. All around him Christians and Muslims grappled together, engaged in terrible combat for the very ground upon which they stood.

There is nothing holy about this land; it's just dirt and grass and the things that grow in them, he thought.

The crusaders were losing the battle for Damascus. He could see it in their pained faces, feel it in the surge of intensity from the infidels. Still, the French troops would not give ground easily. Gabriel noticed one knight in particular standing surrounded by dozens of bodies. As Gabriel watched the man turned and beheaded one of his comrades. He shook his head. Such was the tragedy of war. A moment later, though, he saw the same knight deliberately sink a knife into the chest of yet another crusader. Gabriel took a deep breath as anger rose inside him. Death didn't distinguish between Christian and infidel, and clearly neither did the knight.

Gabriel was close enough that he could hear the dying man gasp, "God forgive me."

"Better you should have prayed to me," the knight said as he pulled his knife free.

Gabriel narrowed his eyes. He turned aside and headed for one of the lords who was presiding over the battlefield. The man sat arrogantly astride his horse, a magnificent stallion that was clearly more eager to join the battle than his master.

Gabriel rode up beside him, and the man inclined his head slightly. Gabriel indicated the knight he had just observed. "That man seems to have a taste for blood."

The other man grunted. "He likes to fight, that one."

"Who is he?"

"Name's Raphael. He hails from the Decazeville region."

"So, you are his lord."

"Yes."

"You should watch your man; he doesn't seem to care which side he's on."

The lord cursed. "The devil take him," he concluded.

"You never know, he just might," Gabriel said. He turned his horse and touched his heels to the beast's sides. The horse jumped forward, and Gabriel quickly left the battlefield behind.

The king was in an encampment eight miles away, where he spent his days negotiating with his allies— although *bickering* was a better way to describe it. While kings were busy quarreling with one another their armies were losing the battle. Rumors of retreat had begun to circulate, but Gabriel paid them little heed. Unlike the crusaders, he was there for a very particular purpose that had nothing to do with popes and kings.

Gabriel arrived at the king's camp on the heels of Jean. As he slid off his horse and tossed the reins to a servant he observed Jean dismount. The knight was stiff from the long ride but both he and his mount seemed to be in one piece. Gabriel slipped past him, unseen, into the tent of the king and took his customary place in the back corner to the left of Louis where he could observe all who came and went. Everyone in the room shifted a couple of steps away from him.

Gabriel smiled as he usually did. They were afraid of him and yet they had no idea why. Some instinct prompted them to move out of his path, to not meet his eyes, and to speak about him but never to him. He came and went as he pleased with none to question him. He knew that they were happier when he was absent.

EUROPE, PRESENT DAY

Despite the fact that she was still a captive, Wendy was nearly breathless with excitement as she wondered what it could possibly be that Jean had found. A nail, a thorn? The parchment didn't say. She couldn't help but feel, though, that everything that had happened in the past and everything that was happening in the present were far more connected than all of them could guess.

What is it they say about history? Those who don't remember it are doomed to repeat it? She shuffled through the pages, her eyes scanning here and there, but nothing jumped out at her. She'd just have to keep reading from where she'd left off.

THE HOLY LAND, 1148 AD

The king's guard stopped Jean at the entrance to the tent and demanded to know his business.

"I have found a holy relic; it is for the king's hand alone," Jean said.

He was ushered into the tent. The floor of the tent was covered with rugs, many of which looked to have been picked up on the long journey to the Holy Land. The smell of perfume hung heavily in the air, making him slightly sick with its dizzying sweetness. It was cooler than outside and it felt good to the dry, cracked skin of his face and hands, which had been too long exposed to wind and sun and sand.

The king was holding court at the far end of the tent, sitting on a throne. One of the guards approached the king and whispered in his ear. King Louis waved Jean forward.

Jean willed himself to believe the best possible outcome as he knelt before his king.

"What is it you have brought?" Louis asked.

"A gift worthy of a king. I have brought something touched by the King of Kings, something Your Majesty could present to His Holiness."

"Let me see this gift," Louis said.

Jean pulled the small box from inside his tunic. He held it up toward the king.

When he opened the box, he heard murmurs as people surged forward to look and then dropped to their knees in reverence. A chill touched him. Lord Avignon stared at him with intense, inscrutable eyes.

Louis reached down and picked up the relic. Jean tried not to wince. It was divine, not for man's touch, but kings could do as they willed.

The king held up the object and smiled as he stared at it. Jean wondered if he could feel the power coming from it. As Jean saw the greed dancing in King Louis's eyes he realized he had been right to keep back the second one. Louis had no intention of giving his prize to the pope. As the king held the relic Jean could feel tears stinging the backs of his eyes. If the king would not surrender it to the pope, then he would have to find another way.

"Well done indeed," the king said at last, breaking the silence.

Those in the tent slowly stood, though they spoke only in whispers to one another.

"Thank you, Majesty," Jean said.

"You shall, of course, be rewarded."

"I did not bring this to you in hopes of a reward," Jean said, trying to hide the bitterness in his voice.

"No, you brought it out of duty and nobility. Well, you shall find that while you sought no reward one shall yet be yours."

Jean took a deep breath. "The only reward I would seek is the privilege of removing this relic from this place of battle to the safety of Your Majesty's palace in France."

The king looked thoughtful as he placed it back into the box that Jean still held and snapped shut the lid. "I will think on it. For now, since you have brought it safe this far, I entrust it to your keeping."

Jean bowed deeply. When he turned to leave the tent he saw Lord Avignon still staring at him. Jean shivered in fear as he met the other's eyes. There was something about them that wasn't right. The lord broke eye contact with him and walked silently to the king's side and bent to whisper in his ear. He could still hear the man's words.

"I know of a knight who would be perfect to carry your prize safely home," he purred. "His name is Raphael, and he is the fiercest of your warriors."

Once outside the king's tent, Jean took charge of his horse and led the animal away to where he could unsaddle him and let him rest for the night. He had just finished rubbing down the horse when a squire approached him timidly.

"What is it?" Jean asked.

"You are to dine tonight with His Majesty," the squire said.

"I'm hardly dressed for it," Jean said, wishing to stay with his horse in case he needed to take the relics and run.

"There are fresh clothes waiting for you, my lord, in your tent."

"I don't have a tent," Jean said. While Jean was a knight, he was a poor one, with only a single horse to his name.

"You do now."

Jean turned.

"Please come with me," the squire said, ducking his head.

Jean patted his horse's neck and then turned to follow as the squire led him to a small tent. Inside there was a new suit of clothes, finer than any he had ever owned. He raised his eyebrows in surprise. "Are you sure we're in the right place?" he asked.

"Yes. I will wait for you and then escort you to His Majesty," he said, backing out of the tent.

There was a washbasin, and Jean moved to it gratefully and began to wash the blood and the dirt from his skin and hair. When he had finished he put on the new clothes and then emerged from the tent.

Moments later he was sitting down to a feast. His stomach growled loudly at the sight of the food and he closed his eyes and inhaled the rich fragrances.

Before they could start to eat the king called for silence and raised his goblet. "To our new Marquis de Bryas."

Jean glanced around, trying to figure out who had been named a marquis. It only took a moment for him to realize everyone else at the table was staring directly at him. He turned bewildered eyes back to King Louis. "For your faithful service in securing a most precious gift for the glory of France we honor you tonight, Lord Jean."

Dinner passed in a haze as he struggled to come to grips with what had just happened. He was a marquis. He wished more than anything that his beloved Marie was there. She would have reveled in the moment even as he felt conflicted. He would have rather been sent home with the relic than have all the titles in the world. Nothing had gone as he had envisioned since he had made his way to the king's tent with the precious box.

At the end of dinner the king returned to his throne, summoning his court around him. Once they were settled, a filthy man entered and knelt before the king. He must have come straight from the field of battle. He reeked of blood and death, and gore was caked onto his hands, clothes, and face.

When the king called, Jean stepped forward. As he drew closer, he could feel evil coming off the man. This, he realized, was Raphael, the man to whom he would be asked to surrender the box and its precious cargo. Jean presented the box with the relic. Then he watched in disgust as Raphael pretended to pray. Jean fingered the cross that Marie had given him and wished he was riding home to be with her. He had left her as a knight, poor and ill prepared to provide for her. Now he was a marquis, an honor that he had not sought but would do his best to live up to. He would far rather switch places, though, with the ruffian who even now was taking possession of the box without feeling its power, its significance.

Lord, make him worthy of carrying that which You once carried, he prayed.

As Raphael walked past him on his way out of the tent and King Louis looked smug, Jean pledged his life to keeping the second relic safe.

He shivered suddenly and was not surprised to see Lord Avignon, the tall man with dark hair and blazing eyes. As a count, there were many in the tent who outranked Lord Avignon, but there was still something terrifying about the nobleman. Jean watched as others moved instinctively out of his way. He was dressed in black, but there was a further darkness about him, as if no light touched him. When he had knelt before the relic earlier, though, there had been real fear in his eyes. As much as Jean disliked him, he found himself still wishing that it was Lord Avignon, and not Raphael, who was safeguarding the box on its way to France.

"And now, Jean, I have a special task for you," Louis said suddenly, interrupting his train of thought.

"Your Highness," Jean said, stepping forward.

"The battle here is lost, curse that German fool. We are withdrawing to Jerusalem."

"How may I assist?"

The king leaned forward and smiled as though losing the battle mattered nothing to him. "I want you to find me something."

What more could any man want than what he had just brought him? He glanced after Raphael. "But, Your Highness, I've already found you... *everything*."

Louis smirked. "Yes, well, now I want you to find me everything else."

CHAPTER THREE

*Blotting out the handwriting of ordinances
that was against us, which was contrary to
us, and took it out of the way, nailing it to his
cross.*

—Colossians 2:14

PRAGUE, PRESENT DAY

Susan lay on the bed in her room upstairs, unable to fall asleep. She had left David downstairs. He was working on the computer, running Internet searches, hoping to figure out where Pierre might have taken Wendy. He had been doing property title searches to see if he could discover any other buildings owned by the vampire, since he wasn't to be found at his home or office in the city. She had offered to help, but there was nothing she could do and he had insisted that at least one of them try to get some sleep.

David was a computer programmer who had been transferred to Prague from his home back in the United States for a three-month assignment. His injuries had kept him from reporting to his new job. She was guessing it was only a matter of days, perhaps less, before he was finally fired. Somehow, though, she had the impression that this was the last thing that he cared about.

What he did care about was Wendy. Her vivacious

cousin had often been the object of men's affections, but never in such a dangerous, explosive way. Their first night in Prague Wendy had been nearly killed by a vampire and things had just gone downhill from there.

And another vampire might have killed her already.

Susan thought of the times she had been in Pierre's office and sensed, *known,* that there was something wrong. He'd had a large portrait of her grandmother as a young woman on one of his walls and he'd been very eager to find the cross necklace her grandmother had given her, which Susan had taken pains to conceal from him. Of course that didn't matter much now that he had the necklace along with Wendy.

She squeezed her eyes shut, angry with herself for not having been able to figure out that he was a vampire. It seemed so obvious now that it was almost laughable. And it was a sad, terrible thing that in all the hours they'd spent reading their ancestress Carissa's diary never once had she mentioned the name of the man who'd tried to have her killed. Had they read the name Pierre in that diary maybe they would have been suspicious in time.

The diary itself now sat untouched downstairs. It was in medieval French and neither Susan nor David could read it. Wendy had been their translator. Susan felt more anger and frustration bubbling up in her. She knew there was more the diary could tell them, not just about Carissa and what fate ultimately befell her, but also about things in the present. Because their present seemed completely intertwined with that past.

Maybe she had the vampires to thank for that. Her thoughts slid to the three in the other room. She had sent up many prayers in the last couple of days while sitting at the bedside of the vampire monk. But Paul hadn't gotten any better, only worse. Now what was left of him was the color of ash and she worried that the slightest touch would cause his body to disintegrate. God Himself had to be keeping the vampire alive because no one else had any other possible explanations for how he could have sustained such massive burns and not crumbled instantly into dust.

Even though she'd learned much about Gabriel from Carissa's diary, the vampire was still largely a mystery to her and terrified her. She could tell he frightened Paul and Raphael as well.

Raphael.

She felt her heart give a little leap at the thought of him. He was dark and dangerous but struggling so hard to be good. It had been him who had saved Wendy before and she had to believe he would save her again. She thought of the way he had held her when she cried. He had been so tender, so gentle. It was a different side to him and it had made her care for him even more than she already did. And that, of course, was dangerous and stupid because nothing could change the fact that he was a vampire.

After a couple of hours lying there unable to sleep she went downstairs. David, it seemed, had finally passed out on the couch. She tiptoed quietly to the computer and looked at some of the websites and documents that he had up. He had typed in a few addresses in a document file and put several question marks after them. She felt her heart lift at the sight. Maybe he had found something important.

She turned to wake him up so that she could ask him more about them, but his face was scrunched up in pain in his sleep. She paused. All of them were truly exhausted, and when they found Wendy they were going to have a fight on their hands. It would be a fight they would most certainly lose if they weren't rested and prepared for it.

Reluctantly she got up quietly and returned to her room upstairs. This time when she laid down it was only moments before she was fast asleep.

EUROPE, PRESENT DAY

Wendy couldn't help but think about everything she had read so far. Their grandmother had left Susan a letter to Carissa from her father, Jean, detailing what the secret of the cross necklace was. The letter had been stolen, though, before Susan could have the French translated.

Stroking the old cross around her throat she thought about Jean wearing it during the crusade. She kept thinking that maybe, somewhere in the pages she was reading, he would reveal the secret. She was also wildly curious to know exactly what relics he had found in the box inside the mosque. He had mentioned Christ on more than one occasion and she couldn't help but wonder if those relics were some of the ones they had suspected Richelieu was after.

THE HOLY LAND, 1148 AD

Jean was weary to his bones. His horse plodded along, barely managing to pick up its hooves and stumbling every few steps. He patted the sweat-soaked neck. "I know, boy, me, too," he said.

They were limping their way back to Jerusalem, empty-handed again. This time the king had sent him to Nazareth to search for the missing bones of John the Baptist, the ones that had not been burned by his followers years after his death. At one point they had been rumored to be in Jerusalem but they seemed to have long since left the city. He had found nothing that could be identified as the bones of the prophet.

Jean was regretting his decision to ever reveal the truth of the relic he had found to his king. He had spent weeks trying to find the bones of the apostles, the spear that had pierced Christ's side, and anything else the king thought of and desired.

He had found none of those things. He had hoped to spend Christmas at home in France with family and his beloved Marie. That hope was beyond him. The war was being lost and Jean felt the fool trying to chase ghosts while his comrades died by the hundreds. Worse, a messenger the king had sent to France had returned a week earlier with the news that the knight Raphael and the relic never made it to the palace. Jean wondered what had befallen them.

He pulled his horse up short and the exhausted animal stopped with a groan. Jean glanced at the sky. The sun had just set on the horizon and darkness was edging its way across the land.

He would never have admitted it to any man, but Jean feared the night. Since coming to this place he had been having nightmares again, reliving every tale his grandfather ever told him of demons who dwelt in the darkness waiting to prey on lone travelers. "God defend me," he whispered.

He urged his horse forward. He had intended to stop for the night and camp, but the fear he was feeling was more than what the night usually brought.

He rode for an hour, the moon steadily climbing in the

sky shining brightly and illuminating his way. The horse began to walk faster and he did nothing to slow him. Off to the right he saw something. He turned to look but there was nothing there. Nothing he could see at any rate. He let his hand drop to the hilt of his sword. There was a sound like wind sighing... or someone laughing.

He could feel his horse's muscles begin to quiver and tense. When the animal reared, Jean was ready for it and he kept his seat long enough to see eyes flash in the darkness. He dismounted in one step, drawing his sword and keeping the horse between him and whatever it was that had come for him.

He could hear nothing beyond the frightened whinnying of the beast. He looked to either side, waiting for someone to come around the horse after him. The smell of blood made his pulse quicken. Suddenly something seemed to hit the struggling horse, toppling it to the ground.

Jean scrambled, trying to get clear, but the falling horse knocked him down and crushed his legs beneath it. Pain washed through him, and he struggled to stay conscious. An animal threw itself through the air and landed, perched on top of the horse, fangs gleaming in the moonlight. For a moment all Jean could see was a mane of tawny hair, flashing eyes, and the fangs. A sound that was half snarl, half scream rent the air.

It has to be some kind of lion, he thought.

The moon shone full on the creature's face as it raised its head and Jean realized that the beast snarling and spitting at him was a man. He gasped and reached for the sword that had been knocked from his hand in the fall. His fingers closed around it and he brought it to bear.

The man knocked it away as though he were batting at a

child's stick. "I know you," the monster growled. "You're the one who found *it*."

He must be talking about the relic, Jean realized. He looked closer at his attacker. The face was contorted, the eyes gleamed with madness, and he looked inhuman. Still, there was something familiar and when Jean recognized the man, his blood froze. "You are...were...the one who carried it, the knight Raphael," he said.

"And I still do," the man hissed, licking his fangs.

"You lie, demon! The likes of you could not touch it."

"I don't have to touch it, not when it comes in such a pretty box."

"What happened to you, what made you this way?" Jean asked, stalling for time. He knew he was going to die. If he died, though, the monster before him would continue to carry the holy relic and his own secret would be lost forever. He moved his hand to his chest where it closed around Marie's cross.

Raphael laughed. "God made me this way, of course, and you know what that makes me? The son of God!" he roared.

EUROPE, PRESENT DAY

Wendy gasped. She knew that once Raphael had been a monster, but the description Jean wrote was so vivid, so utterly horrifying, that it made her heart pound. She thought of her cousin Susan, who had spent so much time with Raphael. Susan, who she was sure was falling in love with the vampire. She deserved to know the truth. How evil he had been. How evil he still might be.

She stood up and paced for a moment while she tried to process everything she had read. She couldn't put down the pages for long, though, and she had soon sat back down and picked them up.

The blasphemous monster glared down at me, saliva dripping from its fangs. "You lie," I told it.

THE HOLY LAND, 1148 AD

"God didn't make him like this; I did," a voice said out of the darkness.

Raphael jerked and turned his head toward the sound. Jean thrust the cross he was holding upward toward Raphael's forehead and the demon screamed and fell back, rolling in the dust to put out the flames that had suddenly engulfed his face.

Jean struggled to free his legs, but he was trapped by the body of his horse. He couldn't tell if the animal was injured or merely frozen with fear. A shadow passed before him and suddenly the body of the animal was lifted off him like it was a child's toy. As soon as the horse's hooves touched the ground it was off and running. Jean tried to get up, but his left leg flared in pain and the sudden movement sent a wave of nausea through his body.

"Be still!" the shadow commanded before falling on Raphael.

"Did you kill him?" Jean asked as Raphael went limp. The shadow stood slowly, revealing itself to be a man.

"No, but he will be still until I decide what I'm going to do."

"With him?"

"No, with you."

And suddenly the man was crouching on the ground next to Jean and he could see his face. He recognized Lord Avignon, the adviser to the king, and he knew in a moment that he'd been right to fear the man, to sense something dark and unnatural about him.

Jean was still holding the cross and Gabriel glanced at it.

"The man who made that cross does excellent work."

"It belongs to the woman I love."

"Then you'd better put it away before you lose it," Gabriel said.

Jean let go of it. He could feel its weight on his chest and he took some comfort from that.

"Well, if you want to kill me all you have to do is leave. I have no horse and am unable to walk."

Lord Avignon smiled at him and somehow it frightened Jean more than all of Raphael's growling. "You are a clever man, I think you would work out a way to survive," he said.

"You have no reason to harm me."

"It doesn't pay to have people walking around who have seen what you have seen."

"My grandfather saw such things. People thought he was mad," Jean said, realizing the truth.

Gabriel tilted his head to the side. "I cannot take a chance that they will think you the same."

"Then give me the relic the monster has, let me go, and I shall give you my word not to speak of this."

Gabriel shook his head.

"You do not believe me?" Jean asked.

"I believe you. I cannot do that. Besides, why do you need it? You still have yours."

"How...how did you know of that?"

"I have been watching you a long time, Jean."

Jean was getting desperate. The pain was getting more intense and he had the feeling that the longer the discussion went on the more likely he was to end up dead. "Then let me battle the monster when he wakes; whichever of us wins gets to live."

"I cannot take that chance. You might kill him."

"And that would be a bad thing?"

Gabriel nodded solemnly. "If you kill him, then he will not learn."

Jean had no idea how to respond to that as he groaned, trying to quell a wave of pain and nausea that washed over him.

"Let me look at your leg," Gabriel said.

Jean considered refusing.

"You think you can fight me." Gabriel seemed to expect no answer to this.

Jean grit his teeth as Gabriel inspected the damage. Gabriel found a shirt in Jean's saddlebags and tore it into strips to bind up the wounds. While he worked Jean slid in and out of consciousness.

When he had finished Jean was once again awake. "It was you who I sensed in the mosque that day," he said.

"Yes."

"Are you the same as him?" Jean asked, looking toward Raphael.

"Yes, but much older."

"Why are you helping me?"

"Because the world needs more people like you. I have decided, therefore, to let you live. I will even get you somewhere that you can mend. But you must promise me one thing."

"What?"

"As soon as your leg is well enough to ride, you must return home. Have your children. Teach them to be good people."

"That seems like a strange request."

"Do you agree or not?" Gabriel asked, his fangs showing.

"Yes," Jean said. He was a fool not to make that deal, especially when going home, getting married, and raising a family was all he wanted. Gabriel nodded, and then Jean slipped into darkness.

When Jean awoke he could tell before opening his eyes that it was daytime. His body jolted to the side and he snapped awake as pain seared through his broken leg. He opened his eyes and saw that he was in a wagon.

A man was sitting beside him and he smiled.

"Where am I?" Jean asked.

"On the way home to France, my lord, courtesy of the king."

More like courtesy of Lord Avignon, Jean thought. *Not that I'm complaining.*

He touched the cross around his neck and was relieved that it was still there.

"How long have I been unconscious?"

"Three days—you had the fever, but you are better now."

"Who are you?" Jean asked, looking the man over. He

was dressed better than a peasant but did not look like a nobleman or a soldier.

"Will, my lord. Your manservant."

Jean jerked in surprise. "I have no servant," he said.

"You do now," Will said with a smile. "Quite a few. Courtesy of the king. Most have gone ahead to prepare the castle."

Castle. Servants. Jean closed his eyes and wondered if he was dreaming still. Or perhaps he was in heaven, killed by the monsters. Then again, he imagined if he was dead his leg wouldn't hurt nearly as badly. Why had Lord Avignon spared him? It couldn't be a bribe for his silence, it would have been far easier to kill him. And why would he care how Jean lived the rest of his life?

"How long will it take us to get there traveling this way?" Jean asked.

"About three months, my lord."

Jean sighed. He wasn't going to make it home for Christmas, but he would make it home for Easter.

Marie, I'm coming. I'll be there as soon as I can, he vowed.

The journey was tedious but from the moment they made it onto French soil Jean could barely contain his excitement. His leg was nearly healed and he took time to walk on it a little each evening when they made camp. He knew it was vanity but when he came face-to-face with Marie he didn't want her to see him limping.

He still had not become accustomed to having servants, but he had found Will's help to be invaluable. The man had a rudimentary education and experience managing households that Jean was sure would prove invaluable in the months ahead.

Will had offered to travel ahead and prepare his family for his arrival and their move to Bryas, but Jean wanted to surprise them himself. As the day grew closer he grew increasingly anxious, praying often that he would find his family well and Marie would still feel for him as he did for her.

On the last night they had to make camp the waiting became intolerable. He lay awake long after the others were asleep, staring up at the stars and wondering what the future held. He thought about the relic he carried, as he had every night since he had found it. After struggling with the decision for the entire journey he finally determined not to surrender it to the king. Maybe one day. Maybe to a different king or to the pope. God had delivered it into his hand and he believed there was a purpose for that even if he did not see it. With that determined, he finally slept a little.

The sun was high overhead when his home came into view. It was a lovely stone structure that had housed his parents, his brothers, and himself during the happiest years of his life. It had always been a castle to him, though it would doubtless pale in comparison to the new home he would be moving to.

Jean could see his parents and one of his brothers come outside as the group approached. Visitors were few and far between and always excited interest. He smiled at seeing them all alive and looking well. The wagon rolled to a stop and before Jean could reveal himself Will had jumped down.

"Greetings to the people of this good house," Will said, bowing with a flourish.

"You are more than welcome," Jean's father said, his voice deep and warm.

"My master, the Marquis de Bryas, is traveling to his

home and he was wondering if he might share a midday meal with you and your family." Jean shook his head in amusement at Will's introduction.

"He may, and most welcome," his mother said. "Tell him to come in and rest himself."

Will turned to the wagon and said, "May I present his lordship, the Marquis de Bryas."

Jean stepped down and faced his family. His brother was the first to comprehend and, with a shout, flung himself forward and hugged Jean fiercely. Then Jean was facing his parents and hugging them both and they all cried.

"What is this trick?" his father asked at last, dashing away the tears.

"It's no trick, sir," Will said, stepping forward. "Your son is the new Marquis de Bryas."

"It's a long story," Jean admitted sheepishly.

"Well, then come on in and tell it while I make us something to eat," his mother urged, waving Jean and his companions inside.

The midday meal took the rest of the day and bled into supper. By the time night had fallen Jean was worn out from talking and laughing. His mother had determined that he and his men would spend the night there before continuing on to the castle. Jean had insisted that they come to live with him and they had agreed.

He told them everything he could about the things he had seen and done, always making sure never to touch on the subjects about which he was sworn to secrecy. They, in turn, caught him up on all the news and happenings that he had missed. At last he found the courage to ask the question that burned most brightly in his heart.

"How is Marie?"

His parents exchanged a quick glance and he felt fear prick his heart. "I suspect she'll be much better now that you've come home," his mother said.

"She's been to see us several times," his father added. "She loves you."

"Then what's wrong?"

"Her father has been trying to force her to marry before you returned. There is a baron whose wife died in childbirth who needs an heir. There's talk of him coming here."

Jean had known Marie's father had always wanted a marriage for Marie that would increase his status. Having no title of his own, being the father of a baroness would raise his station. The man no doubt resented Jean for interfering, but it had always seemed he disliked him on a personal level as well.

"It's never made sense, her father being set against you," his mother said.

"Will, I have an idea and I need your help," Jean said thoughtfully.

The next morning, early, Will rode out for Marie's home. Several hours later Jean followed. It felt good to be on horseback again, even though his leg still hurt. The ride was not a long one, but it still felt the longest of his life.

When the farmhouse Marie lived in came into view Jean headed his horse for her favorite spot. It was a small rise behind the house covered with trees. On one in particular he had long ago carved a heart for the two of them. He hoped that she would be there and not inside the house. When he spotted a lone figure sitting beneath the trees his heart leaped.

She stood as he rode up, eyes wide. As he dismounted in front of her he prayed that she would still feel the same as he did. He walked slowly, ignoring the pain in his leg. Before he could walk very far she ran forward and threw her arms around him.

He held her close, buried his face in her hair, and tried not to cry. When she finally let go of him he could see the joy in her eyes and he breathed a sigh of relief.

She put her hand on the cross around his neck. "Did it help protect you?" she asked.

He nodded. "It certainly did." There was so much to tell her, and so much he shouldn't. It could all wait though. The important thing was they were both alive and now they could get married.

"Are you back to stay?"

"Yes. I made a promise and I intend to keep it. I've come home, Marie, and now we can be married."

Her face fell and she dropped her eyes to the ground.

"What's wrong?" he asked her.

"My father has always harbored ill feelings toward you," she confessed.

"I don't care. I'll go and speak with him." He turned toward the house and she grabbed his arm.

"What's wrong?"

Tears filled her eyes. "He's going to force me to marry. First I thought it would be to a baron, but now the new Marquis de Bryas has come from the crusade and has sent his man to inquire after me."

"Then I'm too late," Jean said. Her tears hurt him, but he pressed on, needing to know the truth.

"I don't have a choice."

"I know the marquis. He is a kind man, rich and handsome. I'm sure he will make you very happy. You'll have anything you could ever want."

"But what I want is you."

"Do you still love me?" he asked.

She nodded. "More than ever. You don't know how many times I dreamed of this day. You would come home and we would be married."

"It can still happen," he said.

She shook her head. "My father—"

"Run away with me, Marie. I love you. We might not have an easy life, but whatever I have is yours. What do you say, will you come with me right now?" He put his hand under her chin and lifted her face so that he could see her eyes.

"Yes," she breathed.

He kissed her and all the pain of the war seemed to fade away. Finally he pulled away and turned back to his horse. "I will go speak to your father right now."

She grabbed him with a cry. "No, you mustn't! Our only chance is to go right now."

He smiled at her. "We will go in a moment. And we will be married today. Now that I know you still love me, I have something I need to tell your father."

"What?"

"Dearest Marie, I am the new Marquis de Bryas."

She stood for a moment, staring wide-eyed at him. He moved forward, afraid she was going to faint. Instead she sobbed with joy and threw her arms around his neck.

"Do you think he'll like me once he finds out I'm the marquis?"

"I think he'll love you so much he'll try to marry off my sister to your brother."

Jean laughed. "God help us all."

EUROPE, PRESENT DAY

A sound at the top of the stairs made Wendy jump. She hastily shoved the parchment papers underneath the mattress and crossed the room so she was by the table, waiting. She tried to disguise the fact that her hands were shaking by clenching them into fists at her side.

She could see the massive door at the top of the stairs, and she heard a key in a lock. Then, at last, with a great groaning sound the door swung open.

CHAPTER FOUR

*And whosoever doth not bear his cross, and
come after me, cannot be my disciple.*

—Luke 14:27

PRAGUE, PRESENT DAY

Raphael woke and strained for several agonizing moments against the sleep paralysis that gripped him tight. He could smell blood and that only heightened the sense of urgency he was feeling. When he finally sat up with a gasp he was irritated to find that Gabriel had already left the room. He stood and glanced at Paul.

It hurt him to look at the vampire that was his grandsire. Susan had been right. The little flesh that was left had turned gray, the color of ash. There were drops of blood on his lips and Raphael realized Gabriel must have already tried feeding him some more that night.

Which meant his sire had been up for a while. One of these days he had to get him to teach him how to do that. It made no sense that Gabriel was forced into the same sleep coma with the rising of the sun that the rest of them were but then was able to cheat it by waking while the sun was still up. He had never heard of another vampire who could do it. It was just one of the many things that made Gabriel so terrifying, even to his own kind.

Raphael left the room and stood on the landing for a moment, listening. He could hear voices downstairs and after a moment he recognized both David and Susan. So everyone who could get up already was.

He took the stairs in a flash, irritated at feeling like he was coming late to the party. He didn't see any sign of Gabriel. David and Susan, though, were huddled together, heads nearly touching as they both stared at something on the computer screen.

A flare of heat ignited his blood and he blinked at the sudden, uncontrollable feelings of jealousy that threatened to overwhelm him.

"It's okay," David said softly to Susan, placing his hand over hers on the desk.

Raphael wanted nothing so much as to rip that hand from David's body.

He forced himself to unclench his fists. Susan didn't belong to him and, even if she did, David had eyes for Wendy, not her.

"Evening," he said, to announce his presence. David and Susan turned quickly from the computer screen. There was surprise on their faces, but nothing more.

"You're up," Susan said, and there seemed to be genuine relief in her voice.

"Look what I've found," David said, gesturing to the screen.

Raphael didn't have to move closer to read it. Being a vampire had certain advantages. It was a list of addresses, all over Europe it seemed.

"What is that?" he asked.

"Properties owned by Pierre or one of his companies," Susan said, her voice tinged with excitement.

"Since you didn't find him or Wendy at either of his places in the city, I decided to see if we could expand the search," David said eagerly. "So far I've found a dozen places that they could have reached by dawn if they were driving."

"He's drawing up a secondary list of places that they could have flown to," Susan added.

Raphael squeezed his eyes shut in frustration. He and Gabriel had just returned from chasing all over Europe after holy relics they thought Richelieu was after. He didn't relish the thought of doing the same in an attempt to find where Pierre might have stashed Wendy.

If she was even still alive.

"How can we be sure he doesn't have her somewhere else in the city?" he asked.

David shook his head. "I haven't been able to find records of Pierre or his company owning any other buildings in Prague."

"What about hotels, abandoned buildings, or someone else's place?" Raphael asked.

"From what I've seen of Pierre he seems very private, I doubt he'd trust any place too public. There was, of course, the blond vampire who was helping him," Susan said. "We haven't figured out who he is or where he might be yet."

"The Baron. He lives in Germany," Gabriel said suddenly from behind them.

Even Raphael jumped. "Where did you come from?" he asked.

"Leipzig, Germany. That's where the Baron lives. It's about a hundred and twenty miles, definitely within driving distance last night. Though he hasn't been seen there in the past week and it seems too obvious. He wouldn't take Wendy there."

"Who is the Baron?" David asked.

"I saw him with Pierre before," Susan said, her voice tight with fear. "But are we sure he works for Pierre? Could he have kidnapped Wendy for himself?"

"Doubtful," Gabriel said darkly. "It would not be the first time that Baron Erik von Bayer has worked for Pierre. The two have a very long history together. And it involves your family as well." He stared straight at Susan.

"What do you mean?" she asked.

Raphael could smell the fear coming off her and it saddened him greatly. He had been wrong to drag her into all this. It was too much for anyone to take. It wasn't just the burden of what was before them, but it was also the burden of knowing what lay behind them.

"When Carissa and I escaped the prison where Pierre had sent her to die, he released one of the other prisoners, accused of being a German spy, to kill her. Erik was promised his freedom and the ability to return home. Before the prison he had been a celebrated singer in his homeland. But years in there change a man. He emerged ready to destroy anyone he had to in order to avoid going back."

Susan visibly shuddered. "The man who attacked you with fire on the road, forcing you to split up," she said.

A shadow passed over Gabriel's face. "She wrote about that?" he said, his voice soft.

"Yes, she was terrified, sure that you had been killed

when you made her leave. I don't know what happens next. Wendy was the only one able to read the old French the diary is written in."

Gabriel turned away from the rest of them. "Things got...worse...after that," he said simply.

Raphael stared intently at his sire. Gabriel rarely spoke of Carissa, certainly not to him except for those few moments where he had admonished him to look after Susan, to be unafraid to love her. The truth was Raphael didn't even know most of what had happened to Carissa.

He turned back to Susan and saw that she had gone completely white. She had risen slowly from her seat in front of the computer. "Wendy...Wendy looks like Carissa. It's not possible that Erik, or Pierre, thinks that she is Carissa, is it?"

"No!" Gabriel said, forcefully turning around. "They both know better than that," he said, dropping his voice slightly.

But Susan had taken a quick step backward at the aggressive tone and the fierce look in Gabriel's eyes.

Raphael couldn't help himself. He moved to her side and touched her elbow ever so briefly. He didn't know why. To show his support? To try and comfort her?

He turned and glared at Gabriel.

David cleared his throat. "I think we should try looking for Wendy at some of these places," he said, attempting to draw attention back to the computer screen.

"We should focus on finding and destroying Richelieu," Gabriel said, glaring at Raphael.

He blames me for creating this entire mess and he's right. Raphael hunched his shoulders and bared his fangs. Just because the older vampire was right didn't mean

Raphael wanted to hear about it. He'd done several life-times of self-flagellation on that topic already.

"No!" Susan said, her voice rising in panic.

Raphael reached down and wrapped his hand around hers and gave it a gentle squeeze. "We will find her. We need to find her. She's part of this, too. And she has the necklace," he said, daring Gabriel to contradict him.

And a moment later he realized that had been a bad idea.

Gabriel thought about killing Raphael. They'd been leading to it for centuries and now seemed like a good time, regardless of what Susan and David might think. After all, Raphael had been Gabriel's mistake. He should never have turned him. He had been nothing but trouble.

They hadn't been able to spend much time together before he himself had been imprisoned and Raphael had been left to his own devices. He was still grateful that Paul had tracked him down the way he had and taken him in hand. It seemed that, just as in the human world, vampire sires were constantly cleaning up their children's messes.

Still, it had been a mistake to take Raphael back to civilization as soon as he had. He should have stayed with him in the Holy Land longer. Instead, just a few months after he had cursed him, the two had returned to Gabriel's home in Avignon.

AVIGNON, 1149 AD

Home. Gabriel smiled as it came into view. Avignon glittered under the moonlight, lovely, ancient. The partially completed Cathédrale Notre-Dame des Doms d'Avignon stretched skyward, seeking to protect those in her shadow. The Rhône River shone like a ribbon in the moonlight and on the opposite bank he could make out Villeneuve-lès-Avignon. One of these days he decided he should erect a bridge over the river to connect the two towns.

Gabriel thought back on the long history of Avignon. Celts, Romans, Arabs, and the French had all claimed it at one time or another. Recently it had been under Germanic control although that had been mostly in name only. Now it was independent, but it was only a matter of time, in his opinion, before it was pulled in again under French rule. Being the Lord Avignon came with special challenges but also gave him more autonomy than most.

His horse moved restlessly, sensing its journey was nearing completion. They had picked up the horses at the last village. While a few of his servants knew what he was, the majority did not and Gabriel wanted to keep it that way. He glanced sideways at Raphael, who fidgeted on his own horse. He didn't like bringing him to his home; it was like inviting a fox into the henhouse. Still, there were few alternatives and none of them better. He sighed in frustration.

"The people here are mine. They are under my protection," Gabriel said, slowly and with emphasis. "You are not to touch them."

"Sheep," Raphael said, sneering.

"Maybe, but they are *my* sheep," Gabriel said, allowing the menace to fill the sound of his voice.

"One of these days I'll kill you," Raphael said.

It was an idle threat and Gabriel didn't bother responding to it. Instead he stared his fill at his home. He had been gone for a year and that had been far too long. He wondered what things he would find changed. Who would have died, who would have been born. It never ceased to amaze him how a single year could bring so much change with it.

He touched his heels to his horse's flanks and headed down the hill, Raphael behind him. He took in every house, every field as he rode. He inhaled the air, so much cleaner and more alive than the air in the Holy Land. Grass and trees, birds and all manner of beasts surrounded him. He could smell the people inside their houses, the wood of the fires, the aromas of roasting meats and baking bread. No sand, no dust, no stench of war. He allowed himself the luxury of breathing it all in.

Finally they neared the castle and the horses stepped faster, eager for a rest and food. Their hooves clattered on the stone of the forecourt and Gabriel heard the cry of the night watchman announcing the arrival of visitors. He smiled to himself. There would be surprise indeed when they discovered that he was no common visitor, but the lord arrived home.

A stable boy came running, the smell of hay and horses and mead wafting around him. Gabriel stepped down and tossed the reins to him and Raphael followed suit. The boy took a good look at Gabriel and then a grin split his face. "Welcome home, my lord."

"Thank you, George."

The boy led the horses off as several people poured out of the main building and scurried forward. In the lead was Andrew, his most trusted servant, the one who ran his affairs when he was gone, the one all the others answered to, and one of the few who knew exactly what his master was.

Andrew's eyes widened in surprise. "Hail, the lord has returned!" he bellowed in a deep voice.

The cheer was picked up by others and soon everyone had poured out into the courtyard to greet them. He recognized maids, grooms, footmen, kitchen staff, and many, many others. He lifted his hands high in the air and silence descended.

"I must say, I have seen the wonders of the Holy Land, beheld its treasures and secrets, walked in the very footsteps of Christ. And yet, I tell you now there is nowhere I want to be other than here, at home in Avignon."

Cheers and laughter greeted that and soon they were being escorted inside. Every time he touched a shoulder or a hand he would smile and silently will them to stay as far from Raphael as possible.

He knew well the danger of bringing Raphael here only a few short months after he had been changed. But Gabriel had desired this homecoming more than anything and could not bear the idea of spending the years it would take to train Raphael away from the home he loved and the people he cared for. Besides, it was not good for a lord to be too long absent. There were always others, vultures, fearmongers, and thieves, ready to steal what belonged to another. Avignon had been his for far too long for him to ever let it go.

"I'll have some supper prepared for you quick as you please, my lord," the mistress of the kitchen declared once they had moved into the great hall.

"They have dined on the road and I'm sure wish nothing more than a good night's sleep in real beds," Andrew interjected smoothly.

Gabriel nodded to the woman. "He is right, but do not worry, we shall enjoy your cooking soon enough."

A sudden growling caused Gabriel to turn. His

wolfhound was staring hard at Raphael and approaching slowly, teeth bared.

"Gaston!" Gabriel called the dog sharply.

The dog turned to him, whining, and Gabriel snapped his fingers. Gaston bounded joyously to him and Gabriel scratched behind his ears. "That's a good boy."

"You named the beast?" Raphael asked, the contempt thick in his voice.

Andrew had been staring hard at Raphael and he spoke up quickly. "I've often accused the master of having more love for that dog than any of us. Worst thing a person could do is underestimate that. While he was gone the old boy has gotten quite spoiled, I'm afraid."

"We'll go hunting tomorrow," Gabriel promised the dog, who licked his hand.

A few minutes later Gabriel escorted Raphael to the room he would be using, one just down the hall from his own. He wanted the other where he could keep an eye on him at all times. No sooner had Raphael thrown himself down in a chair than Andrew arrived with two goblets. He handed them both to Gabriel.

"I'm assuming he has similar tastes to yours," Andrew said, clearly not wanting to get close to Raphael.

Gabriel nodded. "He does. And as you've guessed he's not entirely learned to control them. See to it that the others give him a wide berth." He drained his own goblet and handed the other to Raphael, who followed suit.

"I'll take my leave of you," Andrew said, bowing and turning to go.

"Wait," Gabriel commanded. "I want to talk to you." He glanced at Raphael. "Settle in, I won't be far away," he told the younger vampire.

Raphael snarled in reply. Gabriel turned and left the room, closing the heavy door behind him.

He and Andrew moved to Gabriel's room, where they talked at length about the happenings at Avignon in the months he had been away. As dawn approached Gabriel yawned. He could tell when Raphael finally stopped pacing his room and fell asleep. He looked longingly at his own bed and felt his eyelids growing heavy.

"There is one other thing you should be aware of," Andrew said.

"What is that?" Gabriel asked.

"Shortly after you left the bishop began to ask questions. I caught him grilling one of the scullery maids one Sunday after services. He passed it off as nothing."

"But you suspect otherwise?" Gabriel asked.

"I do not know," Andrew admitted, shaking his head. "After that he seemed to stop, or at least, he became far more discreet."

"Perhaps I should pay the bishop a visit," Gabriel suggested.

"It would probably be a wise idea, my lord. You could...reassure him...that all is well, especially now that you have returned from the crusade."

"Thank you, Andrew," Gabriel said, permitting himself a rare smile. "I don't know what I'd do without you. Now go, we'll speak more tomorrow night."

Andrew bowed and left the room. Gabriel undressed and finally laid down. He closed his eyes and savored all the familiar feelings of being home before flipping on his side and falling asleep.

At night when he rose he attempted to go about his duties, but every hour he and Andrew were interrupted by something else Raphael had done. First he slaughtered half the pigs Gabriel owned and sent the swineherd running for his life. Then he attempted to escape on Gabriel's own warhorse and Gabriel had to run him down on foot.

Gabriel had finally locked him in the dungeon, but Raphael had escaped and killed another prisoner in the process. Gabriel didn't know if he'd have the patience to control the young vampire for much longer.

And no matter how many times he tried to reason with him, he couldn't dissuade Raphael from his desire to return to his own home in Decazeville. To let him do so would mean the destruction of many. It would be easier to kill him.

It was times like this when he wished he could talk to Paul. His sire would surely have some sage advice on the topic. But he had locked himself up in a monastery years ago and Gabriel had no desire to go seeking him out in that place.

PRAGUE, PRESENT DAY

Gabriel was still staring at Raphael, still weighing what his fate would be. Again he wished he could have the counsel of his own sire but was denied it.

"Why is it I feel like both of you have been keeping things from me?" Susan asked, interrupting his musings. "Secrets? Why are there so many of them? I mean, why couldn't my grandmother just have told me why that cross necklace was special? Now I might never know with that letter stolen. Does one of you know why it's special? My grandmother said the vampire who saved the knight Jean's life knew the secret. I'm sick to death of secrets! I get that our family is connected to this, but what is it you're not telling me?" She was practically shouting at the end.

"We're *all* connected," Gabriel said suddenly.

"I get that, but how?"

"Why don't you tell her what she wants to know?" Raphael demanded, staring at him with eyes filled with hatred.

They would never have the same relationship that he and Paul had shared, Gabriel knew that, but the younger vampire still lacked respect.

"You are not the only one from whom secrets have been kept," Gabriel said to Susan. He glanced at David and then at Raphael.

If it was possible, a look of even more intense hatred flashed across Raphael's face. "It's not your place," he hissed.

"He deserves to know the truth before the end," Gabriel said.

"Me? How could I possibly be connected? I chose to help, but…" David trailed off, looking from one vampire to the other.

Raphael was shaking from head to toe and looked stricken. He was trapped, though, and he clearly knew it. He pulled away from Susan and paced across the room, putting distance between himself and the others.

Finally Raphael cleared his throat. "I killed my entire family when I was a young vampire. It's something that happens often, unfortunately. I wanted to spare Richelieu from the same pain. Before he joined the clergy he sired a child, a daughter. She grew up and had a son of her own by the time I had decided to curse Richelieu. I sent them away and then told him that they had been killed so he'd never go looking for them, never risk harming them. I figured in a few centuries' time when he gained some control over himself I would tell him the truth, help him find his descendants. But, he never came to that point and so I kept his family a secret."

David had gone completely white. "What are you saying?"

Raphael wouldn't look him in the eye. "You are descended from the man, the monster, we're trying to kill. I have kept tabs on you, your entire family, for centuries."

"And you brought me into this fight?" David asked, tight lipped. "On purpose?"

Raphael shook his head sharply. "I hadn't seen you since you were a little boy, when you were very ill once. You were dying. I was standing outside your building in the dark, struggling with what to do, helpless, when a woman came and prayed fervently for you. Her prayers healed you. I haven't seen you since then. I didn't even realize who you were until I heard your name. Then, it just seemed like fate, that you were meant to join in the battle."

Raphael slid his glance over to Susan. "The woman who prayed for David, for his healing, was your grandmother."

Susan sat down abruptly on the couch and after a moment David joined her. "She was always being called to go and pray for people, half the time she didn't even know them," she said in a shaking voice.

Gabriel nodded slowly. "We have all been connected for so long and I believe that Paul would say that God has been planning what's coming since before the world began. It's a strange thing when you begin to learn that there truly are no coincidences in this life."

CHAPTER FIVE

But God forbid that I should glory, save in the cross of our Lord Jesus Christ, by whom the world is crucified unto me, and I unto the world.

—Galatians 6:14

EUROPE, PRESENT DAY

Wendy stood, waiting, heart hammering in her chest, as the door at the top of the stairs opened. She prayed that somehow it was David who had come to rescue her. Her hopes were dashed, though, when a tall, broad figure filled the doorway and slowly descended the stairs.

She sucked in her breath. It was the man who had abducted her outside the cathedral, the one with the long blond hair. He had another tray of food with him. She forced herself to stay put as he set it down on the table. She was relieved, though, that he didn't seem to want to move any closer to her.

She lifted her hand and grasped the cross necklace. It was the only weapon she had that she could use against him. His eyes followed the motion and narrowed to slits.

"Do you know what the hardest thing about being a vampire is?" he asked.

She shook her head.

"Remembering the passage of time."

"I don't understand," she said.

"How could you? You're human, after all."

He folded his arms across his chest and shook his head. "It's easy to forget how much time has passed, how fleeting life is for others. I look at you and my first thought is to ask you why you bleached your hair."

Wendy touched her blond hair self-consciously. "This is my natural color."

"Of course it is. But you look so much like Carissa and her hair was dark."

"Who, who are you?" she gasped.

"I am the Baron—my apologies, that seems a bit formal under the circumstances," he said, interrupting himself. "You may call me Erik."

"How do you know I look like Carissa?" she demanded.

"When you spend weeks chasing someone, you're unlikely to forget them," he said, with a small chuckle.

"You! You're the one Carissa wrote about in her diary. The one sent to kill Carissa when she escaped from prison with Gabriel!" Wendy said, the knowledge seeming to come to her in a flash. For a moment she felt like she was almost there, like she could see him battling Gabriel as Carissa rode away. There was more, bits and flashes of Erik years later, after he was a vampire, hunting, killing.

She pressed her fingertips to her forehead, which had begun to ache. It felt so real, like some sort of vision she was having.

Come to me, a voice seemed to whisper inside her head.

She glanced suspiciously up at Erik, but he was regarding her with a quizzical look.

He inclined his head slowly. "I am the one."

Wendy thought of the unread pages in the diary back in the safe house in Prague, the rest of Carissa's story that was unknown to her. "Did you kill her?" she asked.

"The events you're speaking of happened centuries before you were born. Does it really matter to you who killed her?"

Wendy felt her heart stutter slightly. Although logically she knew that she'd been reading a dead woman's diary, it still saddened her to hear it and sickened her to realize that Carissa had, indeed, been killed.

"Yes, it matters very much to me who killed her," she heard herself saying.

It was probably the wrong thing to say, wrong to admit it to the vampire standing in front of her. But she couldn't help herself. It was the truth.

He narrowed his eyes as he seemed to pierce her very soul with his gaze. "Then I suggest you look no further than Gabriel."

"Gabriel! He can't have killed her," Wendy gasped in despair.

"Those who fall in love with a vampire come to a bad end," he said.

Susan! she thought wildly. Her cousin was falling for Raphael and she didn't know what had happened to Carissa.

No wonder Gabriel terrifies me so much, she thought.

She stared at the vampire in front of her. "What do you want from me?"

He shrugged. "For myself? Nothing."

"Then why am I here?" she asked.

"The man who once sent me to hunt down Carissa asked me to bring you to him."

"I-I don't understand," Wendy stammered. "How is that possible?"

"Pierre, her husband?" the Baron said, with a lifted eyebrow.

Pierre, the lawyer from Prague whose name she'd found on the letter across the room. She felt sick to her stomach as she realized the truth.

"But, but when, how did he become a vampire?" she asked.

"Ah, that was Gabriel's doing as well. It seems you do not know your ally as well as you should."

She sucked in her breath and took a gamble. "Maybe you don't know yours either. He wants to destroy the world."

The Baron shook his head. "Pierre may be a monster, but he is not insane. We want nothing to do with the lunatic Richelieu."

Wendy gripped the edge of the table, prepared to seize her chance. "Then help us fight him, help us stop him."

"The enemy of my enemy?" he asked, a smile twisting his lips.

"Something like that."

"It rarely works with nations, even less rarely among people," he said.

"But it would be far better to be my friend, *our* friend, when the others come for me."

"And where will they be looking for you?" the Baron asked. "You are not even in the same country that you were."

Fear flared in her. She knew she'd been unconscious for a long time, but just how long? How far had they gotten?

"Help me, please," she whispered.

His smile faded. "You are not the first to ask for my help."

She felt the faintest stirrings of hope. "Will you give it?" she asked after what seemed an eternity of silence on his part.

"Not today," he said, very quietly. Then he turned and walked back up the stairs, closing and locking the door behind him.

Wendy sat down abruptly before her knees could give way and realized she was still gripping the cross. Wrong, all of this was wrong. She should still be safely home in California. Susan was the hero, not her.

"God, I can't do this," she moaned before sinking her head onto the table. She sat that way for a few minutes as the terror worked its way through her system.

Finally she realized she could smell bacon. Eagerly she turned her attention to the tray of food. Eggs, bacon, and toast greeted her when she lifted the lid. Apparently, even though she believed it was nighttime, it was breakfast time as far as the vampires were concerned.

She quickly ate her food, half expecting Pierre to show up at any moment. She had met him in the cathedral; he had been the one who had looked at her so strangely. Even without knowing what he had done to Carissa he would have terrified her.

She finished eating and sat waiting a few more minutes. Maybe he wouldn't be paying her a visit, at least not yet. Her eyes flitted over to her mattress. There was no way she was going to sleep even though she was getting tired.

She'd sleep when she was sure they were asleep. She just hoped she could trust her body to tell her when it was day.

Until then, she had more reading to catch up on. She'd have to be careful, though. The last thing she wanted was to be caught with the papers.

FRANCE, 1149 AD

Jean couldn't help but smile at the excitement on Marie's face as their carriage pulled up outside the Château de Vincennes. They had been married a month and if possible she grew only more beautiful by the hour. When the news had come that the king had returned to France and requested their presence at the château she had clapped her hands like a child.

He had told her how it was that the king had made him a marquis. He hadn't told her, though, about the relic in his possession. It was a decision he had wrestled long and hard with, but he had ultimately decided she was safer not knowing. To the best of his knowledge only Lord Avignon knew he had it and he wanted to keep it that way. The piece was now safely concealed.

The carriage rolled to a stop and a liveried servant helped them out. Marie's eyes widened as she took in her surroundings. The château was a hunting lodge in the forest of Vincennes. It was humble by royal standards but far above and beyond anything either of them had ever before seen.

They were escorted to their rooms and servants immediately began to unpack their bags. The man who led them inside turned to Jean. "Milady has more than enough time to refresh herself before dinner. I was asked to escort you to a meeting once you had arrived."

Jean glanced at Marie and she waved him away with a smile. He nodded and followed the servant, who led him deeper into the château and eventually stopped before a closed door. "You are to go in," the servant said, before bowing and taking his leave.

Curious, Jean opened the door and stepped inside. Several men wearing white mantles who were seated before a fire stood up and greeted him by name. He recognized them from the battlefields. One, Bernard de Tramelay, strode forward and embraced him.

"Jean, how have you been?"

"Well, although I confess I am surprised to see Templars so far from Jerusalem."

Bernard laughed and clapped him on the back. "Unfortunately not all battlefields are in the Holy Land."

Jean smiled.

"We wanted a chance to speak with you for a few minutes. We wanted to invite you to join our order."

Jean stared at him for a moment before slowly shaking his head. "I'm married."

"Marie?"

"Yes."

"Congratulations! That is great news."

"Thank you. It does, however, present an insurmountable obstacle."

Bernard exchanged a look with the other knights. "Not entirely. We are a monastic order, yes, but in rare instances we do invite married men to join us."

"Provided their wives agree," one of the other knights added.

Jean wasn't sure why but something did not feel right to him. He had fought beside Templars, seen them on and off the battlefield, and they were fierce fighters and loyal companions who feared God. Had he not been in love with Marie he would have long before joined them. Something about their demeanor now troubled him, though. They wanted something from him, he could sense it. Why else would they be willing to make an exception?

"I will have to discuss it with my wife then," Jean said, being careful to smile when he said it.

He left a couple of minutes later and rejoined Marie in time for the evening festivities. After a magnificent feast the grand hall was cleared for a ball and musicians began to play. Jean watched as the dancing began. Women in brightly colored gowns paraded around the room on the arms of swaggering men. At the far end of the hall the Templar knights observed but did not participate in the frivolity. King Louis sat upon his throne above the crowd watching and laughing.

He took Marie's hand and began to escort her onto the dance floor. A couple moved out of their path and Jean found himself suddenly face-to-face with Lord Avignon. Jean felt his heart plummet and for one terrible moment he was sure that the monster had come for him.

"Lord Avignon," Jean managed to say.

"Marquis. Please call me Gabriel. You are looking well, much better than the last time I saw you," Gabriel said.

His tone was pleasant enough but Jean saw the dark look in his eyes and knew that his life hung by a thread. He smiled. "And you look very much the same. Although I must confess I am glad to see that you have gotten rid of that protégé of yours."

The corners of Gabriel's mouth turned up briefly. "Not quite, but he is ill-mannered and would be a nuisance at an affair such as this."

"This is my wife, Marie," Jean said, introducing her. "I took your advice; I came straight home and married her."

"Ah, I have heard lovely things about you," Gabriel said, kissing her hand.

Jean stiffened but knew there was nothing he could do to stop him.

"I am afraid, sir, that you have me at a loss," Marie said with a glance at Jean.

"I am sorry, my dear. This is the Count of Avignon."

Marie curtsied.

"You may call me Gabriel, dear woman."

Gabriel turned his eyes back to Jean. "I see he has never managed to give you back your cross."

Marie smiled. "I wished him to keep it and wear it always. He said it saved his life just as I hoped it would."

"Indeed, it did," Gabriel said, amusement creeping into his eyes. "Did he tell you how exactly?"

"No."

"Well, then maybe someday I will tell you that story."

"I should very much like to hear it."

"Another time then."

"Have a good evening," Jean said, guiding Marie away from Gabriel and breathing a sigh of relief when they had put some distance between them. It was only then that he realized that he had been holding the cross tightly in his left hand.

"He frightens me," Marie confessed a moment later.

"He is not a man to be trifled with and I would not call him a friend. However, try to think more favorably of him. The man saved my life."

"Then I shall keep him in my prayers tonight."

Jean smiled and fought back the urge to laugh.

He watched Gabriel carefully, but the monster seemed far more interested in staring at a bishop who had just been talking with the king.

The music stopped suddenly and they turned to see that the king had risen from his throne. "I have asked you all here on this very special occasion to join me in celebrating a mighty victory for France. We have rescued a great treasure from the Holy Land." An aide stepped forward and handed the king a pillow on top of which rested a small, dark object.

"Behold! A holy relic of our Lord."

Gasps rose around the room and people slowly began to sink to their knees in reverence. Jean looked across the room and his eyes found Gabriel's. The creature moved his index finger to point at Jean, a question in his eyes. Jean shook his head slowly and then returned the gesture. Gabriel shook his head as well. They both turned back to look and joined the last few people in the room in sinking to their knees.

Jean's thoughts raced as he bowed his head. It wasn't the true relic. Surely the king must know that. Why the charade then? Once again he reached up and his hand closed over the cross around his neck.

"Jean, the Marquis de Bryas, found this in Jerusalem. It was sent back here to France, but on the way the knight who carried it was captured, tortured, and killed by infidels."

Horrified murmuring arose around the hall. Once again Jean glanced at Gabriel and noticed that the count looked just as confused as he was.

"Praise be to God, though," the king continued. "A group of Templar knights happened upon them, ascertained what they had done, and retrieved this most sacred item. They killed the infidels who dared to touch it."

Cheers went up around the room as all attention shifted to the small group of Templar knights who had positioned themselves close to the king. Jean found Bernard's eyes and the knight smiled at him.

Jean shifted his eyes to the king, who was smiling as well, basking in the glory of the moment. It was a lie, and the Templars knew it. And so did the king.

"Darling, are you ill?" Marie asked so suddenly that he jumped.

"Sorry, dear, I am just tired."

"You are exhausted from the journey," Marie said.

"Yes, I am sure that is it," Jean said, forcing himself to smile as he took her hand.

He was very grateful she was by his side. He was also grateful that the true relics were safely hidden. At least, the one he kept secret was.

EUROPE, PRESENT DAY

Wendy dropped the pages in her lap and stared into space. She remembered Susan had told her about the letter from their grandmother and the letter from Jean to Carissa: Both had been stolen from Susan at the airport. Their grandmother's letter had said that the cross necklace she was handing down held a great secret. She'd meant for the truth to be read in Jean's letter, but Susan hadn't been able to read the French.

Their grandmother had also said that the vampire who'd saved Jean's life knew the secret. She hadn't thought about it before, but she had to be referencing Gabriel since he had saved Jean from Raphael. All this time Gabriel knew what they had been trying to figure out about the cross she was wearing around her neck.

Wendy reached up to grasp it again. A key chain of Susan's supposedly held the key to unlocking the cross and its secret, but they hadn't had a chance to work on it. She continued to stroke the cross as she thought about everything she knew about it and everything she'd been told. Susan had thought Pierre was awfully keen to see the cross and she had managed to hide its whereabouts from him until he saw Wendy wearing it in the cathedral the night before.

In the club where Susan and Raphael had first rescued Wendy from a vampire, Susan had killed the vampire by touching the cross to it. Wendy knew that crosses were supposed to burn vampires, not incinerate them. What made this one so different, so special? It couldn't just be its age. It had to have something to do with the secret, whatever it was.

She thought of what she'd just read about Jean and his time in the crusade and his encounters with Gabriel. Apparently he had discovered two relics in the mosque, one of which he had concealed. He hadn't given dimensions for the box that housed the relics, but she had the impression it was small.

What had he done with the second relic? Was it possible that whatever it was he had concealed it inside the cross necklace itself?

She glanced down at it. The necklace wasn't tiny, but

neither was it enormous. If there truly was something hidden inside it would have to be very, very small.

Frustrated, she picked up the papers and shuffled to the next one. She realized with panic that it was the last piece of paper. She prayed it gave her the clue she needed. The first thing she noted about it was the date. It had been written several years after the rest.

I buried my Marie today and my heart has broken. She was everything to me and I do not know how I will carry on without her. I nearly buried the necklace with her, but I couldn't extinguish the tiny flicker of hope within me. And I cannot shake the feeling that someday the necklace will help save my beloved child, my Carissa's life.

FRANCE, 1185 AD

Jean hadn't written his thoughts down in years. He had been too busy most days to think, let alone write. But the days had been happy up until the very end. Now he sat at his desk and thought about his wife, and her death, and wondered what the future had in store for any of them.

Carissa had fallen asleep in her bed hours earlier, crying in his arms. He had finally left her. Carissa was his treasure, his gift that God had bestowed upon him and Marie in their old age. She had come as a complete surprise and they had thanked God every day for her. God had granted both Marie and him long, full lives, more than they could have ever dared hope. He had often wondered if it was because it was his task to be the steward of the relic until he could find another to entrust it to.

He fingered the cross around his neck. At the end he couldn't bury it with Marie. The relic, the treasure hidden inside, belonged to more than just him. The trouble was, he had never found a way to ensure that the right people got control of it.

With all the political unrest he had finally decided to hold on to it, as a bargaining chip if nothing else. What he had would be greatly desired by kings and knights, popes and bishops. Things were happening that made him uneasy. A storm seemed to be coming; evil was brewing in France and he feared for the safety of all when it struck.

Religious fervor was running high, but somehow there was a hard, frightening edge to much of it. Accusations had been made against some of heresy. These things troubled him, but not so much as the actions of the accusers.

No, it was best to hold on to his relic, for the day might come when he would need it. He thought of his daughter, lying asleep upstairs, still so young and innocent despite her sorrow. Someday she might have need of the necklace and so he must keep it safe for her sake.

She was too young still to tell her the secret, the secret he had never even shared with Marie. But could he risk something happening to him and the secret being lost forever?

With a heavy heart he picked up his quill and began to write on a second parchment, this one a letter to his daughter. He told her the entire story of the finding of the relic, of how he had hidden it, and how she might access it. And when he had finished he took the paper, rolled it tightly, and sealed it inside the hollow opening in the right front leg of his writing desk where he had concealed the pages he had written while he was in the Holy Land.

When he was done pouring out his feelings for Marie he would seal away that parchment, too. Before he died he would need to tell Carissa about the hollow leg. But, if he never could, he was sure she would discover it for herself when she became lady of the castle and settled herself at the desk to take care of the affairs of running the estate.

Hopefully by that time she'd be married with children of her own. He smiled at the thought. A sudden sound startled him and he glanced up. There in the doorway was a tiny figure. For a moment he thought it was his daughter but then realized that it was too small.

He hastily screwed the leg back into the table and then waved the child forward. The little girl was barely four and she stared at him with great, tearful eyes.

"What's wrong, Fleur?" he asked his grand-niece. She and her parents lived at the castle. In the end his brother had indeed married Marie's sister. Both of them had gone to be with God many years before, though. Their son had eventually taken a wife, and Fleur was their daughter, only slightly younger than his own Carissa.

"Mommy won't stop crying and Daddy won't tell me why," she said.

"Come sit with me," he said.

Fleur scrambled up onto his lap and he held her close.

"What's wrong with your desk?" she asked.

He winced, wondering how much she had seen. "Nothing, I just thought I saw an insect and I was swatting at it," he lied.

She nodded, apparently satisfied, and a minute later she was fast asleep.

CHAPTER SIX

He saved others; himself he cannot save. If he be the King of Israel, let him now come down from the cross, and we will believe him.

—Matthew 27:42

PRAGUE, PRESENT DAY

David felt like he was going to be sick. He turned and glared at Raphael. "You knew that Richelieu was my many times great-grandfather and you never said a word?"

"I wasn't sure you would want to know," Raphael said, face inscrutable.

Rage poured through David's veins. "When you recruit a guy to kill his own ancestor, then, yeah, that's something you should share."

He buried his head in his hands. It was too much. All of it.

"I'm so sorry," he heard Susan whisper.

And somehow, knowing everything she had gone through and everything she had lost, to hear her tell him how sorry she was just made it that much worse.

He couldn't think about any of this right now, let alone begin to deal with it. There were bigger, more important things that had to be dealt with first.

"Richelieu still needs to be stopped," he said, lifting

his head to look at the others. "But we are going to find Wendy first," David continued, hearing the way his own voice had risen to a shout.

Gabriel nodded. "Print out a copy for me of that list, I'll find her."

"Not without me," David said grimly. "I'm going with you."

"I can travel faster alone."

"But you'll need someone who can keep fighting when the sun rises."

And the truth was he didn't trust Gabriel to bring Wendy back. Saving her wasn't his first priority. Stopping Richelieu was. David was going with him to make sure they searched under every rock until Pierre, Erik, and Wendy had been found.

Gabriel gazed intently at him and David stared back defiantly, not caring if the vampire could read his thoughts. At long last the other gave a short nod.

"What about Richelieu and the relics?" Susan asked quietly.

Everyone turned to look at her. She was pale and looked like she was on the verge of losing it any moment, but her fists were clenched at her sides and she was holding her head high.

"I want Wendy back more than anyone," she continued. "But shouldn't we be trying to figure out what Richelieu is going to do next? Is he going to hunt us down looking for the sudarium or is he going to be going after some other artifact now? We still can't let him take the blood of Christ into himself, right?"

There was silence for a moment. Gabriel finally broke it. "We have no way of knowing if he's still in the city and what artifact he might target next, if any. It's possible that he was only planning on going after the sudarium and now he has to rethink his entire plan. Since we can't guess what he's going to do next, the best thing we can do is try to find Wendy while she may still be alive."

While she may still be alive. The words cut David to his very core.

"We still don't know what his plans are," Raphael said quietly, "or if we have hours or weeks before he sets everything in motion. Gabriel is right. If Wendy can be found quickly then that is a good use of time. Besides, Pierre might know more about Richelieu's plans than we do and finding him and interrogating him is not a bad idea. I can stay here and continue to search for Richelieu."

"It's settled then," Gabriel said.

Five minutes later David and Gabriel left. Raphael half wished that Susan would have gone with them. It may have been safer than for her to be here in the city when Richelieu knew who she was.

There was nothing he could do about that, though, except try to find Richelieu before he found them. One way or another he felt in his bones that things were about to come to an end.

He turned and glanced at Susan, who was still standing, staring at the closed door. He could smell her fear, feel the anxiety she had for her cousin. He wished there was something he could say to ease her suffering, but he didn't even know if Wendy was alive or dead. Every little while he tried reaching out to Wendy with his thoughts, summoning her to him, since he had never released her from his mesmerism. Even if a distance did separate them, she should be able to hear him and be compelled to come to him if she was able. He just wished he could hear her thoughts so he'd know where she was.

"You're exhausted, you need to get some sleep," Raphael said softly to Susan.

She turned large, dazed eyes on him. "I don't want to sleep. I just want to know what to do. I feel helpless and I hate that. I can't help Wendy, I can't find Richelieu. I can't even use this to figure out what's so special about that cross," she said, holding up a key chain that she had pulled from her pocket.

"What is that?" he asked.

"I don't know!" she wailed. "But apparently it holds some way to unlock the cross or something and reveal whatever secret it has." Tears began to streak down her face. "Too many secrets," she whispered.

Raphael reached out and folded her into his arms. He held her as she cried and he could feel the front of his shirt being drenched with her tears. He could smell the salt in them mingling with the scent of her skin. Next to his chest he could feel her heart beating, strong and fast. She might feel like her heart was breaking, but it had never sounded more powerful to him.

He closed his eyes and rested his chin on the crown of her head. She had been through so much and all he wanted was to take away the pain, but he didn't know how. He knew so much about pain—how to give it, how to withstand it—but not how to take it away.

Finally her crying stopped and she pulled back slightly. He looked down at her and even with her swollen eyes and tear-stained face she was the most beautiful thing he had ever seen.

He bent down and kissed her before he could think about it, before he could stop himself. And after a moment she kissed him back. Her hands moved up and twisted in his hair and her kisses became more intense, more desperate, like she was trying to lose herself in the kiss.

More like escape her own fear and pain, he realized.

He should put a stop to it. He knew he should. Before one of them did something they'd both regret. But nothing in him wanted to stop because he could feel her in his arms, so warm, so passionate, so alive. And he had been so afraid for her, too, ever since everything that had happened in France.

He wrapped his arms around her tight and kissed her harder. A buzzing began in his head, though, and he remembered their last true kiss, one shared with the taste of her blood in his mouth. And as much as he wanted her, he wanted her blood even more.

He pulled away and she said nothing, just looked so sad and lost that it made him ache deep inside. He had to get away from her and clear his head.

"I'm going out, see if I can't find Richelieu's new hiding place," he told her.

She didn't say a word, just watched him go.

Raphael was gone for hours, leaving Susan alone with her own tortured thoughts. She spent time praying for Wendy and for Paul. She sat vigil for a while next to the monk and talked to him, but he seemed even worse to her.

A dozen times she picked up Carissa's diary and berated herself for not having taken French in school. She knew that the parchment papers stuffed into the diary marked the place where Carissa had stopped writing in the diary and her cousin Fleur had begun. Wendy had read everything Carissa had written through the first part of the book and the parchment sections she'd written after she had been imprisoned. They had not yet read anything, though, of Fleur's thoughts upon discovering her cousin was missing.

She needed to know how the story ended for all of them. If she asked, Gabriel would just tell her to keep reading, she was sure of it. He was the one who had given her the diary in the first place. Was his reluctance because something had happened that was too painful for him to talk about? He revealed so little emotion, it was hard to guess his motives.

Everything, everyone, they were all connected. That's what Gabriel had said. The more she learned the more she believed it to be true. Perhaps Fleur's part of the journal held a missing piece of the puzzle somehow.

She finally went and spent some time at the computer, too upset to sleep. She wished she knew what she was looking for, though. She had no idea where Richelieu would be, but she felt sure he was still nearby. She was also sure he'd be looking equally hard for them and the sudarium that they had kept him from stealing.

She looked up the location of relics that Raphael and Gabriel had not had time to go and check on. Then she ran Internet news searches related to the churches that housed them looking for any stories of break-ins or other odd events that might signal a relic had been stolen. She didn't find anything that seemed promising.

She then did searches on different things related to Prague, including churches and other places considered to be holy. She was dealing with a vampire with a messianic obsession and she couldn't afford to overlook anything.

Again she came up empty and her frustration built. How was she supposed to help fight a war when she couldn't even figure out what the enemy was planning? She checked on the sudarium half a dozen times, her own paranoia getting the better of her in a house that creaked and groaned and kept her on edge.

When Raphael finally returned there was at least an hour left before dawn. He looked grim and haggard and she could tell without asking that he hadn't found anything.

"Is there anything I can do?" she asked.

He shook his head. "Anything I can do for you?"

An idea came to her and she sprang up from her chair and crossed to the coffee table. "Yes, actually. You can translate this for me. I can't read the French," she said, picking up the diary.

He hesitated. "What is that?"

"A diary, used by both Carissa and Fleur."

"Gabriel would not want me reading Carissa's innermost thoughts."

"This section seems to be written by Fleur. I don't know what happened to Carissa after she and Gabriel parted ways when the Baron attacked. All I know is that she was on her way to Bryas to confront her husband, Pierre. But Carissa left this journal behind on her wedding night, before she met Gabriel. Fleur wouldn't have known anything about him."

Raphael's lips tightened.

"If they're Fleur's words, thoughts, surely you can read them," Susan said, feeling desperate. "She was Carissa's cousin, my ancestor. Please, I have to know."

She held out the diary, opened to the right page. He still

looked agitated, but finally he sat and gently accepted the ancient book. "Okay, for you," he said.

"Thank you," she whispered, and sat down next to him on the couch. She had an almost uncontrollable urge to lean against his shoulder but forced herself not to touch him. That way led only to danger.

He glanced at the page and then began to read: "'God help me, something has happened to my cousin Carissa. It has been three days since her wedding and no one here at the palace has seen her or Pierre since. She would not have left without saying something to me. I fear that something terrible has happened to her. I will ask Étienne for help in finding out the truth.'"

FRANCE, 1198 AD

Fleur was sick with fear. It had been three days since Carissa's wedding. Not only had she not heard from her cousin since the wedding banquet but no one in the palace seemed to have seen either Carissa or Pierre since then.

She had been eager to discuss things with her cousin, particularly the growing feelings she felt for the knight, Étienne, whom she had been spending so much time with since their arrival at the palace. He was loyal and passionate and kept proclaiming his feelings for her at every opportunity. When she caught the merest glimpse of him she was happy. When she was with him her heart would sing. She was eager to tell Carissa, but her eagerness soon turned to fear and worry.

On the third day, when she met Étienne in the garden for their daily rendezvous, she had decided to ask for his help, but before she could even get a word out she began to cry. He stood there, face flushed with anger.

"My lady, is there a wrong that has been done to you? I told you, I am yours. What can I do? Who shall answer for your pain?"

She dried her tears quickly. "I hope that there is none to be punished but that my fears may be placated in another way."

"Say the word, I will undertake any quest for your sake."

"My cousin, she is nowhere to be found."

He relaxed visibly. "Perhaps she has returned home."

Fleur shook her head. "We had not planned to depart until Monday. She would not have gone without saying a word; I was meant to travel back to Bryas with her."

"Marriage has a strange effect on some. Perhaps she and her groom needed to be alone."

Fleur shook her head. "Then someone would have seen them go."

"Not if they left under cover of darkness."

Fleur sighed. "All of her clothes, all of her possessions are still in the rooms we shared before her wedding night."

That brought Étienne up short and he stared at her with a puzzled expression. "All of them?"

She nodded and watched as his face hardened. "I will help you search and we shall discover what has happened to her. I promise you that if it is within my power you shall be reunited."

Fleur believed him, but she had a terrible feeling that they were already too late to aid Carissa.

The afternoon passed and the evening and Fleur retired to bed early, still sick with worry. It was the middle of the night when a voice spoke to her.

"Milady, please wake up."

Fleur sat up, startled to find a maid hovering by her bed. Behind the woman Fleur could see through the window, it was still dark outside.

The maid held a candle that she used to light the one on the table near the bed.

"What is it?" Fleur asked.

"A certain young gentleman sent me straight here, claimed it was an urgent matter," the maid said with a sly look.

In a moment Fleur was out of bed. "What did he say?"

"That if you want to have some of your questions answered, you'll meet him in the courtyard as fast as you can dress."

"Help me," Fleur commanded, flying to grab her clothes.

Fifteen minutes later she was standing in the cold and the dark, watching as a carriage drew up and two men she recognized as Carissa's drivers approached it.

"Pierre is leaving for Bryas," a voice said in her ear.

She jumped and turned to see Étienne, his face grave. "And what of my cousin? That is her carriage, her horses, even her drivers."

He shook his head. "Of her I've heard not a word."

A man strode forward from the palace and Fleur recognized him as Pierre. Before she could even think about it, she was running toward him. "Sir!" she called when he arrived at the carriage a hair before her.

He turned and a look of annoyance crossed his face.

A thousand questions crowded Fleur's mind, but only one was important. "I have been searching for several days for my cousin, your wife, and have not found her. Do you know where she is?"

"In hell."

Fleur gripped the door of the carriage to steady herself. She glanced up at the two drivers and they turned their faces from her. "What do you mean?"

"I mean this: Your cousin was a witch. Out of respect for any family she had left, her execution was a private one. She's dead. Now, unless you wish to draw suspicion upon yourself as well, you will put the wicked wretch from your mind and concern yourself with the destination of your soul."

Fleur was stunned, barely able to comprehend what he was saying. Dead? Carissa? She couldn't be. The witch part was ridiculous and she couldn't even begin to fathom what kind of cruel joke this man was playing on her.

She stood there, staring dumbly at him, a thousand thoughts colliding in her mind.

And then she felt a hand on her elbow.

"My lady, let me escort you back inside," Étienne said.

Fleur turned to him. "It's a lie," she whispered.

He nodded so slightly that she wasn't sure she had even seen it. "We should do as the magistrate says."

Pierre took to the carriage. He leaned his head back out and called up to one of the drivers, "What about the other horse that arrived with you, the mare?"

Fleur turned. "She is my horse, Dancer." She glared at the two servants, daring them to contradict her. They said nothing. For a moment Pierre hesitated and then shrugged.

"Drive on," he called. A moment later the carriage rolled away, leaving her and Étienne standing alone.

She had lied about the horse but she didn't feel guilty. Carissa would never have wanted Pierre to have the mare, and if he had killed her cousin then she would not permit him to have the horse that Carissa had loved. She felt tears stinging her eyes. "She can't be dead."

Étienne shook his head. "Something sinister has happened, but just what I do not know. I do know that you need to avoid Pierre lest you share her fate. He is a powerful man."

"I do not believe she is dead," Fleur said, taking a ragged breath. "I should speak with the king."

Étienne shook his head fiercely. "Who do you think he will believe? Even the king would not move against a magistrate of the Inquisition without proof."

"How will we find such proof?"

"I undertook this quest for you and I will not stop now. If she is alive we will find her. And if she is dead we will do what we can to seek justice."

Days later Fleur sat on one of the stone benches in the gardens and waited. It seemed like her life was spent waiting. She didn't know what to do. She did know that she couldn't keep idle much longer. She heard footsteps and she stood up hastily but was disappointed to see a young couple strolling nearby. She sat back down, closed her eyes, and prayed to find Carissa. So fervently did she pray that she didn't realize Étienne had arrived until he sat down next to her.

She opened her eyes and studied his face. "Well?" she asked.

"My uncle will arrive at the palace in five days. We can speak with him then."

It seemed so long to wait but she nodded her head. If he couldn't help then she had no idea what they would do next.

"Thank you, Étienne, you have been so kind."

"It is not kindness that motivates me," he said.

"Do you remember when we stood in this very garden the first night we met?" she asked.

"Sorrow has made it seem long ago but my feelings have only grown deeper," he said.

She smiled at him. She had needed no proof of his love other than his word. Her eyes dropped to the stone bench. Their hands were close, almost touching. It would be improper to touch and, depending on who saw, it could prove dangerous as well.

He shifted his hand ever so slightly. The very tip of his index finger touched the very tip of hers. She looked up at him but he was looking out across the gardens. She followed his gaze. It was a beautiful vista. If all she could do was wait there were worse places to do so and she let herself for a moment enjoy his barely felt touch. She prayed that if Carissa lived that she, too, could find some small measure of comfort.

When he finally arrived at the palace, Fleur couldn't help but like Étienne's uncle, Marcus de Molay. With his dark, wavy hair, straight nose, and brown eyes he looked like an older version of Étienne. The man was warm and sympathetic and she found it hard to believe he was actually a magistrate. He listened carefully while they explained everything that had happened.

"I have heard nothing of this," he confessed at last. "A couple of magistrates do live nearby, though, and it would have been an easy thing for Pierre to call them to a secret trial." He sighed deeply. "I do not like the way things are," he confessed. "I should not say that aloud, but it is true."

"Do you think Carissa is dead?" Étienne asked.

Fleur leaned forward, holding her breath, as she waited for the answer.

"Well, normally the Inquisition likes public executions because they serve as a warning to others."

"Could he have had her executed privately?" Fleur asked.

"Not without the other magistrates agreeing to it, which they might have if he had provided a compelling reason. Still, it seems unlikely to me."

"Then where is she?" Fleur asked.

A sudden light dawned in the older man's eyes. "I think I might know. I must warn you, though, if my suspicions are correct she very well may be dead already."

"We must take that risk," Étienne said.

"There is a prison a day's journey from here. It houses every manner of criminal and heretic. If he accused her as a witch but did not have her executed, she would be there."

"Then there I will go," Étienne said, rising to his feet.

"There is more." He looked uncomfortable and the words seemed to come with effort. "There is a prisoner there who is…unnatural. Sometimes, if they do not want someone to be found, they put him in the cell with that other prisoner."

"Why?" Fleur asked.

"He kills them. It allows the men who so ordered it to go home and sleep in peace, telling themselves they had naught to do with the death."

"Then we must go now," Fleur said, standing to join Étienne.

"It is not a journey nor a place I would recommend for a woman," Marcus said.

"If my cousin is there, she will need to see a face that she knows. I must make the journey. I cannot continue to sit here and wait for news," Fleur said.

Marcus chuckled. "I like your spirit," he said. "That is doubtless one of the reasons my nephew admires you."

Even through her haze of fear and anxiety, Fleur still managed to blush. She took her leave of them and hurried to her room, where she bundled up a couple of things she might need, including a dress for Carissa.

Half an hour later she met Étienne at the stables. He had saddled Dancer and his own horse and held them both at the ready.

"Are you sure about this?" he asked as she tied her bundle onto Dancer's saddle with shaking hands.

"Yes," she lied. Just touching the gentle mare was making her tremble. All the years she had been afraid of horses stretched behind her and a long, torturous road stretched before.

"You and I, we are going to save your mistress," she whispered to the mare. "I cannot do it without your help."

The horse nickered softly, and, only slightly reassured, Fleur accepted Étienne's help into the saddle. Étienne mounted his own horse. She took a deep breath. What she was about to do, there was no turning back. She knew that she should not be leaving the palace without a chaperone, but she couldn't risk telling anyone else her plan or brook delay.

"If you get into trouble, let me know," Étienne instructed, his eyes doubtful.

She forced a smile. It had to be obvious that she knew very little about horses. "I will," she reassured him.

"Good, now let us go get your cousin."

His horse lurched forward and Dancer followed suit. Fleur let out a little shriek and held on for dear life.

The ride was interminable and a couple of hours later Fleur's bones felt like they had all been jarred loose when Dancer jumped a small tree that had fallen across the road. She let out a whimper and beside her Étienne twisted in his saddle.

"Do you need to stop?" he called.

She shook her head grimly. "I just need to get there!"

Something terrible was about to happen, she could feel it. She wanted to tell him, to explain, but there was no time. From the way he urged both of their horses faster, though, she wondered if he already knew.

Even at the increased rate of speed it was hours before they saw the gray building looming on the landscape. Forgetting all her fears and sore muscles, Fleur urged Dancer into a gallop and only reined in the horse when they were in front of the massive gate.

"Ho within! Open the gate," Étienne called.

"What business have you here?" a sentry called.

"We are here with a message for the warden."

A few seconds later the gate began to rise. They rode slowly in and it was closed behind them.

"The warden is occupied but I can take you somewhere to rest and wait for him," the guard said.

"Very well," Étienne assented, "but let him know that it is an urgent matter."

As Étienne helped her dismount Fleur could feel evil coming from within the prison and she didn't want to step inside.

Ahead of them some other horses were being attended to. "Someone else has arrived tonight," Étienne said.

Fleur looked over the horses and then stiffened. She made a soft hissing noise.

"What is it?"

"The horse nearest us, it belongs to Carissa, to her family. It is one of their fastest horses."

"Pierre must be here," Étienne said.

"I pray we are not too late," Fleur said.

To her relief, they were escorted to the warden's private quarters and the door was closed behind them. She paced back and forth, wondering what Pierre was doing there. Étienne looked equally worried but they both agreed that showing themselves could result in a fight at the very least and their execution at worst. Finally Étienne stole out of the room to try to find out what was going on.

After a while Étienne returned with a tired-looking man he introduced as the warden Marcelle.

"Prisoners have escaped," Étienne said.

"Was one of them the lady Carissa?" Fleur asked swiftly. "Please tell me. She's my cousin, falsely accused by that monster, Pierre."

"I had feared as much," the warden said heavily. "She did indeed escape with her cellmate tonight. But that doesn't mean she's safe. She was locked in with a monster, a demon."

Fleur's heart skipped. It was as Étienne's uncle had said.

"You have no idea where they are heading?" Étienne asked.

"There's no way to know."

"And they may have separated," Étienne added.

"If he hasn't killed her," Marcelle said.

"I believe that God has seen her this far and that He will

continue to protect her," Fleur said. "Where they would go, I do not know. I know she would want to go home."

"But she would believe that Pierre might be there," Étienne added.

"What about the palace, to try to speak with the king?" she asked.

"She might, but it's just as likely that the demon has convinced her that no one will believe her story," Marcelle said.

"Will they?" Fleur asked bluntly. "Or will the king just send her back here?"

Both men were at a loss to answer her.

Marcelle sighed heavily. "If I was running, though, I'd not stop until I knew no one was following me."

Fleur shook her head. "So, we know nothing. How will we find them?"

Marcelle cleared his throat. "The magistrate has sent another one of the prisoners to hunt them down."

For a moment Fleur felt faint, but she took deep breaths to clear her head. "What do we do?"

"We follow him," Étienne replied.

CHAPTER SEVEN

And he that taketh not his cross, and fol-
loweth after me, is not worthy of me.
—Matthew 10:38

R aphael looked up with a pained expression.

"What's wrong?" Susan was quick to ask as she studied his face intently.

He shook his head. "He told me, recently, that he had been imprisoned. But for years I thought he had abandoned me."

She reached out and put a hand on his arm. It still unnerved her. He wasn't hot or cold, he was just there, the same temperature as his surroundings.

He was gazing off into the distance and his lips curled, revealing his fangs. She wanted to know more. There was so much about his life that he hadn't shared with her.

"What happened?" she asked.

He hunched his shoulders and when he turned to look at her his eyes seemed to be glowing.

"You mean after I left his castle in Avignon and slaughtered my entire family? My entire village?"

She forced herself not to flinch under his gaze even though she could feel his anger. "Yes."

He turned away from her. "I went to Africa. I found a tribe there I could bend to my will. They treated me as a god, sacrificing their blood and their lives to me. And I reveled in every unholy moment of it until he found me."

"Who?" Susan asked, guessing he couldn't be referring to Gabriel.

"Paul," Raphael said, casting his eyes toward the ceiling for a moment. "He introduced himself as my grand-sire."

"Then what happened?" Susan asked.

"He showed me that I was not a god." Raphael shuddered as though reliving some terrible moment. "He set me on fire. I thought I was going to burn to death, but at the last moment, he saved me."

He glanced toward the stairs. "He was always more of a sire to me than Gabriel and now he's lying up there burned and lingering somewhere between life and death and there's nothing I can do to save him."

He turned back and she noticed with a start that blood tears were streaking their way down his cheeks.

"I'm sorry," she whispered.

"So am I," he said, wiping at the tears. He cleared his throat. "Let's see how Fleur and Étienne are getting on."

Susan bit her lip but didn't say anything as he picked the book back up and found his place. "'It seemed we traveled forever, pushing our horses and ourselves as hard as we could. We eventually found an inn where the others had been seen and we continued on without ever dismounting. When we finally reached a monastery we knew we had to rest and to change our horses if we could. We never dreamed who we would find there, almost as though he were waiting for us.'"

Fleur practically fell from her horse when they stopped in front of a monk outside a monastery. Étienne dismounted and gave her the support of his arm. She blushed at the contact but gratefully leaned on it.

"You are far from home," the monk observed with quiet humor.

"I am," Fleur admitted.

"I am Brother Paul. You remind me of someone I met recently, a very beautiful lady, great of spirit. Like you, there was sorrow upon her."

Fleur felt her heart begin to race. "I have traveled far seeking such a lady, my cousin." She stopped, not sure how much she should say.

"The lady I knew told me she had a cousin, sweet as a flower and just as wild."

Fleur couldn't contain her joy. "Then surely your lady is my cousin. I am Fleur and I have been trying to find her before something... worse... happens to her."

"It would be difficult to imagine greater calamity befalling a young bride."

Étienne stepped forward. "I praise you for your caution and your discretion. We have a need of finding my lady's cousin before others who wish her harm. It is possible one has already arrived here before us seeking her."

"Praise God there has not been another seeking her and

her companion. If there is, they have not stopped here," the monk answered.

Fleur's heart began to pound even harder. "Then she still travels with him?"

"Yes, and they have now found a way to travel during the day."

"Any help you could give would be greatly appreciated," Étienne said.

"I think the greatest help I could offer would be to give shelter to your lady while you search for her cousin," the monk said.

"But I need to do this, I have to aid her," Fleur protested.

The monk touched her hand briefly and she felt suddenly calm and more at peace than she had been since leaving Bryas. "There are other ways in which you can aid her, equally important, and I can assist you there," he said.

"I would be very grateful," Étienne said, face anxious.

"Then I will stay," Fleur agreed. She was tired and she was slowing him down. He could search faster if he didn't have to worry about her. And if the monk meant what he had said then she would not have to sit idly waiting for word but could do something. It seemed like the best idea.

"Let me get you some food and a fresh horse," the monk said to Étienne. "Then I can point you in the right direction."

"It has been hard to follow their trail," Fleur said.

The monk chuckled lightly. "I know where they are going and that is all he needs to know. Well, there is possibly one other thing, but I shall tell him when he is ready to leave."

Fleur gazed earnestly at Brother Paul. "Do you really think there is a way we can help my cousin?" she asked.

He nodded slowly and she felt her spirits lift.

After Étienne departed, she spent an hour telling Brother Paul everything she could about what had happened. The only thing she left out was that the man who had escaped with Carissa was some sort of demon. She didn't know what the monk's reaction to that would be or if he would even help her if he knew.

All the while she talked, fear gnawed at her and she wished she had not let Étienne ride on to Avignon alone. Even knowing he would make far better time without her, she hated not knowing how he was.

"You care for him very deeply, don't you?" Paul asked suddenly.

"Étienne?" she replied, startled.

He nodded. "Your thoughts are for him, yes?"

"Yes," she admitted, feeling slightly guilty. She had spent weeks consumed with worry for Carissa, but now that Étienne was gone from her side she found it hard to think of anything but him.

"There is a deep bond between the two of you. I can feel it."

She blushed deeply.

Paul continued. "He believes you when you tell him what you think and feel."

"Yes, he does," she said, staring at him in wonder. "How do you know these things?"

"It is in your face for any to read who have the skill."

"And what is in his face?" she asked.

"Devotion and single-minded purpose."

"To find my cousin?"

"No, to make you happy. The two of you are excellently matched and I would recommend marrying as soon as is feasible."

"Thank you," she murmured, not sure what else to say.

"You are welcome. Now I suggest we work on two plans to help your cousin."

"Why two?" she asked.

Paul looked at her grimly. "One plan if Pierre is killed and another plan for if he is not."

"You don't think she would—"

Paul shook his head. "It wouldn't surprise me. What he did to her was terrible and I know she thinks about revenge. Besides, even if she does not kill Pierre, Gabriel might."

"Who is Gabriel?" Fleur asked.

"The creature traveling with her."

She gasped. "You know? I never said anything about a demon."

Paul chuckled. "My dear child, you didn't have to." He smiled slowly and revealed wicked-looking fangs. "Gabriel and I have known each other for a very long time."

Fleur stared at Paul for a long moment, paralyzed as her instincts battled within her. The natural response was to flee, but before she could move, a calm feeling washed over her.

"You have nothing to fear from me. Your cousin knew what I am and I helped her. You should trust me now so that I might help you all."

His voice was soft, persuasive, and she felt herself yielding to it. "Just tell me what to do."

"Every man has before him many paths that he may

travel. Each decision made leads to new paths and puts others permanently out of reach. The best thing Carissa and Gabriel could do is leave this country and begin anew elsewhere. However, I believe it unlikely that either of them will choose that path."

"Carissa loves Bryas and wants to return," Fleur said.

Paul nodded. "A magistrate accused her, she was sentenced and imprisoned. Not even the king would cross the authority of the church...without good reason."

"So, the idea is to provide the king with a reason to set things right."

"Yes, and it must be compelling enough that he can justify his actions not only to himself but also to the church if need be."

"But she was falsely accused. Is that not enough?" Fleur asked.

Paul shook his head. "Can you prove that? Can she?"

"No," Fleur said, frustration welling within her. "I do not see how when she cannot have been convicted on anything beyond her husband's word."

"If we cannot prove her innocence, then we must prove someone else's guilt."

"Pierre."

"Yes," Paul answered. "He is the villain; now all we have to do is show him as such to the king."

"But how do we prove he is the villain without being able to prove Carissa's innocence?"

Paul smiled. "We prove him guilty of something far worse than lying."

Fleur stared at him for a long moment and then comprehension began to dawn. "If we could prove that he was some sort of...monster...and that he got rid of Carissa because she had found out his secret, then the king would be able to jail or kill Pierre."

"And restore to Carissa what has been taken from her," Paul finished.

Fleur lurched to her feet. "Then we have to stop her from killing Pierre. If she does that—"

"It will be all but impossible to convince the king of her innocence. Pierre needs to be alive and in no position to contradict what we are going to accuse him of."

EUROPE, PRESENT DAY

Taking David with him was only going to slow him down, Gabriel realized, as they drove through the night. David had told him that the closest of the possible locations where Pierre could be holding Wendy was a house in Vienna. If he had to obey the speed limits it would take him hours to get there.

Fortunately, he didn't have to. He drove with all the car's lights off, his eyes seeing clearly for miles around them despite the dark. In fact, the dark was better. He might have taught himself to wake during the day, but the light was still painful to his eyes.

Beside him David said nothing, staring intently out the window, jaw clenched.

He's riding to save the damsel in distress, Gabriel realized. It reminded him of another knight from years before, right after his first fight with the Baron. *So many things change, but so many things stay the same.*

FRANCE, 1198 AD

Gabriel had left the assassin far behind. He rode with the robe shielding his body from the sun, but his blistered hands hadn't yet healed and the pain tore at him more with each passing minute. He thought he saw a rider ahead, and his heart surged, hoping it was Carissa, but a moment later there was nothing but empty road again.

When he saw a small, run-down building a ways off the road, he turned his horse and made for its shelter. They were not far from Avignon and he prayed Carissa could find her way safely to the castle.

He slept fitfully most of the day and as the sun began to set he was startled awake by the sound of a rider approaching. He rose and waited quietly, senses alert.

"Hello inside," an unfamiliar voice called out. Gabriel relaxed slightly. He crossed to the door and pulled it open. A young knight with wavy hair and earnest eyes sat on the back of a black horse.

"Hello, my son," Gabriel responded, mindful of his own appearance. The monk's robes Paul had loaned him had been very useful. "What has brought you here and how may I assist you?"

"I am Étienne de Molay and I was looking for shelter for the night for my horse and myself."

"You will find shelter here but not much else," Gabriel said. "As it happens, I was just about to depart so you will have the place to yourself."

"But it will be too dark to travel shortly."

"I do not have far to go."

The knight's eyes narrowed in suspicion and Gabriel tensed himself to attack.

He eased his horse back a couple of steps. "It is possible you may be able to help me in my quest."

"And what quest is that?" Gabriel asked, breathing deeply.

"I am looking for a noblewoman, falsely accused of a crime and recently escaped from prison. I bring word to her from her cousin, who is deeply troubled."

Gabriel hesitated. It was likely that Pierre had sent more than one assassin after Carissa. Still, the knight before him didn't strike him as a killer. He shook his head slowly. "I'm just a poor monk traveling to my monastery. I know nothing of this woman."

The knight smiled. "You match the description of her traveling companion."

"She is traveling with a monk?" Gabriel asked.

"According to the warden of the prison she is traveling with a demon. And according to Brother Paul, a monk I spoke with, he is a vampire dressed as a monk. Am I correct in assuming that you are he? The vampire Gabriel?"

"I think you should come inside. It seems we have much to discuss," Gabriel said coolly.

The knight dismounted and, after tying up his horse, followed Gabriel inside.

"I am Gabriel," he admitted after studying the man for a moment. "But Carissa and I were separated this morning when an assassin sent by her husband found us. She should be heading to Avignon but I do not know how far ahead of us she is."

"Then she is still alive?" Étienne asked, relief flooding his face.

"She was this morning," Gabriel confirmed.

"Sir, this is good news."

"What of her cousin?" Gabriel asked.

"She is at the monastery with Paul. Together they are trying to figure out how best to help Carissa once we find her. We had been following a German since he left the prison in search of you. We ourselves arrived there shortly after Pierre. It had taken us so long to find her that we feared the worst."

"She is still in terrible danger," Gabriel reminded him.

"I am here to help, just tell me what to do."

"How did you get involved in all of this?" Gabriel asked.

Étienne smiled. "I am in love with Fleur."

Gabriel could see the truth shining brightly in Étienne's eyes, but he did not look long, afraid of what the young knight might see in his own eyes. He made his decision. "The sun is down and this is the best time for me to travel."

"Then by all means, let us go," Étienne said.

They pushed their horses hard and an hour before sunrise they rounded a bend in the road and in the distance Gabriel saw his castle.

Gabriel reined in his horse to a walk, staring at the hulking structure. It had been fifty years since he had seen it. He heard the hoofbeats of Étienne's horse as they came around the bend and then the change in cadence as he broke stride.

"It is beautiful," Étienne said.

"Thank you."

The moon was setting. The Rhône River was barely visible in its fading light.

"The bridge is new," Gabriel commented.

"Keep a dragon in the dungeon?" Étienne joked.

"Don't you think one monster is enough for a castle?"

He said nothing in return. Half an hour later they rode into the forecourt.

Two men approached. One was tall, a good six inches taller than his companion, and much slimmer. The short man held Étienne's horse and took the reins when he dismounted.

Gabriel dismounted and with a flick of his wrist tossed his reins to the shorter man as well. The man scurried off toward the stables, both horses following eagerly.

The other turned toward Gabriel. The two men faced each other for a long moment and then the servant said, "Welcome home, milord."

"Andrew?" he growled. No one should have been alive to recognize him, but Gabriel remembered this man well.

"No," the other man said with a shake of his head. "I am Alenon. Andrew was my grandfather."

Gabriel wanted to kill him. He closed his eyes briefly, fighting for control. He leaned slightly forward, fists clenched at his side.

"How do you know who I am?"

"My grandfather spoke often of you and described you in perfect detail. Until the day he died he was consumed with guilt for having betrayed you, and he always expected that one day you would appear again to reclaim that which you had lost."

In one blinding movement Gabriel was upon him and hoisted Alenon into the air. "What is to stop me from killing you in his place?"

"Nothing, milord. I will not cry out if you do. You see, I, too, carry my grandfather's shame."

Slowly Gabriel set him back upon his feet. "An honorable man? We shall see."

Alenon bowed deeply. "I look forward to proving my allegiance."

Étienne let out an audible breath and stepped forward. "Is your master home?"

"He is now," Alenon said meaningfully. "But if you are referencing that pretender who has been here these many years, he is."

"Take us to him," Gabriel commanded in a cold, hard voice.

"As you wish," Alenon said with a bow. He led the way to the castle with Gabriel on his heels.

"Has a young woman arrived within the past day?" Gabriel asked.

"No, milord, you two are the first arrivals in the last fortnight."

It was not the news for which he had been hoping. However, it was possible that Carissa would arrive within the day had she been going more slowly and cautiously.

At last they came into the presence of the current master of the castle. He was a swarthy-looking man with brown hair and a large, hooked nose. He peered at them disdainfully from across a table covered with papers and ledgers.

"Alenon, who are these people?" he asked, practically spitting the last word as though it were distasteful to him. "You knew I did not wish to be disturbed."

Before the servant could answer, Gabriel stepped forward. "Who we are is unimportant," he said, his voice a low purr. "You need to secure your place at court, make sure you do not fall out of favor. You want to go to the palace and stay there for quite a while. You will tell your servants to obey me and after you leave tonight, you will have no memory of me or my companion."

The man blinked twice and then rose to his feet. He looked at Gabriel with a mildly perplexed expression. "You must excuse me, I have to leave. I must go and finish making arrangements. Please, stay as long as you like."

"You are too kind," Gabriel muttered.

The man nodded and turned on his heel, pacing quickly from the room. After a quick glance at Gabriel, Alenon followed after him.

"So, this was once yours?" Étienne asked quietly.

"And it will be again," Gabriel said, fighting hard to control the anger that threatened to overcome him.

"He is doing as you have told him," Alenon announced as he came back into the room.

"Excellent. Now if you would be so kind as to show us to the hall. We are famished from our journey."

A feast was brought for Étienne, and Gabriel watched in amusement as the younger man fell upon the food with an appetite. At the last Alenon set a goblet before Gabriel. He picked it up, swirled the liquid inside gently, and then drained it in a single gulp.

The blood that coursed over his tongue was warm and fresh and familiar. He set down the goblet on the table very carefully before looking up at Alenon.

"It's yours," Gabriel said.

"Yes, milord," Alenon answered quietly.

Gabriel nodded. "Step away from me slowly," he commanded.

Alenon did as he was ordered.

"While I appreciate the gesture, please bring me animal blood in the future," Gabriel said in even, measured tones.

Alenon nodded and then backed slowly from the room. Étienne raised an eyebrow but did not ask any questions, choosing instead to return his attention to his own meal.

So many nights in the dungeon Gabriel had dreamed of killing Andrew, of drinking his blood. He had remembered the taste of it he had had accidentally after Raphael attacked him. Alenon's blood was similar enough in taste that all the old dreams came flooding back. His vision swam as he struggled to control the overwhelming rage and bloodlust that threatened to destroy him.

For so long he had managed to drink only the blood of animals. That had been taken away from him in the dungeon. The first time it had taken decades to break himself of the need for human blood. He hoped it would not take decades this time lest all those near him should die.

"Would you like a tour of the castle?" Gabriel asked.

"I would love one, but to be honest, I am very tired."

"Alenon can show you to a room. I have business to attend to," Gabriel said.

Étienne nodded and rose from the table. "I am sure she will arrive later today," he said.

"I pray for all our sakes that you are right," Gabriel said. It was likely that she was riding slowly, using caution on the road and hiding often. She had no way of knowing that he still lived. His thoughts turned to the Baron and he couldn't help but wonder if he had somehow managed to track and kill Carissa.

Gabriel found his own room. The decorations of the

current occupant would have to be removed, but there was time enough for that later. The sun was up and it compelled him to sleep. He succumbed but was able to wake himself a few hours later. He was disappointed to discover that Carissa had still not arrived.

By the time night fell he was convinced that something had happened to delay her. When the last of the sun's rays slipped below the horizon, he left the castle on foot to search for her. When he returned just before dawn to meet Étienne's questioning eyes he had to admit that there had been no sign of her.

"Get some sleep; we can decide what to do tonight," Étienne urged.

When Gabriel finally closed his eyes an hour later they flew back open immediately. "She thinks I'm dead," he whispered to himself. "And so she's going to the only place she knows, the place where she can take her revenge.

"Étienne!" he called, running down the corridor.

"What is it?" Étienne asked, appearing from his room.

"She's heading for Bryas. I'll be leaving tonight."

"I'll go with you."

Gabriel shook his head. "She's got a day's head start on us and if she beats us there she'll get herself killed. No, I will chase her down on foot."

"I'll leave now, see if I can find her trail," Étienne said.

"You should return to the monastery and tell them what is happening," Gabriel urged. "If Fleur is that sick with grief she at least deserves to know that Carissa is likely alive. As far as we know."

Vienna, Present Day

David was exhausted, but he was determined to find Wendy, no matter what it took. The moon was low in the sky when they reached their destination. The house was completely dark, but he let Gabriel lead the way. David followed, a stake in one hand and a cross in the other.

Once inside the house, Gabriel swept up the stairs while David crept through the first-floor rooms. It was still night so any vampires present would be awake.

Moments later Gabriel rejoined him, shaking his head. They finished sweeping the main floor and then found a door. There was the faintest glow of light coming from underneath it.

Gabriel pointed downward, indicating that he thought the door might lead to a basement. David prepared himself. Gabriel kicked down the door and they surged inside. What he saw stopped David dead in his tracks. "Wendy," he whispered, shock rippling through him.

CHAPTER EIGHT

And Pilate wrote a title, and put it on the cross. And the writing was, Jesus of Nazareth the King of the Jews.

—John 19:19

EUROPE, PRESENT DAY

Wendy heard something, noise just outside the door at the top of the stairs. She jumped to her feet, making sure that all the pages she had read were safely tucked under the mattress. Then she moved to stand in the center of the room as she had done before, wondering if the Baron was about to pay her another visit. She had no idea how much time had passed. Maybe he was bringing her another meal. At least she wouldn't starve to death.

The door swung slowly open and she felt herself tense. For a moment no one appeared and she felt a surge of hope. Maybe she was being rescued.

She heard a footstep and a figure came into sight.

Pierre.

The magistrate-turned-attorney was walking down the stairs toward her, a strange half smile on his lips. She fought the urge to retreat even as he advanced. If he wanted her dead, why bother feeding her?

Unless he's planning to feed on me, she thought with

a shudder. Vampires terrified and repulsed her. All of them. She didn't know how Susan could be attracted to Raphael.

Pierre made it to the bottom of the stairs and continued toward her, eyes roving over her in a way that made her sick inside. She stood her ground, though, and glared at him. Finally he stopped right in front of her, invading her personal space. She didn't take a step back, though. She didn't want to show this particular predator any signs of weakness he could use against her.

"It's uncanny how much you look like her," he said finally.

"So I've been told."

"I wish I'd known sooner that Susan's cousin bore such a striking resemblance to Carissa."

"My name is Wendy and don't get too comfortable talking to me. Gabriel will be here any minute."

Hatred flashed across his face and she knew she'd struck the nerve she had aimed for. Gabriel was the one he'd intended to have kill Carissa. Instead Gabriel had fallen in love with her and the two of them had shared a fantastic love story. At least, Wendy hoped it was fantastic. She had no idea how the story ended, although somewhere in there Pierre getting turned into a vampire must have been part of it.

"He's a monster," Pierre said, turning his head to spit at the floor.

The gesture startled Wendy, but she remained still by some miracle. "Well, look at the pot calling the kettle black," she said.

"Oh, I well know the evil that lurks in my own heart, but it is nothing compared to his."

Wendy's stomach did a little flip-flop. She remembered what the Baron had said about her needing to ask Gabriel how Carissa had died. Why was it she felt that not knowing the end of that story was going to get her killed?

Because this has all happened before, all of it, she thought suddenly. Pierre had had her imprisoned here and the Baron was here as well. Now all she needed was for Gabriel to show up. Only when he did would he be there to rescue her as he had helped Carissa escape from her prison? And then what?

That's if they are *trying to rescue me. They may think me dead. Or they might be still contending with Richelieu.* Wendy felt her heart sink. Until that moment she had been sure help was on its way. Now she realized she had no way of knowing if they were alive, just as they might not know whether she was still alive.

Had Susan and David escaped Richelieu outside the cathedral? Had Gabriel and Raphael made it back in time to help? And what of Paul? Was he still alive, turning more gray with every passing hour?

She swallowed hard. She couldn't live with this uncertainty, she realized, as fear and grief tore at her heart.

"Did David and Susan escape Richelieu?" she asked.

Pierre stared at her for what seemed an eternity. Finally he blinked. "I don't know," he admitted. "And at the moment it will not be easy for me to find out."

"Susan would take your call."

"Yes, I'm sure she would. But I won't give my brother the satisfaction or the opportunity to track me. Although I'm not sure he could. He's never been very fond of technology from what I understand. It's a pity, really. There's so many useful things you can do with it."

"Your brother?" Wendy asked, taken aback.

Pierre frowned for a moment. "Raphael. We share a sire, so that makes us brothers of a sort."

So Gabriel had cursed him. Why? If he had killed him hundreds of years ago, she wouldn't be here. But since she was, she needed to keep ahead of him. Not say what he'd expect. "By that logic, you are Richelieu's uncle. I think you should go and teach your nephew a lesson."

Pierre smiled again. "I like your spirit. But only a fool would go near that diseased mongrel."

"That diseased mongrel is a threat to everyone, humans and vampires. He has to be stopped," Wendy said, clenching her fists at her side.

"You feel quite strongly about that, don't you?"

"Yes."

"Are those your true feelings or someone else's feelings?" he asked her.

She blinked at him. "What do you mean?"

Quick as a snake his hand moved, brushed her left temple, and then fell back to his side before she could even blink.

"You've been mesmerized. A vampire has you under his spell."

Fear rocketed through her. The lapses in memory, the sudden compulsion to return to Prague to help Susan, these and other things had been nagging at her, making her feel like she wasn't truly her own woman but being controlled, manipulated somehow. Hearing him say she was mesmerized played on the deep-seated fears she had been wrestling with for days.

"By who? Gabriel?" she asked.

"No. Raphael's the one who has touched your mind."

"Raphael! When? Why?"

"That I don't know. But I can tell you that the anger you're feeling right now is completely understandable and normal."

As he said that she realized she was shaking like a leaf and that it was anger that she felt pouring through her veins. "How...how do I know you're not the one doing this to me?" she said.

"You don't. But think about this. I have your body captive. Why would I need to hold your mind captive as well?"

"So I won't try to escape."

"You are more than welcome to try, but you should know that it would be quite impossible."

There were other reasons she could think of, but there was no way she was going to voice them out loud to him. No need to give him any more ideas than whatever he already had.

"What do you plan to do to me?" she asked.

He blinked slowly and a look of puzzlement crossed his face. "You know, to be honest, I hadn't really thought that part through yet."

"Let me go then," she urged.

"No, I'm afraid that would be quite impossible. I captured you and I have every intention of keeping you."

"For how long?" she asked, feeling desperation surging through her.

"For as long as we both shall live, of course," he said with a smile that widened his eyes.

She stared at him, not quite sure if she'd heard him correctly. And he was staring at her, his eyes softening ever so slightly.

"I can't believe you're here, after all this time," he said quietly.

Wendy gaped at him, her mind racing even as he reached out and brushed a strand of hair out of her face.

"You know I'm not her, right?" she asked, her own voice barely more than a whisper.

He continued to stare at her, and she could swear she saw madness lurking behind his eyes. "I don't know what you're talking about, Carissa," he said. Then he turned, climbed the stairs, closed the door, and locked it behind him.

PRAGUE, PRESENT DAY

"You should get some rest," Raphael said suddenly as he put down the diary on the coffee table. "You have to be exhausted."

Susan blinked at him. "I can't. Not until they find Wendy. You get that, don't you?"

He scowled. "You are like Fleur. You refuse to rest when you should. You might be called upon to help your cousin and how will you have the strength to do so?"

Susan laid a hand on his arm. "Please, tell me that you do understand. I can't rest, I can't sleep. And this diary, it connects us ... *all* of us."

Raphael's eyes narrowed in suspicion. "*All* of us?" he asked.

Susan nodded, feeling a tingling deep inside that seemed to be spreading throughout her body. It was because of the way he was looking at her, that was it. They just had some chemistry, animal attraction. It couldn't possibly be more than that.

But she knew she was lying to herself. She reached out and took his hand, lacing her fingers through his. He stared at their two hands, fingers entwined. When he looked back up at her she couldn't read his expression.

"I'm a monster."

"No, you're not."

"The things I've done—"

"Are in your past. Everyone has baggage, skeletons. Yours are just more literal." She smiled and hoped her tone was as lighthearted as she was trying for.

"It's not a joke," he said. "I've killed people. *Hundreds* and hundreds of people. Did you not hear what I said earlier, what Gabriel made me tell you? I slaughtered everyone I knew."

"I know."

"And that doesn't mean anything to you?" he asked. His eyes were burning intently and his lips were twisting. She thought it might be in anger, but she could feel her attention drifting, fixating on his eyes, his mouth, remembering what it was like to kiss him.

She put her free hand on his chest. "*You* mean something to me," she said, shocked at her own boldness.

He looked at her and there was such raw pain in his eyes that it broke her heart. But slowly it was being replaced by something else, by a smoldering fire that only served to fan the flames of the desire she was feeling.

He put his hand over hers. "No heartbeat. Susan, I'm not human."

She leaned closer to him. "No, you're not," she said, feeling like she couldn't quite catch her breath.

"And you're so young, barely more than a child."

"I'm a woman and old enough to know my own mind."

"You don't know what you're saying," he said. He let go of both her hands and grabbed her around the waist. He picked her up and set her down on his lap. She put her arms around his neck and gazed into his eyes.

"I'm a creature of darkness."

"Then let me be your light."

He kissed her then, full and deep, and she let herself savor it as she closed her eyes. There was so much death, so much fear. All she wanted was to feel loved and needed.

And the more Raphael kissed her the more she felt both.

"We are all connected, you're right," he was whispering to her. "All of us, more than you can possibly guess. You, me, David, Carissa."

"Do you know what happened to Carissa?" she asked.

He stood abruptly and she slid off his lap onto the floor. She stared up at him in shock, not sure what had just happened.

"You should worry more about yourself than her," he said with a growl.

But looking up into his eyes she could see fear there, terrible, crushing fear. She realized that whatever had happened to Carissa, Raphael was terrified that it was going to happen to her as well.

"Just tell me," she whispered.

He stood, staring down at her, agony burning in his eyes. "I can't," he whispered at long last.

"Then at least tell me what happened to you."

He cocked his head to the side. "What do you mean?"

Susan took a deep breath. "Bryas."

"What about it? You know that I was kidnapped while we were there."

"No, tell me what happened the first time you were there."

His lips curled, revealing his fangs. "I don't want to talk about it."

"But I want to hear about it."

"Not now," he said with a quick shake of his head.

She picked up the diary. "If you won't tell me your story, then at least continue to read me Fleur's."

He hesitated. "You yourself have pointed out that the diary connects us all. What have you read of me?"

Susan licked her lips. "The only thing so far about you in here was a conversation Carissa overheard between Paul and Gabriel. Paul told Gabriel that you had set yourself up as a god to a primitive culture and that he set you on fire."

Raphael shuddered. "All true," he said, his voice sounding hollow.

"You told me about that yourself already. So what is it you're afraid I'll find out?" Susan asked.

Raphael looked away and the act sent shivers up her spine. Whatever it was must be terrible, but worse than killing hundreds of people? "Please, just read to me a little longer," she asked.

Slowly he sat down. He picked the book back up. "'There is nothing worse in this entire world than waiting, except if it's waiting to hear word about the ones you love.'"

FRANCE, 1198 AD

Fleur sat on a small rise, watching the road below for signs of Étienne or Carissa. She had suffered with nightmares all night and awoken with a feeling of dread. As the day wore on she found her anxiety heightened instead of lessened. The sun had just set when she heard a step behind her.

"You look troubled," Paul said.

Fleur looked up at him. "Something is wrong, I can feel it. It is like there is a storm coming. There is not a cloud in the sky but I just know it is going to rain."

"I have felt it, too," he said quietly. "Something is about to change. Not all change is bad; oftentimes change can be a good thing."

"And now?"

He shook his head. "I cannot read the future."

"But you can read minds," she said.

"That is a fanciful belief on your part."

It just happens to be true, she thought.

So it does, he answered. Out loud he said, "What do you want to do?"

She sighed. "I want to go back to Bryas, but I do not see how I can with Carissa somewhere out there and Pierre holding court in her castle. It's not right."

"Maybe you should return to Bryas regardless," he suggested.

She turned and looked him in the eyes. "Tell me what you are thinking."

He laughed deep in his chest. "I think you already know."

Fleur and Paul left the monastery a half hour later. Fleur couldn't help but marvel at her own brashness. Twice now she had found herself on a journey alone with a man with no one to chaperone. The fact that Paul was a monk did little to ease her mind since there was also the vampire side of him to contend with.

She had no idea how her cousin had survived traveling with a vampire, let alone locked in a cell with one. No sooner was the monastery lost to sight than she began to wonder if she had made the right decision to venture out into the dark with a creature from a nightmare and her beloved Étienne searching for her cousin in the opposite direction.

"Étienne will find us soon enough," Paul said. "And then I think you will find that it is I who is the chaperone."

She flushed. "Can all vampires read minds?" she asked.

"No. All vampires can manipulate a person's thoughts but not all of them can actually read thoughts."

She felt her blood run cold.

"Don't worry, you're on this journey of your own free will, I promise you."

"How do I know that is true?"

"I am a man of God," he said, looking at her solemnly.

"There are those who claim to be men of God who are not."

"Then I guess you will just have to trust me," he said.

She thought about that for a moment. "Perhaps it would help if I knew more about you."

He laughed. "You are a curious one, aren't you?"

"I like to understand things."

"It seems we share something in common then. What do you want to know?"

"What are your abilities?"

"Speed, strength, immortality, the ability to read and sometimes manipulate thoughts."

"And your weaknesses?"

"Forgive me if I am not overeager to share those," he said with another laugh.

"And yet I am to trust you with my life?"

He stopped his horse abruptly and when he turned to her his fangs glistened in the moonlight. "If you wish to turn back, now would be the time. I have no particular desire to leave the monastery. No love for your home or your cousin drives me onward. I would be just as happy not to miss morning prayers. I avoid leaving whenever possible. I like it there."

"Why?" she couldn't help but ask. "You have so much and you could do anything you want, why would you choose to stay there?"

"Because I love God and have little tolerance for the foolishness of man. Since I cannot live out the rest of my existence with no human contact, though, I choose to live among those whose devotion to God rivals my own."

She could not say why exactly, but she believed him. "I am sorry for asking what I did. It was quite rude. Please, will you escort me home?"

He inclined his head.

"May I ask why?"

"Because Gabriel loves your cousin."

She gasped. "How do you know this?"

"I have known him for most of his life. I was the vampire who created him. He may hide his emotions well from most of the world but to me they are as plain as words on a page. He loves her and out of my friendship for him I choose to keep you safe as long as I can."

"Thank you," she said, not trusting herself to say anything else.

"You are welcome," he said, before urging his horse forward once more. "Now, let us go, we are wasting moonlight."

VIENNA, PRESENT DAY

David walked slowly down the stairs, heart thudding painfully in his chest. On the wall beside him was a massive mural of what he had at first thought was Wendy with dark hair but quickly realized it must be Carissa instead. Susan had told him that Wendy bore a striking resemblance to their ancestress and it was true. Except for the hair color they could be twins.

In front of him he could hear Gabriel breathing and the sound set him on edge. From what he understood, vampires only breathed if they were contemplating attacking something. It was their equivalent of growling he guessed. Only the sound was so loud, so powerful, from one who was usually so silent that the effect was eerie, far worse than had he actually been growling.

David stayed a couple of steps behind him, giving them both space to maneuver should they need it. The rest of the house was dark, empty, but there was light coming from this basement so it stood to reason that someone or something was down there. It took all the restraint David had not to push past Gabriel and rush down the stairs to see if this was where Wendy was being held prisoner. He forced himself to hold back, though, because if there was a vampire waiting for them Gabriel would be far better equipped to handle him.

At the bottom of the stairs they turned and were able to take in the entire basement, which seemed to be crammed with art and display cases.

There was no one there.

David felt himself relax only slightly. His mind was already racing ahead to the next house on the list. Wendy had to be in that one. They would find her.

He turned to go, but he heard a strangled sound escape Gabriel. He turned back and saw the vampire standing in front of a display case perched on top of a marble pedestal.

He glanced at Gabriel and was taken aback when he realized there were bloody tears glistening on his cheeks. Gabriel looked completely shaken, like he'd seen a ghost. He lifted a hand and placed it against the glass, so gentle it was almost a caress.

"Are you okay?" David asked.

The vampire didn't answer, didn't move.

"What is it?"

"A lock of Carissa's hair."

David turned and looked back toward the mural that had startled him when they first opened the door. The lock of hair in the case matched the dark-haired image of Wendy, the famed Carissa.

He turned and slowly began to take in the rest of the objects in the room. The walls were covered in portraits of Carissa. From the looks of them they had been painted in different time periods by different artists. One in particular caught his eye, filled with light and swirling colors. He walked up to it to study it more carefully and saw the artist's signature.

"Van Gogh? He had Van Gogh paint a portrait of her?" he asked. The painting had to be worth millions and yet no one knew it even existed or would ever guess if they did who the woman pictured in it was.

He looked around the room and began to recognize

the work of other masters. He even saw a sculpture of her that could only have been done by Michelangelo. He began to inspect the glass display cases that were scattered around the room. In one he saw an ancient-looking hairbrush and comb. Another contained a pair of sapphire earrings. A third held a piece of parchment with a large, ornate seal on it.

There were more, but his eyes were finally drawn to one very large display case. A white dress was draped on a mannequin. There were dark spots on the neckline of the dress on one side, some much larger than others. He stared at it, an uneasy feeling settling on him.

Gabriel finally came to stand beside him.

"Did this belong to Carissa?" he asked at last.

"Yes. She was wearing it when she died."

David felt sick deep inside. Those stains had to be blood then. He closed his eyes, struggling with emotions that threatened to overcome him. He, too, had become caught up in her story as he'd been sharing it with Wendy and Susan. To see artifacts of the real woman, including this, was almost more than he could bear. Especially given that Wendy had been kidnapped and might also be dead.

He forced himself to look away from the dress. From the rest of the house he never would have guessed that this shrine existed in the basement. The lights had been on. Had someone just left it before they arrived?

He didn't know. He just knew that they needed to go, head for the next place on their list. Still, the enormity of everything around him was overwhelming.

"What is…all of this?" David asked in hushed tones.

Gabriel stirred at that. He turned and looked at everything in the room with hard, narrowed eyes. His expression had changed and if anything he seemed even sterner, more intimidating.

"All of this? Obsession. Wendy's in even more danger than I thought."

CHAPTER NINE

And he bearing his cross went forth into a place called the place of a skull, which is called in the Hebrew Golgotha.

—John 19:17

"Paul was the strangest traveling companion I have ever known,'" Raphael read.

He turned the page and paused. "There's a couple of loose pages folded up in here."

Susan sat up immediately. "Are they written by Carissa? The last pages we found like that were."

He glanced at them. They were certainly written in a different style handwriting and the sick, twisting feeling he had in his gut made it easy to believe that she had written them.

"I can't read these pages," he whispered.

"You have to, please."

"No, not Carissa's words. It would be wrong."

"Gabriel meant for me to know everything she had to say."

It was true. If he hadn't, he would not have given the diary to her.

Raphael hesitated, but her eyes were so pleading. It was

possible that one or both of them would soon be dead. And if these pages were written by Carissa, there was no way they could contain an account of her death in them.

"Okay," he said, and was rewarded with a brilliant smile.

He stared at the words and they seemed to swim in front of his vision for a moment and he felt dizzy.

It's just nerves and guilt, he told himself. *Push through it.*

"Okay, here goes."

Susan nodded eagerly.

" 'My heart grieves for Gabriel, but I am fixated on the task that lies before me. I am comforted by the knowledge that soon I will join my father and mother in heaven. I only pray that God in His mercy sees fit to let Gabriel join us there.' "

FRANCE, 1198 AD

Carissa didn't know how many prayers she had sent up for Gabriel's soul, but it seemed the only thing she could do for both of them.

At the rate she was traveling Carissa calculated that it would take her one week to reach Bryas. As soon as she had set on the road heading north she had been overcome with impatience. One way or another it would all be over soon and she found herself pushing her horse faster than she normally would.

The horse was powerful and his stride was aggressive. Unlike her beloved Dancer there was nothing smooth or gentle about his gait. All that she had suffered, though, had hardened her, body and mind, so that she barely noticed.

The farther away from Avignon she rode the more she wondered what it would have been like to return with Gabriel to his home. Tears began to fall as she thought of him. She was sure he was dead. She had come across the body of the horse of the man who had killed him. There had been burn marks on the ground that had to have been where Gabriel died, the sun burning his body at the last. Of Gabriel's horse or the German there had been no sign.

She thought bitterly of how the man had said that he only had to kill her, at Pierre's orders. He was still alive, which meant somewhere he was hunting her. She prayed he had continued on the road toward Avignon and wouldn't discover until too late that she was not there. If he caught her before she could reach Bryas then Gabriel's death meant nothing.

Her horse suddenly pricked his ears forward and she instinctively slowed, straining to see or hear whatever had caught his interest. In a minute a couple of riders came into sight, coming toward her.

There was no cover of any kind, just flat land to either side of the road. She thought of turning tail and running, but that would only excite their interest and invite pursuit. If she continued on, they would be suspicious of a woman traveling alone. She opted to continue riding, forming a story in her mind and hoping to entreat their aid.

She kicked her horse into a canter and the two men pulled to a stop, waiting for her to reach them. As soon as she drew abreast of them, she stopped her horse. Both men were a few years older than her, their faces hardened by years in the sun.

"Please, can you assist me? Thieves attacked my brother and me. I think they killed him," she said, allowing her own grief for Gabriel to come through.

The two men looked at each other and then the nearest one turned back to her. "Sure, we can help you," he said, reaching out casually to grab at her horse's bridle.

She looked into his eyes and shivered. She saw what he had in mind for her. She kicked her horse into a run. The man fell back with a cry. She gave her horse his head. A moment later she heard the pounding of hooves behind her and she leaned lower across her horse's withers, urging him on with hands and voice.

The wind whipped past her faster and faster. She focused on the sensations, trying to quash her fear. The speed was exhilarating and yet, somehow, she found herself comparing it to the night that she and Gabriel had raced through the fields, with her on his back. She remembered the sensation of soaring through the air as he leaped. In that moment she realized that racing along upon a horse would never be the same again.

She heard shouts behind her that faded. She risked a glance backward and saw that her pursuers had stopped and one of them was on the ground inspecting his horse's leg. She turned her eyes back to the road but did not slacken her horse's pace for several more minutes.

She finally pulled him into a fast trot. Nearly an hour later when there were still no more signs of pursuit she began to relax and she let her horse slow to a walk. "Remind me to find you a special treat," she said, patting his neck.

He nickered and she smiled.

"Of course, we still have to figure out the safest place to spend the night."

She suspected that so long as he got his promised reward he would have no opinion on the topic. She would dearly love to stay at an inn and sleep in a bed after a hot meal. It was risky, though, and as much as she didn't like it she realized she would probably be safer finding a patch of forest to sleep in. She shivered.

The last couple of days with Gabriel she had begun to believe that there might one day come a time when she felt safe again. The dream had died with him, though. Now the best she could hope for was to stay alive long enough to find and kill Pierre for what he had done to her, for what he had done to them.

Just before sunset Carissa turned off the road into a stand of trees. An hour before, with a heavy heart, she had given a wide berth to an inn. Now she found herself a place to rest for the night that was likely far more safe, even though it didn't feel that way. Sleeping outside left her feeling vulnerable and exposed.

After she laid down she closed her eyes and prayed for sleep. Every sound seemed to startle her, though, until her heart was beating fast. If Gabriel had lived she was sure he could have found her just by the sound. She wrapped her arms around herself and tried not to give in to the grief that threatened her.

She wished she could feel relief. With Gabriel gone she no longer had to worry about him drinking her blood someday. She had often thought she would part company with him at her first opportunity but without him she felt more alone than she ever had.

She turned her thoughts toward home, just a few days' ride away. She would give anything to be there, safe and secure. But hatred filled her as she reminded herself that where Pierre was there was neither safety nor security. So many nights she had lain in that cell and dreamed of revenge.

Now revenge was within her grasp and even as anger continued to surge through her she realized she had absolutely no idea how to carry it out. *What is it I want?* she asked herself. *Do I merely wish him dead? If so, that is easily enough accomplished. I just have to find a way to get close to him with a dagger or poison.* In her mind she imagined what it would be like to cut his throat or to watch as he choked to death.

She shook her head. It wasn't enough. Death was better than he deserved. He hadn't done her the courtesy of allowing her a quick, clean death, and she wouldn't allow him one. *But if not death, then what?*

She wanted him to feel pain, she wanted him to know the same terror that she had faced inside that prison. She wanted him to be stripped of everything he was and have everything taken from him. Only then could she rest. Only then could she die.

I am going to die.

She took a ragged breath. Death was the natural end for her. She was already thought dead and whatever good reputation she might have had Pierre had long since destroyed. Even if she survived her encounter with Pierre she would not be able to escape her own doom. She might escape Bryas castle, but she would never escape the other magistrates. Their power reached well beyond the borders of France.

She might elude capture for a day, two at the most, but she had no illusions that she could escape. The only reason she was still alive was that Pierre hadn't wanted to draw attention to the fact that she was, else he would have sent a dozen assassins after her.

But I do not want to die, she thought. It was true. Despite everything she had lived through she wasn't yet ready to lose her life. *What if I do not go to Bryas? What if I head to England or Germany instead?* She let herself think about it for a minute before letting go of the idea. It wasn't possible. She was a woman alone with no name, no money, no family. She would be reduced to doing anything she could for food. She would have to sacrifice the last vestiges of her soul and become the very thing Pierre had accused her of being. She couldn't do that. Of the two, death was preferable.

So on to Bryas, but what I am going to do once I get there I do not know. Minutes later she drifted to sleep and dreamed dark dreams with faceless monsters who drove her to her doom.

VIENNA, PRESENT DAY

Gabriel and David were back in the car and heading for the next destination. Gabriel had been shaken by what he'd found in that basement far more than David even guessed. To see a shrine to dear, dead Carissa had shattered him. The fact that it was Pierre's shrine made it so much worse. The monster had no right to think of her at all let alone erect a monument to her memory and gather things that she had owned in life.

He had thought about burning the entire place to the ground. David had argued, though, that it might somehow alert Pierre and cause him to do something rash. He had also argued that the portraits and other items should right-fully go to Wendy and Susan when this whole mess was over.

Although the paintings themselves were worth millions, it was all little compensation for the hell that they had been sucked into.

"Where next?"

"Vaduz in Liechtenstein," David said.

He felt the frustration building inside him. It wasn't the first time he'd had to go chasing after a woman of Bryas. He remembered what it had been like when he realized Carissa had abandoned the plan to go to Avignon and had instead turned and begun to head home to Bryas. He had been terrified that he would not find her before she got herself killed.

AVIGNON, 1198 AD

A quarter of an hour before sunset Gabriel left the castle at a dead run. Étienne had left early in the day for the monastery. Gabriel moved far faster than a horse could have and with his full strength finally regained and nothing to carry he could move at a speed even Carissa would not have believed. He knew he would be able to run without tiring until sunrise. He hoped he would find her before then.

He ran for quite a ways before coming to a forest not that far from where he had battled the Baron. On a hunch he swerved and plunged into the trees, probing with all his senses for any sign of her.

He was about to give up when the faintest hint of her

scent reached him. He twisted and turned through the forest until he came to a spot where she had rested. He was able to follow the footsteps of her horse back out of the forest and noted that the animal had indeed turned north toward Bryas before its hoofprints were lost on the road.

It was almost dawn when Gabriel saw the inn. His first instinct was to go around it, but he slowed. He wondered if Carissa might be there or at least stopped sometime within the last day. The last thing he needed to do was arouse local suspicion by asking about a woman traveling alone. It was about as far as he would expect her to push her horse, though.

He hesitated and then decided to push on a little farther. He stopped and settled just inside the edge of a forest. He would keep watch during the day. If she had stayed at the inn she would have to pass by him. If not, then he would have to assume that he was still behind her.

He stretched out on the soft earth and rested while it was still dark. The sounds of the forest soothed him and he breathed in its rich scents. Somewhere nearby a rabbit had been recently killed and the smell of blood was so strong that it overpowered almost everything else. He settled down to wait.

It was just past midday and Carissa was looking for a place to rest both herself and her horse. As the day had worn on she had passed a dozen travelers and had discovered from one that she was close to Vézelay, which meant that most of the people she had seen were pilgrims. They were heading to the abbey, which was said to house the bones of Mary Magdalene.

For her, though, the thought of Vézelay conjured memories of her father. It was in Vézelay that Bernard of Clairvaux had preached the crusade and from there that her father had embarked upon the journey to Jerusalem. He had spoken of it often and the thought of seeing it stirred something deep within her.

When she was little she had often wished she could accompany her father on some grand adventure. Now that she was on her own grand adventure she found she would give everything to have been able to live out her years in peace at Bryas.

She did find herself breathing easier, though, as she realized she could pass as a pilgrim and draw much less attention to herself. She stopped looking for places off the road to hide when other travelers came in sight. Instead she smiled and greeted them in the name of the Lord and found that the time passed pleasantly.

At last she saw a large shady area with plenty of grass that looked inviting. Clearly her horse thought so as well, as he turned toward it with no urging from her. She hailed a stranger heading toward her.

"Sir, how much farther until I reach Vézelay?"

"A little more than half a day's journey. I left there with the dawn."

"Thank you," she said. He nodded and continued on.

"You hear that, boy?" she said, as she dismounted. "So, what do you say, ride hard and chance reaching there late tonight?"

The horse shook his head.

"Or should we find some place to sleep tonight and arrive there tomorrow?"

The horse had turned his attention to eating the grass. She sat down, settled her back against a tree, and thought about her father. He had told her many stories about the crusade, but she suspected she had not heard them all. He had often said that one day he would tell her a very special story. She wondered what it would have been and was sad that she would never know.

Out of long habit she reached for the cross that wasn't there. When she realized what she was doing she swore again that she would take it back from Pierre no matter the cost.

She leaned her head against the tree and watched as a small group of pilgrims passed by. She could see the devotion on their faces, hear the joy and excitement in their voices. Her own pilgrimage was much more grim and far from holy. She closed her eyes and fell asleep.

Gabriel shouted in frustration. He traced the spot in the earth where Carissa had slept the night before. He had been minutes from catching up to her at daybreak. Now she was gone again. He rose to his feet and began to run, swearing to let nothing, not even the cursed sun, keep him from her.

He made it to the road and had taken a dozen steps when he stopped and spun around. The road was empty and the woods were still and dark. And yet there was . . . something. He closed his eyes and strained his ears but heard nothing that should not be there. He had spent enough time hunting, though, to recognize when he was being hunted.

He continued to run but kept his senses alert for any signs of pursuit. Whoever the hunter was he could wait. Gabriel had to find Carissa before something happened to her. Even if she managed to make it safely to Bryas, once there she could still be killed.

It wasn't his battle; he knew that. But he had pledged to aid her in finding revenge. In his heart, though, he knew that wasn't the real reason. Something had happened in that prison cell that he never could have foreseen. He had come to know her better than he had ever known another. It was more than just the stories of her life. It was the qualities of her character, the subtleties of thought and action that he had learned. And somewhere amid all of it he had fallen in love with her.

That was why he had to find her. That was why he had to help her. And, ultimately, that was why he had to save her.

He ran for a couple of hours, stopping twice to look for signs of Carissa or the hunter. He could find evidence of neither. When he stopped a third time he could smell the presence of people close by, but none of them appeared to be Carissa. They seemed to be camped just off the road. He made to give them a wide berth when sudden screaming caught his attention.

He headed toward the sound and a moment later a man, his body engulfed in flames, staggered onto the road and fell. The smell of burning hair and flesh filled his nostrils as more screaming reached his ears. He ran around the man who was beyond help and saw the camp. There were a dozen people, half of them dead, their throats torn out. Two more were on fire and the remaining ones were running for their lives.

Gabriel spun in a circle, looking for the threat, but could find nothing. A teenage boy ran past him and Gabriel grabbed his arm. The boy spun around, eyes wide with fear, and blood gushing from his nose. He began to babble incoherently and Gabriel shook him.

"Calm yourself and tell me what happened here," he demanded, voice slow and deep.

The boy went slightly slack and Gabriel found himself holding him up. "We are pilgrims traveling to Vézelay. We were attacked by some kind of monster. He killed some, he burned those who tried to help."

"Did you get a good look at this monster?"

"No."

Gabriel wrestled with what to do. He sensed that the immediate threat was over. He wanted to leave, to find Carissa, but the survivors would need his help if they were to make it through the night.

Given the amount of destruction and the speed with which it had obviously happened it was a safe bet a vampire had been involved. On some level that made it his problem. The attacks, so brutal and so public, were the actions of a young vampire. Keeping the existence of their kind a secret was the responsibility of every vampire old enough to know better. With any luck the vampire's mentor would have already found him and would clean up the mess.

I should keep going.

"Did he say anything?" Gabriel asked the boy.

"My cousin was praying," the boy said, licking his lips. "And it said 'Better you should have prayed to me.'"

Gabriel froze.

Raphael.

He had hoped that the vampire would have at least learned some restraint. So many things had changed since those days, but apparently much had also stayed the same.

He stood for a moment, staring into the darkness. Somewhere out there he knew Raphael was watching.

* * *

Carissa awoke to the sound of her horse screaming in terror. She opened her eyes and realized that night had fallen while she had slept. She scrambled to her feet. A short distance away the animal thrashed around and then fell. It staggered to its feet and lurched off.

Carissa moved to go after him when an icy hand touched her back. She didn't know if it was real or imagined but the sensation brought her up short. She spun around and stared up into a snarling, demonic face that loomed in the darkness above her. She started to scream but a hand clamped over her mouth. On it she could smell blood and death and charred flesh. Her body convulsed even as she tried to pull away. He grabbed her with his free hand, though, and pulled her close.

"You are of interest to Gabriel," he growled. "And that makes you of great interest to me."

She struggled against him but he only laughed. "Do you know what they say about little girls who play with vampires?" he asked.

She shook her head.

He leaned down and whispered in her ear, "Sooner or later they get bitten."

CHAPTER TEN

*Then said Jesus unto his disciples, If any man
will come after me, let him deny himself, and
take up his cross, and follow me.*

—Matthew 16:24

Raphael dropped the pages Carissa had written as if
they had scalded him. He cursed himself for being a
fool. He had been so concerned about keeping the truth
of Carissa's death from Susan that he hadn't even
stopped to think about that night in the forest and what
he had done to her. But there it was, in ink on the page.
She had written it down, faithfully recording his sins for
a new generation to discover. He shuddered with the horror of the memory.

So much rage, so much pain. He had vowed revenge
upon Gabriel and he didn't care who he hurt to get it.

"What happened?" Susan asked, in a voice that broke
his heart.

He couldn't look at her. "I found them by accident. I
was traveling to Avignon to see if he had ever returned. It
was the night before the Baron attacked, just before daybreak. The next night I tracked them and then kept on her
trail when the two parted ways."

He took a breath and realized that he was more afraid to tell her the rest than he was to face Richelieu. "You have to understand. I was young. I was very angry. I had no idea what had happened to Gabriel. I hated him for creating me and then I hated him even more for abandoning me, or so I thought at the time. I would have done anything, *anything* to get revenge for that. As it turns out revenge can be the most destructive of all actions, with consequences that reach much further than you can ever dream."

"If hindsight for the average person makes things clear I can imagine what things you can see, connections you can make, looking back over eight hundred years," she said quietly.

"You have no idea," he whispered. That was the heart of the curse of vampirism. You lived long enough that you came to repent of your sins, regret your mistakes. It was more than that, though. You regretted your omissions and your missteps as well. When you could trace so many things and see how one tiny act could have ripple effects that resulted in the death of a dozen people three hundred years later it was devastating, heartbreaking. He suspected it was just one of the reasons why so many vampires who reached this stage turned to God. They were broken, shattered, seeking the comfort and guidance that so many humans seemed to find in their tiny little lifespan. But for some it took so much longer to learn the lessons of life.

"What kills me is that I'm almost nine hundred years old and I'm still making mistakes, still choosing wrongly. I'm still a monster."

He could hear the pain in his own voice and he winced. He'd spent nearly a millennia trying not to be vulnerable to anything and now he was completely undone by a young woman who somehow seemed so much wiser than he was even if she knew very little of the world.

She reached out and put her hand on his arm and he jerked away. Every time they touched it led to danger, for both of them. He couldn't stop being what he was, who he was. But neither could he stop caring for her far more than he should, far more than he'd ever cared for anyone.

Even myself.

"I'm sorry," she said.

She meant it, he could tell. She didn't wish him to be in pain or to feel the burning guilt and agony that he did. He thought about Gabriel. His sire was more comfortable in his own skin than anyone Raphael had ever met. It was truer now than ever before.

He knows he's a monster, but he accepts that.

Raphael wasn't sure he could ever accept himself. He would settle for being able to forgive himself.

"I forgive you," Susan whispered.

He jerked, for a terrible moment thinking somehow she could read his mind, too. But she couldn't. That didn't mean she didn't know what to say. She understood on some deep level what he was going through.

"The sun's rising," he said. He was grateful. He couldn't stand to pick up those papers and read Carissa's story of what had happened next. He was sure that it would kill him to do so, even if Susan did offer her forgiveness, ignorant as she was of what exactly she was forgiving him for.

"Then you'd better lie down," she said.

He nodded and stood. He headed for the stairs and could feel his legs becoming heavy as dawn came closer with each second. He made it into the room upstairs. He could feel the pull of the sun upon him as he lay down on the ground close to Paul's bed.

"We need you," he whispered to the monk.

Only silence answered him as the sun rose and sleep claimed him.

AUSTRIA, PRESENT DAY

Gabriel drove as fast as he could push the car without causing them to crash. His reflexes were lightning swift and he had nearly a century of driving experience to his credit, but in the end there was only so much you could ask of a mechanical steed. In that regard things hadn't changed so much from the old days.

The more things change the more they stay the same.

The horizon was lightening and soon the dawn would be upon them. The one advantage to having both David and the car along was that the journey could continue while he was asleep.

He pulled over to the side of the road. David roused. Gabriel wasn't sure if the human had been deep in thought or asleep.

"What is it?" David asked.

"Sun's coming. Time for you to drive while I sleep and hide from the sun," Gabriel said. He got out of the car and David came around to the driver's side.

"Will you be in the trunk?" David asked.

Gabriel smiled. "Nothing so uncomfortable or so cliché, fortunately. The windows on the car have the strongest possible tint on them and I should be fine in the backseat under a blanket."

"Okay. As long as it's safe," David said absently as he yawned and stretched.

Gabriel hid his smile. David had forgotten, even if for a moment, how uncertain all their lives were. As David climbed into the driver's seat Gabriel got in the back. He unfolded the blanket that he kept there for just such a need and pulled it over himself as he laid down.

He could feel the car accelerate back onto the road. The sun had risen and he could feel its pull. He resisted for a few minutes as he continued to think about Raphael.

The younger vampire still infuriated him, but he had also proven himself quite useful. His feelings for Susan would continue to mellow him out if he didn't suppress them. Gabriel hoped for all their sake's that he did not. A more mellow Raphael was better for everyone. It was a happy change from the hotheaded killer he had cursed so many centuries before. But no matter how much time had passed he did not forget what Raphael had been, what he had done. Gabriel remembered well what the aftermath of one of Raphael's massacres looked like.

FRANCE, 1198 AD

The smell of blood hung heavy in the air over the camp and it made things that much harder for Gabriel. He kept up a string of curses in his mind, all directed at Raphael as he tended to what needed to be done. Every moment he had to spend helping was a moment more apart from Carissa, a moment lost that he might have spent finding her.

If he got his hands on Raphael he would kill him, put an end to this destructiveness. But that couldn't be his focus. He had to find Carissa before it was too late. She might already be dead or captured for all he knew and the thought just made him curse Raphael all the more.

The survivors of the massacre were all in shock, some of them babbling incoherently. Their confusion and uncertainty was a hindrance as he worked but it would serve him well once he left.

The boy who had asked for his help did what he could to assist. He would grow into a fine man someday if he survived the pilgrimage he was currently on.

When the work was finally done Gabriel cursed Raphael as he left behind the survivors of the massacre. He had helped bury the dead, doctor the wounded, and ease the minds of the survivors. He was fairly certain none would remember him or the speed with which he had aided. He had also worked hard to convince them all that they had been attacked by a band of savage men and not a single monster.

Still as the road flashed beneath his feet he began to despair of finding Carissa that night. Worse, he had no idea where Raphael was. The other vampire could be behind him or ahead of him.

There was a time long ago when he would have reveled in such a chase, two quarries, himself hunted even as he was hunting. But that man had died ages before. Paul had seen to that. Now he took no thrill in the hunt. All he cared for was finding the girl and either eluding or killing his cursed protégé. He just hoped that Raphael hadn't found Carissa.

That fear spurred him on even faster and the miles disappeared beneath his feet. Suddenly he heard the sound of a horse walking slowly toward him. In a moment the animal came within view and a cold knot settled in Gabriel's stomach when he realized there was no rider.

Was this another hapless traveler who had fallen victim to Raphael? He strained his eyes, seeking to get a better glimpse of the animal. Fear touched him as he realized that it looked like Carissa's mount.

A thousand thoughts crowded his mind, as everything that could have befallen her played itself out in his imagination. When he reached the horse he discovered that the animal was weak, probably from loss of blood. Tied neatly to the saddle was a parchment. He pulled it free and by the light of the moon was able to read what had been written there in blood.

How important is she?

He began to run again. The horse turned to follow him but he didn't care. *God, let me find her. God, let her be safe*, he prayed as he ran. Finally in the distance he could see fire, what looked to be something much larger than a cooking fire. He headed for it, trying to fight the fear that threatened to overcome him.

He could hear Carissa screaming. And then he saw her. She was tied to a crude cross, surrounded by fire that outlined a giant cross on the ground. Raphael meant to burn her to death.

Carissa could feel the heat of the flames. She screamed, hoping someone, anyone would hear her. The vampire had knocked her out and she had regained consciousness just as he was lighting the giant cross on fire. She was in the dead center of it.

She had asked him what he wanted from her and he had calmly replied that it was nothing to do with her and everything to do with Gabriel. She had told him Gabriel was dead, but he had just laughed and walked away. She struggled against her bonds, her hands growing slick with her own blood until the smell of it filled the air.

Panic flooded her and the terrible irony that she was going to be burned not by Pierre but by a vampire who cared nothing for her was overwhelming.

That she should come so close to realizing her revenge only to be killed by someone seeking revenge against Gabriel crushed her. She couldn't give up, though. She owed it to herself and Gabriel to keep trying, to keep fighting.

"God, help me!" she prayed frantically, repeating the words over and over as she continued to strain against her bonds.

Suddenly a figure appeared just outside the flames. For a moment she thought her captor had returned, but it wasn't him. In a rush she recognized Gabriel.

She sobbed with terror and relief. "Gabriel! You're alive!"

"Carissa, are you unharmed?"

"Yes, but I cannot get free."

He hesitated, and then she realized that even if he could somehow leap over the flames that he would have to walk on the cross to free her, burning himself, perhaps beyond his ability to heal.

"I can't find anything to put the fire out with," he shouted.

She watched as a ribbon of flame snaked toward her. "I don't think we have much time," she said.

"I don't know how I can free you."

"Paul can touch crosses without burning," Carissa reminded him.

"Not me."

"Maybe that's because you really do fight against God," she said.

"I believe in God. I believe He brought you into my life."

The heat was growing more intense and she felt like her skin was on fire. "Gabriel, hurry!" she begged.

"God, give me the strength," she heard him pray.

She watched as he backed up several feet and then leaped over the flames. He landed on his feet and there was a fleeting look of pain that was soon replaced by grim determination. He ran to her and tore the ropes loose. She collapsed into his arms and then they were running, and for a moment flying.

He landed hard beyond the flames, staggered and nearly dropped her. After a moment he straightened and began to move in the direction of the town. She heard a whinny and turned to see that her horse was following. She rested her head against Gabriel's shoulder and allowed him to carry her.

"Are you okay?" she asked, her voice shaking.

"I'm not on fire," he said with quiet significance.

"Does that mean you've stopped struggling against God?" she asked.

"I don't know what it means exactly, I'm just grateful," he said.

"So am I."

She dozed fitfully, only half aware of them skirting the town she had been trying to reach. Sometime close to morning they stopped and Carissa fell asleep under a tree, knowing Gabriel watched over her protectively.

PRAGUE, PRESENT DAY

Susan was able to get some sleep but was awake in the early afternoon. She checked in on Raphael and Paul and sat for a moment, praying over both of them, hoping for some change in Paul's body and some change in Raphael's spirit.

She feared for him. He was carrying around too much anger and guilt and it would destroy him if he wasn't careful. She knew there were things that he didn't want to tell her, but she also knew in her heart that she could forgive him anything in his past. She just needed him to trust her and himself.

After making herself something to eat she called David.

"Hello?" he asked, slurring his words.

"Did I wake you?"

"Yes, thank you."

"Oh, I'm sorry."

"No, it's a good thing. Trust me," he said, his voice grim.

"What's wrong?" she asked.

"I'm driving."

She shuddered. "If you're falling asleep at the wheel then it's time for you to pull over and get some sleep. You're no good to Wendy dead."

"I can't. I have to keep going. I can get there by nightfall, I think."

"I repeat: not if you're dead."

"I get your point. But I'll be okay."

"I very much doubt that," she said.

"Then talk to me awhile."

She quickly filled him in on what else she knew about Carissa and Fleur. "What about you? Find anything?" she asked.

"We found…something," he said. "It was in the house in Vienna. Pierre turned the basement of that house into a shrine to Carissa. He's obsessed with her in a Stalker of the Millennium kind of way."

"What was down there?"

"What wasn't down there? Seriously. He had so many things. He had a brush, a lock of her hair, earrings, even the dress she died in. I thought Gabriel was going to go completely ballistic. He scared me in a way that I don't care to ever be scared again."

"He loved her, and Pierre is the monster who tried to kill her. I can understand him being upset."

"This was beyond upset."

"I can only imagine how he must have felt. To have loved her and then to have seen all that stuff so long after she died."

"Have you figured out what happened to her yet?"

"No, not yet," Susan admitted. She thought of Raphael lying upstairs and his reluctance to read Carissa's diary. Did he know what had happened to her? "I hope whatever happened, she died peacefully at a very old age."

"Somehow I doubt that's how it happened," David said. "The dress she died in? There was blood on one side, by the neckline. It was quite a lot of blood, actually."

Susan could feel herself tensing up. "Do you think she was killed by a vampire?"

"That was my guess when I saw the dress," David said.

Susan glanced at the stairs. She thought of all the times that she and Raphael had kissed and how he had said it was so hard to restrain himself. Then there was the one time he'd had to drink her blood, to save his life. But she had given that blood to him willingly.

She pressed a hand to the side of her neck. Sometimes it was strange, but it was almost like she could still feel him biting her.

"Do you think it was one of Gabriel's enemies, perhaps even Pierre?" David asked.

"Maybe," Susan muttered. Raphael would have been one of Gabriel's enemies in those days. The thought that he could have killed Carissa was horrifying. Yet he had stopped reading abruptly when it was clear he had encountered Carissa on her journey to Bryas. She had to have survived that encounter for her to have been writing about it, though. Was it possible he had killed her, but at some later date?

The thought made her feel sick inside. *God, I know I said I could forgive him for anything, but please, please let it not be true*, she prayed silently.

She cleared her throat, remembering that she was talking to David. "Or maybe she gave her life to save Gabriel."

It was possible. After all, Susan herself had nearly given her life to save Raphael. Carissa could have been trying to do the same for Gabriel but he might have drunk too much.

"I just don't know," she said at last.

"Think we ever will?" David asked.

"Yes. I'll make someone tell me the truth," Susan vowed. "What else did you find in the shrine?"

"Artwork by the masters, all of them paintings of Carissa that Pierre must have had commissioned over the years. It's got to be worth a fortune. I barely managed to stop Gabriel from torching the whole place, though."

Artwork. Something stirred in the back of Susan's mind. She thought of being in Pierre's office. He had a portrait of her grandmother as a young woman in it. She remembered how odd it had been to see that portrait. And what was it Raphael had once told her? *I was not the vampire who was in love with your grandmother.*

Shock rippled through her. Pierre. Pierre had to have been the vampire who was in love with her grandmother.

"Did you find anything that belonged to someone else, someone other than Carissa?" she asked, her voice shaking.

"Not that I saw. Why, what's wrong?"

"I think Pierre's obsession with Carissa extended to our grandmother, Wendy's and mine."

"The woman whose funeral brought you both to Prague?" David asked quietly.

"Yes. There's a portrait of her as a young woman in his office here in Prague."

"Really?"

"Yes."

And just like that she knew what she had to do. She glanced at the clock. She still had a good three hours of sunlight left. It was enough time. At least, she hoped it was. The portrait was important. She didn't know why, but something deep inside her told her that it was. She could feel it. She was learning to trust these urgings more and more as promptings of the Holy Spirit.

"David, I have to go," she said.

"Why, what's wrong?" he asked, suspicion lacing his voice.

"It's better if you don't know."

"Don't play that game with me, Susan," he said, his voice ominous. "We've already got one person missing. I can't deal with a second."

"Okay, I'm going to break into Pierre's office and get that portrait. I have a feeling it's important. If I go now, I can get there and back before sunset."

EUROPE, PRESENT DAY

For a moment David considered asking Susan if she'd lost her mind. He forced himself to calm down, though. Nothing he was going to say was going to sway her; he could tell that much by the sound of her voice.

"Okay," David said, taking a deep breath. "Be careful. I wish I was there to help."

"Just find Wendy as quickly as you can and call me if you see or hear anything else I should know about," Susan said.

"I will as long as you promise to do the same. And please, call me the moment you're back safe in the house."

"I will. And if you start to fall asleep again, pull off to the side of the road or at least wake up Gabriel or something. You know he can be awake during the day, so as long as he's not in the sun it should be fine."

"After what I saw in that basement, I'm happier with him asleep."

"He really scared you that badly?" she asked. "What did he do?"

"It wasn't anything he did. It was the look on his face and the vibe he gave off that were indescribable. I don't think I've ever been that freaked out in my entire life."

"Given what we've been through lately that's saying a lot."

"Tell me about it. I'll be okay. If I start to get tired I promise I'll pull over and at least get some fresh air or something."

"Okay. Wish me luck."

"Good luck, Susan."

He ended the call and focused on the road ahead. He prayed that she would be safe while she was breaking into Pierre's offices. "Why does she have to be so stubborn?" he asked the universe when he was finished.

"Because she's a woman of Bryas."

CHAPTER ELEVEN

For Christ sent me not to baptize, but to preach the gospel: not with wisdom of words, lest the cross of Christ should be made of none effect.

—I Corinthians 1:17

David shouted in surprise and nearly lost control of the car. He managed to straighten it out and then he pulled over to the side of the road. His heart was hammering in his chest and whatever lingering sleepiness he'd had was completely gone.

"I thought you were asleep," he said, twisting in his seat.

Gabriel was sitting in the backseat, staring out at him from underneath his cloak with eyes that seemed to burn and glow in the darkness. A blanket lay crumpled on the seat next to him.

"I was, but I heard you say my name."

David blanched, trying to remember how early in the conversation with Susan he had said Gabriel's name. Whenever it was, it couldn't have been good.

"Next time, make a sound, something. Let me know you're awake and don't wait until you can shock the living daylights out of me."

"It's an old habit, one not easily broken."

"I understand, but please try."

I don't care what you say about me. It matters not.

The words echoed around in his head making him grit his teeth. At least they were nearing the next house on their list. Traffic was getting increasingly heavier as they approached the city. He found himself pressing down on the accelerator more and more while constantly checking his mirrors for police. Of course, he didn't even know what kind of car to watch out for in this country, but he still looked compulsively.

The faster they got to Wendy the better.

Gabriel could tell that David was now embarrassed as well as uncomfortable. It didn't matter, Gabriel preferred the silence to forced conversation. He glanced around them.

"We're close to our destination," Gabriel noted. And at the back of his mind something shifted. "He's completely obsessed with Carissa."

"Yes, I think we've established that already," David said, still clearly rattled.

"We've been looking at this all wrong. He's going to head back to Bryas."

"What?"

"That's where he's going to take Wendy. Where's the closest house to that?"

"There's one in France, I think it's outside of Paris by about eighty miles."

"To the northwest?"

"I think so."

"That's it. That's where he's got her. Change of plan. Drive there."

"Are you sure?" David said. "We're only about half an hour from the house we're heading to."

"I'm sure. It's a waste of time. He's taken her to France. I know it."

A minute later David changed lanes and they went shooting off onto a different road. Gabriel cursed himself for wasting valuable hours figuring that out. It had been there, in the back of his mind ever since he was standing in that basement and realized he was staring at a lock of Carissa's hair.

Bryas. Why was it his footsteps constantly led back there? It had been that way many times across the centuries. Ever since his first visit there with Carissa. They had been seeking Pierre just as he and David now were.

But the road had been long and the journey nothing like he had ever expected it to be.

FRANCE, 1198 AD

They were within a night's ride of Bryas. There had been no further sign of Raphael. Gabriel began to believe that whatever he had planned it wasn't going to materialize immediately. Still, he didn't let down his guard. They had come too far to let anything stop them now. He still wasn't sure why the vampire hadn't stayed to watch and attack while Gabriel rescued Carissa from the burning cross. He was just grateful for the reprieve.

He walked while Carissa rode. It was much slower going than if he had carried her, but she hadn't objected. And he had come to realize he didn't want their journey to end.

What was waiting for her at Bryas would be terrible, no matter the outcome.

And he had grown to enjoy her company, to crave it. When she fell asleep before he did he missed her. It was utterly strange to him the way he was thinking, feeling.

He marveled at the newness of the emotion even as he dawdled on the road. Still, it was a dangerous game they were playing. Just as death and peril waited for them at Bryas, it also lurked here with them in the woods. Raphael had not shown himself, but it didn't mean he wasn't near. The same also held true for the Baron, who had surely found their trail.

As they drew near to Bryas, though, he realized that the time had come for them to finally discuss exactly what was going to happen when they reached her home.

"Another night's ride and we will be there."

She smiled at him. "I have missed my home. It's beautiful, you know."

"I am sure it is," he said. He had never been there. He had always planned to steer clear, leave Jean and Marie alone and happy there. He had been imprisoned before it ever became an issue.

"Your parents must have been much older when they had you," he said at last.

She nodded. "Yes. They didn't think they were going to be able to have children."

"What is your plan once we reach Bryas?" he finally asked her, wishing he did not have to bring it up. He'd give everything he owned if he could convince her to leave this place and go away with him somewhere, anywhere. But he knew that with Pierre alive she would never do so.

"Reach Bryas. Make it inside the castle. I will get close to Pierre and kill him."

Gabriel stared at her in disbelief. "Weeks to think about it and that is your grand plan?" he asked.

She shrugged.

"No escape plan even?"

She shook her head. "I have always known I will probably die, too."

"Sweet, crazy Carissa. I am going to have to do what I can to keep that from happening," he said.

She smiled weakly at him.

"How exactly did you plan on killing him? A dagger? That would be the easiest way, but not so easy for you, I think, unless you are trained to use one or wait until he is asleep, and we have no weapon between us. If you wish to poison him we might spend some time in the forest here finding the right plants to aid you."

"I hadn't thought about it that closely," she said. "I just picture the look in his eyes."

"Killing someone is not an easy thing," he said softly.

It sounded good at any rate. He'd heard others say that many times. It had never been a problem for him, but then again, that was part of the reason why he was cursed now.

"I know," she said. "Remember the man on the boat?"

How could he forget? When Carissa had killed him she had only meant to stop him from doing the same to Gabriel. She'd only been trying to hurt the man. "I remember," he said softly.

"But it has to be done. I will not suffer him to live after what he did to me."

"The Bible says that vengeance belongs to the Lord," he said, trying again.

"And how often does He enact that vengeance through the hand of another?"

"Setting yourself up as God's instrument? That's a dangerous proposition. I believe there are several magistrates who have done the same and look at where it has led."

She stared at him with fury in her eyes. "Never equate me with those villains who did this to me."

"I am sorry," he said, meaning it. He knew he'd crossed a line, but he wished that there was some way he could change her mind.

Then he thought about Pierre. He had heartlessly thrown her into a dungeon with a monster. All kinds of horrible things could have happened to her, and Pierre had meant them to. Gabriel hated him for that.

With a start he realized he hated him far more for something else, however. Pierre was Carissa's husband. He had wanted her fortune and tossed her aside as if she were worthless as soon as he had it. Until he was dead, she could never be truly free. If Gabriel had been in his place he would have known she was worth far more than whatever vast property was entailed to her. He would have treated her as a queen and spent his days worshipping her, striving to make her happy.

Rage flooded through him.

Carissa might not have to worry about how she killed Pierre. He was likely to kill him before she could even lift a finger.

"In my father's study is a dagger that he had with him in the Holy Land. I think I'll use that," she said suddenly.

"Sounds like an excellent choice," he said. "But you will need help getting close to him without raising his suspicion, so that he can't call for help, take the dagger from you, or find a weapon of his own."

"I need you for that," she said.

"I am at your command."

"I need you for so many things," she whispered.

He heard but did not say anything.

They continued for a while more. Mist began to fill the air. Morning was coming.

The sun would be rising shortly. Gabriel could feel it even though he could not see the sky through the fog that shrouded the land.

He turned off the path and Carissa followed. About a quarter of a mile off the path he found a spot where the trees grew together in a thick canopy overhead. He turned to help Carissa but she had already dismounted. He smiled appreciatively. "You certainly do know your way around a horse," he said.

She smiled as she tied her horse's reins to a tree and loosened the saddle. "I love riding. It is the only thing that makes me feel truly free. What makes you feel that way?"

"This," he said, waving his hands to encompass the forest around them as he stretched out beneath a tree. "I love the forest. I especially learned to love it after I was changed. Here, I can be outside in the daylight and yet still be safe."

She walked to him and slowly sank down to a sitting position. She looked around and her expression was suddenly timid. "The forest has always made me feel vulnerable, like there was something out there waiting to eat me."

He laughed. "And this time you are right." He lifted his hand and ran a finger down her cheek.

She jumped and looked at him with wide, frightened

eyes. She moved as though she was about to stand. Suddenly he realized exactly what he had implied. He grabbed her, his hand sliding behind her neck and pushing down gently but firmly.

"I did not mean that. I was joking. I have no intention of harming you." His heart was breaking that she believed otherwise.

She gazed deep into his eyes. He wanted to make the look of fear go away. He suddenly felt more helpless than he had all those years in the cell.

Not sure what he was doing, he leaned forward and kissed her and time seemed to stand still. Her lips were soft and warm against his and he marveled at them.

At last she pulled away and he let her go. She turned slightly and moved so that she was lying next to him with her head on his shoulder. He wrapped his arm around her. He tasted blood in his mouth where the inside of his lower lip had been pressed against his fangs. He smiled and closed his eyes, not sure what had just happened and not wanting to question it.

A moment later her breathing changed, slowing. She was sleeping, which was good. That meant she was no longer afraid.

It was the first kiss he'd ever had. And sitting there under the tree as the sun rose he vowed it would not be the last.

The sun was low in the sky as Carissa awoke. She lay still for a moment, feeling Gabriel's shoulder beneath her cheek. She thought of the kiss they had shared and marveled at it. He had been so gentle and yet she had found it impossible to resist his embrace. It had taken all of her will to end the kiss because she had wanted it to last forever. So many strange things had happened to her that she was surprised that anything could yet amaze her.

Love. It had to be. Nothing else could describe what she was feeling. She longed to say it aloud, to taste the word on her tongue. Love, the magic that poets talked of, had finally found her. She remembered what the gypsy woman had told her, that she would wander long in darkness before finding love.

The darkness had been long and terrible indeed. And yet, just as she had said, Carissa had fallen in love.

How had it happened? How had she fallen in love with a vampire? Looking back she realized it had been no one event, but a series of steps that had led inexorably and inevitably here. A thousand words, a hundred gestures, a dozen acts of thoughtfulness and kindness.

So this was what it felt like. It was a quiet passion within, not the raging storm she had been led to expect by poets and gossips. Maybe they had never truly experienced it and just made up the other to have something to say so that they might seem wise and worldly.

I love him, but to what end? she asked herself as quiet revelation was crushed by stark realities. *He is a monster.*

Though she thought it, her soul did not believe it. There was something too noble, too fine, about him. Maybe that had not always been true, but surely if the sinner could turn from his ways the base man could elevate himself. So what if he outwardly seemed a monster; was it not the quality of his mind and soul that made a man?

If that were true, then Pierre was certainly no man, but rather a monster who wrapped himself in a shroud of self-righteousness.

He was awake. She didn't know how she knew, but she did.

"Are you awake?" he asked softly in her ear.

"You know that I am or you would not have asked," she replied, struggling with her own newly discovered emotions.

"Are you well? Your heart is racing."

She looked up at him. She wasn't ready to answer that. Instead she asked a question she had spent a lot of time thinking about. "Is it difficult to restrain yourself from...from..."

"From biting you?" he asked.

"Yes." She had wondered that for a long time. Now she wondered if it was half as hard for him to keep himself from biting her as it was for her to keep from kissing him again right then.

"Yes, it is," he said. "Very hard."

Her heart skipped a beat.

"Do not worry, I will not."

And she thought of what it would be like to have his lips on her neck, his fangs piercing her skin, and her heart began to race even faster. "What if I wanted you to?" she whispered before she could stop herself.

"Then I would," he growled.

Suddenly he was breathing, long, powerful breaths.

Heart pounding, she lifted her arms and put them around his neck. She looked into his eyes and saw fire dancing within them. She wanted to know that fire, be a part of it.

"I want you to," she whispered.

He picked her up. His breathing had become even deeper, the sound nearly overpowering.

He pulled her hair back from her face and she trembled

at his touch. As he began stroking the side of her throat she closed her eyes and tilted her head away, exposing more of her neck to him.

His touch was electrifying and fear and desire exploded within her. She felt her own breathing begin to slow and deepen to match his. She felt his lips against her ear, tickling and tantalizing her.

"Are you sure?" he rumbled.

"Yes."

His lips trailed from her ear down the side of her neck. He wrapped his arms around her, crushing her to him.

"Please," she begged him.

Then his teeth sunk into her neck, penetrating the skin. She could feel her blood flowing from her into him. As pain and pleasure washed over her she grabbed the back of his head and pushed his fangs deeper into her. She gasped as she felt the connection with him. For a moment she could feel what he felt: all his desire, his passion, his power. Time seemed to stand still, the two of them locked in an eternal embrace.

She groaned and let herself go limp in his arms. When he pulled away she cried out, bereft. He lowered her slowly back onto the forest floor and then laid down beside her, softly stroking first her cheeks and then her arms.

"Don't leave me," she sobbed.

"I won't," he pledged, wrapping his arms around her.

Carissa watched the moon rise with sorrow. Soon they must confront Pierre. She suddenly wished they could run away instead, far away where no one would ever find them. But if they did that, she would never truly be free. Finally she got up and a few minutes later Gabriel helped her up on her horse.

They moved swiftly and didn't speak much. She wanted to make it well before dawn, fearing what would happen if they had to wait another night. Now that the task was at hand she felt a growing sense of anxiety and unease and she realized she would not be able to breathe freely until it was done.

Gabriel trotted alongside her horse and she kept glancing at him, overwhelmed by the feelings she had for him. In such a short time he had become her whole world. Her heart soared one moment and ached the next as she struggled to sort it all out.

They made good time, faster than she would have thought, but the hours were slipping away and the moon was dipping back toward the horizon when they finally topped a small ridge.

She looked down and her chest tightened.

Bryas.

Carissa was home.

She breathed in deeply, smelling the jasmine that grew wild around the castle. Out in a field horses she knew lifted their heads to look in her direction and whinny softly. She longed to go to them, to find Dancer and bury her head in her golden mane. She assumed that her mare had made it back safely. There would be time enough to find out later, though.

"There will be guards," she said.

"Then we would do best to approach on foot."

"There is a secret entrance, a sort of emergency escape route, that Pierre is unlikely to know about."

"Then that is the way we should take."

She hesitated and he looked at her, his eyes so tender that it made her want to cry. "What's wrong?"

"We have only an hour, maybe less, before dawn."

"It shouldn't take longer than that to get in, should it?"

"No, but I don't want to risk being in the middle of things when the sun comes up."

"Then we'll wait. We'll set up camp just off the road. If anyone comes or goes you'll be able to hear them while remaining hidden."

"Thank you," she said, relief flooding her. This way she would know if Pierre tried to leave and she wouldn't have to feel this sense of urgency, of panic, anymore.

"It will be all right."

He led the horse into the forest and a few minutes later they were again sitting beneath a tree. She thought of the last tree they had sat beneath, what they had shared, and she felt herself blushing. She also felt strangely shy around him.

It was just nerves, it had to be. She was so fixated on killing Pierre that all else seemed only half real to her. At least, that was what she tried to tell herself.

"You know what I miss?" she said as she leaned her head on his shoulder.

"What?"

"My nice, soft bed. It seems like all I've slept on for as long as I can remember is stone or dirt."

"There was that nice bed at the inn," he reminded her.

"True," she said, beginning to feel drowsy. It was morning and she was ready to sleep. It made her smile. She'd been keeping company with a vampire so long his hours had become her hours, her body adjusted to them.

"I miss my bed as well. It's soft, warm, beautiful, hand-carved wood made in a faraway place."

"I'd love to see it someday," she said, then blushed

again when she realized how improper what she'd said was.

"And I'd love to show it to you someday," he answered.

She tried to analyze his voice. What did he mean by the statement? She couldn't tell, and she was so sleepy that she didn't want to do anything but continue to sit there, enjoying the feeling of his shoulder beneath her cheek.

Sleepy as she was, though, she still felt slightly nervous and uncomfortable. What must he think of her? She had been so brazen earlier.

"If we survive this, what then?" she asked, realizing that he was right; she had never planned for a life beyond the revenge she wanted to take. She couldn't imagine what would happen to her if she did manage to kill Pierre and somehow escape.

She did know, though, that she didn't want to be parted from Gabriel. Not ever.

He didn't say anything and she wondered if he was already asleep. She could feel herself drifting, floating, her own thoughts growing hazy. She was just about unconscious when she heard him whisper very softly.

"If we survive this, then we'll be married."

CHAPTER TWELVE

Looking unto Jesus the author and finisher of our faith; who for the joy that was set before him endured the cross, despising the shame, and is set down at the right hand of the throne of God.

—Hebrews 12:2

Wendy had been having a bad feeling that had been intensifying over the past few hours. She couldn't help but wonder if this was the same kind of feeling her grandmother used to get and that Susan got now. She wished she knew what was happening with the others. She worried that they were looking for her when they should be trying to stop Richelieu.

Of course, she dearly wanted them to look for her, to find and rescue her, so she was conflicted. Whatever was going to happen, though, she couldn't shake the feeling that time was running out for all of them.

"And what exactly am I supposed to do with this information, this feeling?" she demanded of God at one point, stopping to stare heavenward.

No answer was forthcoming, which was probably just as well. Dealing with vampires was bad enough. If a booming voice had suddenly answered her she wasn't sure she could have handled it.

She systematically went back through the room, looking for anything she might have missed. She didn't find any more documents of interest, nor weapons of any kind.

She sat down on the chair at the table, disheartened, and leaned her head down. The chair creaked underneath her as she shifted her weight and she froze.

She kept forgetting that to her vampire captors there were weapons far different than those she normally thought of. The chair was wood, which meant it could be turned into a stake. Even though she doubted she was fast enough or strong enough to stake a vampire it was better than nothing.

She stood up, picked up the chair, and slammed it down at an angle onto the floor with such force that it made the bones in her hands and arms ache. She inspected the chair but couldn't see so much as a crack in one of the legs.

"Come on," she said as she hoisted the chair up and slammed it down again.

Nothing.

She did it a third time and finally heard a cracking sound. She checked and sure enough one of the legs was loose. She set it down, stepped on the leg, and then yanked the chair up.

With another crack the leg came free. She dropped the chair and picked the leg up to inspect it. The edges were certainly jagged but there wasn't a point sharp enough to pierce a heart, at least it didn't seem like it.

Frustrated she went to work trying to break off the other legs. The second leg broke in half, too short to be of use. Finally leg number three split down the middle and gave her two nice, long, pointed stakes. She broke off the fourth just to be on the safe side, but it, too, was pretty much useless.

At least she had the two stakes, though, one for each of her captors. She just prayed when the time came she would be the David to their Goliath. She sat down on the bed. She knew she should sleep, but she was afraid to. She didn't know if it was day or night and she didn't want them to catch her unprepared.

That meant she had some waiting to do.

"I hate waiting," she told the two stakes she had sitting next to her.

FRANCE, PRESENT DAY

Being a hunter one got used to waiting. Gabriel had practically perfected it to an art, but the last few days had tested him sorely. As he and David raced toward Bryas every minute that ticked by he realized was a minute that all the others were in jeopardy. Still, he was handling it better than David.

The anxiety radiating from the man was overwhelming. It was as nothing, though, when compared with the anxiety Carissa had been feeling when she and he had been about to confront Pierre.

BRYAS, 1198 AD

The sun had set but Gabriel hated to wake Carissa; she was sleeping so peacefully, looking like an angel. Still, it was now or never. He bent down and kissed her. She stirred slightly and he pulled away and watched as she slowly came awake. He knew he'd treasure this moment in his heart for the rest of his life.

When she finally opened her eyes she smiled up at him for just a moment before her face began to cloud over. A few moments later and he could feel the anxiety rolling off her.

"All will be well," he promised, even though he wasn't sure of it at all.

She nodded slowly and stood up, shaking out her dress. There was a leaf in her hair and he moved to brush it out. The smile she gave him in return was strained.

"I fell asleep. I was supposed to watch for people passing on the road."

"Only two came this way," he said, hesitating slightly.

"What is it?" she asked, quickly picking up on it.

"I recognized one of them as the warden who allowed us to escape."

"Why would he come here?" Carissa asked, her face registering shock.

"I do not know, but I am not sure it bodes well for him."

"Do you think Pierre discovered that he let us go?"

"For his sake, I hope not," Gabriel answered. "He passed this way a little more than an hour ago."

"And who was the other man?"

"I do not know, but he was neither peasant nor noble."

"Do you think it was one of the magistrates who . . . who condemned me?" she asked.

"There is no way to tell. If he is, though, I am sure we can pay him a little visit as well."

She nodded, but he saw her fingers twisting in the folds of her skirt, playing with the fabric. He hated to cause her more anxiety, but he felt she deserved to know the truth.

He did know one thing: Both men had reeked of fear as they rode past. It wasn't a happy meeting that either of them was anticipating. Who knew? They might have an opportunity to save Marcelle, the warden, even as he had once saved them. It would be justice of the most divine order.

He looked over Carissa. She was frightened but resolute. "Ten minutes and then we will go."

She nodded and walked off a little ways into the woods.

Carissa's heart was pounding. She distinctly remembered dreaming about kissing Gabriel, only to awake kissing Gabriel. She had wanted it to last forever.

First, though, she had business to attend to. She turned to look at Gabriel, who strode grimly by her side. They had left the horse tied up farther back. She pointed to the right side of the castle. He nodded, his keen eyes no doubt already picking out the path they would be taking.

They rounded the corner of the outer wall, keeping to the darker shadows even though it was unlikely that they would be discovered. After several minutes they reached the back of the massive structure.

Carissa stopped and pointed toward the ground. "There is a trapdoor, here. It provides an escape route for the owners."

Gabriel knelt in the dirt. "Are you certain Pierre knows nothing of it?"

She shook her head. "I never told him and to the best of my knowledge not even the servants know of its existence. My father always said it was our secret."

"That is good."

Carissa knelt beside him and touched the dirt. Weeds grew over the spot. She wedged her fingernails into a hair-thin crack and lifted. The wood door came up slowly, shedding dirt as it did so. Beneath it, narrow steps led down to a dark passageway.

"Where does it lead?" Gabriel asked.

"My bedroom."

"I will have to remember that," he said, sounding amused.

She hit him lightly in the arm but couldn't help smiling.

She started down the stairs and he followed, closing the door behind them and plunging them into darkness. She put her hand lightly against the wall, though, and continued to walk steadily.

She had walked every step of the way a dozen times as a child; her father had seen to it that she would be able to find her way out no matter the conditions. She could feel Gabriel behind her, so close that she could have felt his breath on her neck if there had been any.

At last they reached the end of the tunnel. She paused for a moment before opening the door. It swung silently inward and she stepped out of its way. A large tapestry was before her, hanging on the wall and covering the secret door.

She slid out from behind it, quickly scanning the room. It was empty and the door to the hall was closed. She felt a sharp stab of pain. It was her room but all of her things were gone. Even the bed seemed different somehow. She gripped the edge of the tapestry. At least it had not changed.

She took a deep breath and stepped out into the room. Gabriel followed.

"So this is yours?"

"It was. He's changed it, though. All my things...," she said, walking slowly to the bed.

"We will get them back," he reassured her.

She turned to look at him, tears blurring her vision. "How could he do that?"

Gabriel stepped close to her. "It is still yours," he said, bending down to kiss her.

She wrapped her arms around him. "No man has ever been in this room before except my father."

"Then I feel honored. Should I be on my best behavior?"

"Actually, I think you should be on your worst."

He growled deep in his throat and it sent shivers up her spine. He kissed her again, hard and passionate and it sent her heart pounding.

"First, let us take care of our unfinished business."

Carissa took a deep breath, her passions colliding with each other. Desire for Gabriel vied with hatred and fear at the thought of seeing Pierre. Despite her best efforts to quiet herself, she began to shake.

Gabriel took her hand in his and bit it gently. It wasn't enough to break the skin, but it was enough to startle her.

"What was that for?" she asked, bewildered.

"It was to remind you."

"Of what?"

"Of the fact that I love you and I am going to marry you."

Her breath caught in her throat. She hadn't imagined him saying that earlier. "But, I am already married," she said, unable to think of any other response.

"Not for long," he said, beginning to breathe.

PRAGUE, PRESENT DAY

Susan was terrified. She had to have been crazy to decide she was going to try and break into Pierre's office to get the painting of her grandmother. She thought about turning back half a dozen times but each time she felt that inner prodding, pushing her forward, encouraging her to do the unthinkable. Fear gnawed at the corners of her mind and anxiety slithered through her stomach but she kept moving forward.

The sky was overcast, with slate-colored clouds threatening rain. Though it was afternoon when she left, rush hour had begun. She had needed to walk nearly two miles before finding an available taxi, which she had drop her off six blocks away from Pierre's office. She knew that Raphael had already searched it the night Wendy had been taken and had declared that Pierre had left town.

For all she knew, though, he could have returned already. Or, if not him, one of his vampire associates or a human servant. She realized she was marching blind into a potentially deadly situation, but there was nothing she could do about it.

She had at least packed several weapons in her purse before she left the house, including a lot of stakes, several large crosses, cross confetti, and some vials of holy water. She just prayed that they would be enough to handle whatever it was that she came up against.

I should have waited for night. Raphael would have come with me, she thought. Coming before sunset meant any vampires, including Pierre, would be sleeping. With Richelieu's vampire minions searching for them at night it was safer on that front, too. She just wished it hadn't taken longer to get here than she'd expected. Plus, now that she was here, fears about being discovered by human minions of either vampire flooded her mind.

The sad truth was that she was probably the most

suspicious-looking person on the block. Maybe it had something to do with the fact that she was constantly swiveling her head left and right, checking over her shoulder every five steps, or that she was clutching her purse so tight her knuckles were white.

Calm down, act natural, she kept telling herself, but it was no use. The truth was that she expected someone to jump out at her at any moment and that meant there was no way she could act calm or natural.

When Pierre's building came in sight she started checking over her shoulder even more frequently and she almost made herself dizzy scanning and rescanning everything within sight.

There was a man standing, talking on his phone, right in front of the building. Susan studied him carefully. He was dressed well, like a businessman. He had salt-and-pepper hair and an aggressive air to him. She didn't want to take any chances. She reached inside her purse and seized hold of one of the crosses, then realized that if he was working for Pierre he would be a human servant and not a vampire. She scowled. What she would have given at that moment for a Taser. She hadn't been able to find any weapons in the house that were designed to fight humans. She let go of the cross and grabbed the stake instead. If she had to, she realized she could always stab him.

And if she hit him in the heart, human or vampire, he would die. She closed the gap between them and finally she could hear his side of the conversation.

"What do you mean his assistant called to cancel? When did that happen? Why didn't you tell me before I drove all the way down here? Did he say when Monsieur de Chauvere wanted to meet instead? He didn't? Really."

The man was furious. "Well, who are we going to get to draft these contracts by tomorrow morning? Do we even know if he finished them? I mean, what are we paying for? You don't have any answers—well, you better find some and fast."

He hung up and turned in her direction with a scowl. He glanced her up and down. "In case you haven't heard, the attorney has closed up shop. No one knows for how long."

"Oh, well, thank you, but, I . . . I'm not here to see him," she stammered.

"Lucky for you," he said. He turned and stalked off in the direction of a very expensive-looking red sports car. She kept walking slowly, waiting to see if he would turn around. He didn't. He got in the car and drove away.

She hurried back the few feet to Pierre's building. There was no use trying the front door. She was sure that's how the man who had just left had discovered that the office was closed in the first place.

She ducked down the side of the building, hoping no one saw her. She looked for an open window, something. After all, Raphael had gotten in some way. She wished she knew something about picking locks. When she made it to the back of the building she identified the windows she believed led directly into Pierre's office. Heavy red drapes were pulled inside the building. She tried the windows, but they all seemed to be locked.

She was wasting time. For all she knew Raphael had gone in through one of the windows upstairs, a feat she could never duplicate. She paused, looking for a rock or something else she could use to smash one of the windows. There wasn't anything like that lying around.

She pulled a stake out of her purse. She turned her face

away, shielding it with her left arm as she slammed the stake into the window. It sent a jolt through her arm but the window remained intact. She searched her large purse, and though it was full of supplies, there was nothing in it that would break a window. She eyed the rain gutter, her purse weighing heavily in her hands. She was about to set it down when she had another idea. Grasping the handles in both hands, she swung the purse hard into the glass. It cracked. She hit it again. The sound of breaking glass was like some kind of miniature explosion and she was sure everyone for blocks around could have heard.

She waited for the sound of running footsteps or a burglar alarm, but heard neither. She turned to the window and carefully used the butt of her stake to knock the rest of the glass inside. Finished she reached in and pulled one of the curtains over the windowsill and then hoisted herself up and over.

She climbed into the room, immediately put the curtain back in its proper place, and moved away from the window. She glanced around, praying that the place really was empty. The room was dark with the curtains drawn and no lights on.

She stumbled in the direction of the door and then felt along the wall until she found the switch. The room was instantly flooded with bright light and she squinted as she looked around.

The portrait of her grandmother was hanging where she had first seen it and she moved toward it. The woman depicted in it looked so young and beautiful and in love. Who had she been thinking about when the picture had been painted? Susan hoped it was of her own grandfather and not someone else.

Please let her not have been in love with Pierre, she prayed.

She grabbed a chair and positioned it beneath the portrait then clambered on top and balanced herself precariously as she reached up to grasp the painting. She had to stand on tiptoe to get a grasp on either side of the frame. She grunted as she tried to lift it off its hooks. The picture was heavy, far too heavy to be normal.

It started to tip and she began to lose her balance. She managed to replace it on the hooks before letting go. She half stepped, half fell off the chair.

She would need to stand on something more stable. Her eyes fell on the desk. It was massive and looked heavy. It would definitely be stable enough. The question was whether or not she could move it.

She took a good grip on it and pulled. It didn't budge even an inch. She walked around to the other side, braced her feet against the wall and tried pushing instead. Sharp pain knifed through her abdomen as she strained all her muscles but still the desk did not move.

She stood up and looked around the room. There was nothing else she could use. But she had come for the picture and she wasn't leaving without it. She could knock it off the wall but didn't want to risk damaging it.

She would have to search the rest of the building for a ladder of some sort. She picked up her purse, fished a stake out of it just in case she encountered any human minions, and then crossed to the door. She listened for what seemed a very long time before finally cracking it open.

The hall was dark and silent as the grave. Night was coming and as it crept closer her anxiety grew by leaps and bounds.

She eased out of the door and headed to her left. Back to the right, she remembered, was the waiting room and she didn't remember seeing anything she could use in there. She snuck down the hall, trying to move as silently as she could. She came across a bathroom and a closet full of office supplies, mostly paper and ink cartridges.

She kept going and found herself in another office. She wondered if this one belonged to Pierre's assistant. It was smaller, less opulent, but the furnishings were still antiques. The chairs in the room were the same type as those that were in Pierre's office, though.

She found a massive room devoted to files. Unfortunately, the filing cabinets themselves were built into the walls so she couldn't just empty and move one.

She retraced her steps and passed Pierre's office as she headed for the front of the building. She discovered another hallway she'd never been down, which led to a kitchen and conference room.

She had just about decided she'd have to try looking upstairs when she spotted a door in the kitchen. When she opened it, a cold blast of air hit her square in the face.

It's a basement, it has to be, she realized as her hand fumbled for a light switch. She finally found it, but when the light came on it was incredibly dim. She could only see the first five steps of a staircase that led down into darkness. There were tiny pinpricks of light on the wall spaced out a few feet apart. The nearest one looked like an electric candle and Susan figured it couldn't be more than fifteen watts.

She took her flashlight out of her purse, but it didn't turn on. It must have broken when she hit the window with her purse. She licked her lips nervously. It was either go down or head up to the next floor. As much as she didn't want to go downstairs, she realized it was the most rational place that janitorial supplies would be kept in a place like this. She dug a cross out of her purse and tucked it firmly in the front pocket of her jeans.

Knowing it wasn't long before sunset, she grasped her stake tight in her right hand and then reached out with her left for the banister. It was made out of some sort of metal and was shockingly cold to the touch. She slid her hand along it as she took her first step downward. She was relieved that she could see one step farther down now, but apparently she was only going to be able to make out five steps at a time in the dim, flickering light.

Probably the only person who comes down here is a vampire.

Her heart was racing and she tried to step carefully even as she held the stake ready. She realized that if she lost her footing and slipped she'd have to drop the stake or risk impaling herself.

That just made her feel worse.

She took another step, and another. She lost track of how far she'd come and resisted the urge to turn around and look back. She was terrified that if she did she'd see some evil figure with glowing eyes framed in the doorway behind her. How long had she been searching the building? How soon until the sun set?

She forced herself to keep going, putting one foot in front of the other. Her hand slid down farther and the metal was wet. She resisted the urge to yank her hand away but instead kept a firm grip on the railing.

Just when she was sure that she was never going to make it to the bottom the end came into sight. She could see the last stair and about a foot of concrete floor beyond that.

She looked around, hoping that there was a light switch or something at the bottom of the stairs that would illuminate the rest of the area. She didn't see anything, but there had to be. The house wouldn't have been built with the assumption that vampires and only vampires would use the basement. That was ridiculous. As she made it to the second to last step she began to wonder if it was, though.

Prague was an old city. Vampires could have designed and constructed some of the buildings. For all she knew Pierre was the original owner.

She made it to the ground and moved uncertainly away from the stairs. She still saw no light switches and there were no flickering candles in the basement, just on the stairway. She slid down the one wall, feeling along it for the switch. Darkness pressed in around her and her mind struggled to deal with it even as her eyes kept trying to adjust but couldn't. The darkness was absolute.

She turned to glance back to the stairs, but now even their dim light was lost to her. She felt panic wrap around her heart and begin to squeeze.

"I've been waiting for you," a voice whispered suddenly in her ear.

Chapter Thirteen

For many walk, of whom I have told you of-
ten, and now tell you even weeping, that they
are the enemies of the cross of Christ.

—Philippians 3:18

Susan screamed and swung around, lashing out with her stake at where she thought her assailant was standing. Her hand sliced through air alone. She backpedaled, heading for the stairs. The darkness still covered everything.

She heard a slight rustling sound and she spun toward it, striking out again with her weapon. Again there was nothing there.

But she could see the light from the stairway and it seemed much brighter now that she had spent time without it. She leaped toward it, determined to run up the stairs and out of the building into the daylight.

It should still be daylight. That meant the vampire she was down there with could wake during the day like Gabriel.

Either that or it wasn't a vampire.

Encouraged by that thought she made it to the bottom of the stairs and began to run up them. She was sure that at any moment a hand was going to wrap around her ankle, sending her crashing down. She ran faster, kicking her feet out slightly each time she picked them up as if hoping to ward off unseen hands.

She was getting close. She could see the glow from the kitchen clearly and there were only a few more steps. She put on a final burst of speed and stumbled out into the light. She slammed the door shut behind her and searched frantically for a lock even as her brain registered the fact that it might not slow down her pursuer at all. Suddenly, she froze where she was.

The man from the front of the building with the nice suit and the salt-and-pepper hair was staring at her with a twisted grin on his face.

"It took you a long time to get up here, no?" he asked.

She registered that he was speaking now with a French accent. He hadn't been earlier. Earlier he had been speaking English with no accent. Belatedly she realized that alone should have tipped her off that there was something out of place about him. He had probably worked to sound like her to lull her into a false sense of security.

"Who are you?" she asked, brandishing the stake in her right hand. She had been a fool to come by herself.

"No one of consequence, I assure you."

"I saw you drive off."

"Just around the corner, then I came back to get you. It's so much easier here than out on the street. My master is wise. He knew you would come, looking for your cousin."

"What have you done with her?" Susan demanded.

"Me? Nothing, I promise."

"What do you want with me?" she asked, trying to figure out how she could get past him and make it to either the front door or the broken window in the study. She shifted to the right, but he stood his ground, planted firmly in the doorway between her and the only two ways out of the building.

He was still smiling, his expression somewhere between cool and lazy. "My master wants a word with you."

"Tell Pierre I don't want to talk to him and if he doesn't let Wendy go I won't rest until he's dead."

The man laughed, a chilling sound. "Pierre is not my master."

"Richelieu?" she gasped.

"Wrong again."

"Just how many vampires have I pissed off?" she blurted out before she could stop herself.

"Only one that matters. He'd like to have a word with you concerning his brothers."

That's when it hit her. His master was one of the two remaining Raiders.

The Raiders were four brothers who had ridden with Quantrill during the American Civil War and been famed for their atrocities. As vampires they were fierce, soulless. Richelieu had ordered them to hunt her down and kill her. Raphael had already killed two and in the trauma over Pierre kidnapping Wendy she had entirely forgotten that there were two Raiders still left.

That she forgot in and of itself was a miracle. The second Raider had mentally tortured Susan with terrible images of what he planned to do to her before Raphael had found them and killed him. She hadn't thought she'd ever get over what she had seen in her mind during those minutes.

"Family is more important," she muttered.

"Exactly how the master feels."

"I'm not going anywhere with you," she said.

He shrugged. "I'm human, like you, but much stronger. The stake is a trivial matter. I can make you come with me."

She lifted her chin and planted her feet. "I'd like to see you try," she said defiantly.

He shrugged again. "Or we can just wait here for the master to arrive. Your choice, of course."

There was no way Susan was going to risk an encounter with another one of the Raiders. No, she had to find a way past him and out of the building before the sun set.

She edged farther to the right, then feinted back to the left. He just stood, unperturbed, watching her.

"You don't have to be his slave you know. You can be free," she said, trying a different tack.

"I'm more free than you," he said with another chuckle. "The sad thing is that you do not see your chains for what they really are. The master could have taught you, but he has a different fate in mind."

Knives. She was in a kitchen, which meant there should be knives around. She hazarded a quick glance around the room, hoping to see a butcher's block full of them.

No such luck. The counters were empty. She could check the drawers, but she risked him attacking her while she was distracted.

"May as well give up now. It's better for you this way."

"How do you figure?" Susan asked.

"Eclipse is coming. Balance of power is going to shift forever. You wouldn't want to be on the wrong side of that."

She blinked at him, trying to understand what he was talking about. Even while she was trying to figure it out, a new plan came to her. She had seen windows in the conference room when she had been in there earlier. That was the one place she could run to that he wasn't blocking the way. She could throw a chair through a window and dive out after it.

But there was no way he wouldn't catch her before she could. So, the best plan would be to make him think that was what she intended to do.

She feinted for the conference room. Startled, he lunged forward. She leaped toward him, kicked him in the groin, and then ran around him, heading for the front door.

Just as she reached it, though, it crashed open and she saw outside. The sun had set. Standing before her was the Raider.

She spun and raced for Pierre's office, an insane laugh following behind her.

She slammed the door shut and headed for the windows. The door behind her flew open and a hand grabbed her hair, jerking her to the ground. A cruel face leered above her and for just a moment she had flashbacks to being in the chapel, hiding from this man's brother as he tormented her with visions. More than she feared death she feared having to live through what she knew he was capable of doing to her.

She still had the stake clutched in her fist and she swung it upward. The pointed wood grazed the Raider's cheek as he jerked away. A thick drop of rancid-smelling blood fell and splattered on her forehead. She scrambled to her knees and plunged her hand into her purse and a moment later tossed a handful of cross-shaped confetti into the air.

The Raider hissed and jumped back farther as a couple of the pieces hit him, causing his skin to sizzle. Susan grabbed another handful and stood to her feet, slinging her purse over her shoulder as she frantically tried to figure out her next move.

Running was not an option. He'd be able to catch her in a heartbeat and she would be helpless. There was no reasoning with him if his brothers were anything to judge by. Her only real option was to kill him.

If only she could figure out how. The handful of confetti was the last one she had. There were half a dozen large crosses in her purse, a couple of vials of holy water, and five more stakes. She cursed herself for not having stopped to find some garlic to use. There hadn't been any in the house because the smell of garlic could incapacitate a vampire with a terrible, vomiting reaction.

She glanced around at the antique furnishings in Pierre's office. Out of the corner of her eye she spotted what looked like an old-fashioned oil lamp on a table in the corner farthest from Pierre's desk.

Getting there would mean trapping herself in the corner farthest from both escape routes, but she didn't see that she had much other choice. A second later, the guy from the kitchen came into the room and she knew she was running out of time. She dropped the stake she was holding and launched herself toward the table.

The moment she sensed the Raider was about to give chase she threw her last fistful of cross confetti to slow him down. He backpedaled, but his human minion leaped after her.

She reached the table just as a hand closed around her arm. She snatched wildly at the oil lamp, swung, and the metal base connected with the man's skull, sending him crashing unconscious to the floor.

Susan spun around just as the last of the cross confetti

drifted to the ground. The Raider leaped forward with a roar and when he was steps from her she hurled the lamp with all her might at his chest.

It broke and the pieces tumbled to the ground at his feet. Oil dripped down the front of his shirt and pooled around his feet.

He grabbed her by the throat and lifted her off the ground. She couldn't breathe and she kicked wildly at him. She seized the cross from her pocket and shoved it in his face, but he batted it away with his free hand.

"You humans, so fragile," he said, sneering.

She groped frantically in her purse even as the world was growing dim. Finally her fingers brushed against the thing she was looking for. She pulled the lighter out of her purse and with the last of her strength flicked it on, then pressed it against his oil-soaked shirt.

He dropped her with a roar as flames engulfed his chest. She landed hard on her knees and managed to topple back out of the way as he staggered around, beating at himself.

The flames wrapped around the rest of his body and moments later his head. Then, in front of her eyes, he turned to ash.

"At least we know how to stop, drop, and roll," she wheezed.

A dark figure suddenly crashed through one of the windows and leaped toward her. She scrambled for one of the stakes in her purse and brought it to bear just as the figure skidded to a halt in front of her.

Raphael stared in shock from her to the unconscious man to the pile of ash. "Who was that?" he asked.

"A Raider," she gasped, still trying to catch her breath.

She dropped the stake and touched her fingers to her throat and then winced in pain.

"Did he bite you?"

"No, he just tried to strangle me."

Raphael stared down at her, his eyes wild. "What exactly was here that was worth risking your life over?" he asked in a deep voice.

"That," she said, pointing up to the portrait of her grandmother. "I came for that."

Raphael stepped up on the chair Susan had used earlier and pulled the picture down with ease.

"Okay, we've got it. Let's go."

She stood shakily, discovering that when she fell she had hurt her ankle. "How did you know where to find me?" she asked.

He grimaced. "When I woke up to find you gone I called David."

"I'll have to remember to thank him."

"I didn't think I'd have to remind you that there are vampires after you, too," he said with a grunt.

"I'm sorry. It's just...there's been so much." She bit her lip, determined not to cry.

Raphael sighed. "Okay, let's just get this thing out of here and quickly. I'm not sure how much noise the neighbors will tolerate before deciding to investigate."

He tucked the painting under his arm and extended his hand to her. She took it and he led her back to the window she had shattered to get inside.

"Good job with the window, by the way. I was wondering exactly how you planned to get in here."

"I used my purse. Sometimes you've just got to throw everything you've got at a problem," she said.

"Funny."

Raphael eased out of the window and set the painting down outside. Then he helped her climb through.

"The car's back at the house. I can carry you."

"I think that would be a good idea," Susan said, wincing as she tried to put weight on her ankle. She could already tell it was swelling up. The back of the picture had a wire on it for hanging. He managed to slide it over one shoulder and then he scooped her up in his arms.

Susan put her arms around his neck and leaned her head against his chest. He was so strong and it felt good just to relax and let him take care of her.

She could feel him start to run and wind tore at her hair. It was a jarring ride, but exciting and she couldn't help but think about the times Carissa had described being carried by Gabriel as he ran. It was far more thrilling than she ever could have dreamed.

"Are you okay?" he asked at one point.

"Yes."

Far too quickly it seemed they made it back to the house. Raphael carried her inside and placed her down on the couch.

"Now, tell me what happened," he said as he got ice for her ankle.

She filled him in. At the last she remembered what the minion had said.

"The eclipse is coming and the balance of power will shift," Raphael mused. "What on earth can be significant about the eclipse in Richelieu's warped mind?"

"I don't know, but at least it tells us when he'll make his move."

"But not where or what it will be."

Raphael scowled. He changed out the ice pack and moved the picture to the floor next to her so that she could examine it more closely.

"Why is this picture so special?" he said.

She shook her head. "Stick around and hopefully we can figure that out."

BRYAS, PRESENT DAY

A deep groaning sound reached her ears and Wendy snapped awake, realizing she had dozed off while sitting and waiting. Gone was her chance at catching her captors by surprise. She stuffed one of the stakes under her mattress and after a moment's thought tucked the other into the back of her waistband. Then she moved so she was standing in front of the table and tried to tell herself that she was prepared to face whoever came through that door.

The door opened and a moment later closed again. Pierre walked slowly down the stairs, his eyes fixed on her the entire time. He seemed to be bringing her food since he was carrying a silver tray. She backed away slowly as he approached and he set it on the table. His eyes swept over the broken chair pieces on the floor and she realized she was an idiot for not having at least tried to hide them.

"Good furniture is so difficult to find these days," he said with a sigh.

She stood perfectly still, not trusting herself to do or say anything.

Pierre stared at her for what seemed a full minute before he spoke again. "She lied, of course, about not having it with her. I needn't have bothered having her apartment searched after all. It was here, you see. And you knew that because here you are wearing it. I had it. You know I had that cross necklace in my hands and I let it get away from me. Can you believe that?"

"No, I can't," Wendy said when he stopped, as if he was waiting for her to answer him.

"Well, no matter. It's back now. To be honest, I don't know which of you is the prize and which of you is the icing on the cake. Both so lovely, so perfect, so... mine."

He lifted his hand and trailed a finger down Wendy's cheek and she forced herself to stand still even though his touch repulsed her.

"Carissa, you are more beautiful than the day we met, more lovely than the day we married."

Wendy didn't know what to say, whether she should try to play along or work to get him to see the truth of the situation. If only she could figure out which one wouldn't get her killed quickly.

She pulled away from him, moving so the table was between them.

He smiled at her.

"You can play coy now, but we have all eternity together."

"You tried to have me killed," Wendy said, flipping a mental coin and deciding to play along.

"Never. I only wanted the necklace and to be with you again."

"You did try to kill me. I remember."

He studied her for a long moment, hesitation in his eyes. "Well, that would be quite a trick seeing as how you were only born a couple of decades ago. Wendy, that's your name, isn't it?"

Okay, so he was half lucid, half crazy. How did she work with that? "Yes, Wendy. And you should let me go."

"But I can't do that, you see. You have the necklace. And you bear such a strong resemblance to Carissa that even if you didn't have the necklace, I could never let you go."

"You let her go."

"A mistake. A terrible one. I had everything within my grasp. I could have been a king among men and instead I settled for being a marquis. But you see, I didn't know then what I know now."

"And what exactly is it that you know now?"

"Don't play coy. Surely your cousin told you what Jean wrote to his daughter about that necklace."

"You were the one who had Susan's bag stolen," Wendy realized.

Pierre nodded. "I needed to know what she had found at Bryas and I suspected she would not be entirely truthful with me. Her relationship with Raphael clouded her judgment."

Wendy was on the cusp of pointing out that he was a fine one to criticize someone else's judgment but thought better of it.

"What did the letter say?" she asked.

"You mean you don't know?"

Wendy shook her head.

He smiled. "Give me the necklace and I'll tell you."

And that was when she realized she had power over him. He wanted the necklace just as badly, maybe worse, than he wanted Carissa back, but he wasn't willing to take it from her. Or he wasn't able.

He's afraid to touch it himself, she realized.

"I'll never give it to you."

"I think you will."

She thought of the war coming and made a swift decision. "Help us defeat Richelieu and I will give you the necklace then."

He stared at her for a long minute. "Tempting, but I have no desire to be part of that fight."

"Surely you have to know that he needs to be defeated?"

"I can agree with you there, but I will not participate."

"Why not?" she demanded.

He smiled. "I have always been a magistrate...never a warrior."

"It's not too late to change. Do something good for once."

"I have done much good in this world. And there is no reason for me to involve myself when soon you will be begging me to take that necklace from you." His eyes clouded over again. "You know, I really do love you, Carissa. I just wish you could see that. And I am sorry for...everything. But you should never have left me. You were better than that."

Wendy couldn't think of a single thing to say in reply.

"Now, if you'll excuse me, there are a few matters that I need to attend to. But don't worry, I will return in a few minutes. I promise."

He left, locking the door behind him and Wendy collapsed, shaking, onto the floor.

He was insane, completely and utterly insane. She didn't know how or why, but there was no denying it. He thought she was Carissa. Or, at least, part of him did or he did part of the time. Without knowing what exactly was wrong with

him she didn't know how she could possibly predict his behavior or do anything to protect herself from it.

She just knew that she had to try. He'd said he would be
back in a couple of minutes. She'd be ready for him. She
moved one of her stakes to the stairs where she'd be able
to grab it at a moment's notice.

Then she walked over to the desk and pulled it out from
the wall, looking again for anything else she could use.
On the ground she found a paperclip, a receipt that was a
dozen years old, and a faded picture.

Wendy tightened her grip on the image and stared deep
into the eyes that were staring back at her. It was her
grandmother as she had known her much of her life, not
young, but not yet old. She was still very beautiful. She
was walking next to someone who was just out of the shot
and glancing toward the person taking the picture.

But Wendy could tell she had not posed for this picture.
Someone had taken it of her. Had it been Pierre? No, that
couldn't be, because it was daytime in the picture. It must
have been someone Pierre hired to follow her, a detective
perhaps?

But why would he do that? She looked more closely at
the picture, trying to make out details. In the background
she could see the market where her grandmother had loved
to shop. There was an ice cream store inside that Wendy
had loved as a kid.

What was so special about this day, this moment, that it
had been captured in such a way?

Around her grandmother's neck she could just make
out the image of the cross that she was now wearing. She
touched it, feeling an instant connection to the woman she
loved and for whom she was still grieving. In her left hand

her grandmother clutched a purse, one that Wendy remembered well. It had always smelled like peppermint.

In her right hand she held...

Wendy blinked and forced her eyes to refocus. Her grandmother was clutching a hand, smaller than hers. It was a child. She could just see the wrist at the edge of the photo and she saw a small, dangling star bracelet hanging off it.

She jerked and dropped the picture.

The child was her. When this picture had been taken she had been with her grandmother. Pierre had been spying on both of them, whether he intended to or not.

She felt dizzy and she pressed her hands to her forehead. That day, whenever it was, someone had been watching them. She felt sick inside as though someone were still watching her. Her grandmother couldn't have known. She wouldn't have been smiling.

Wendy reached down to pick up the photo and froze as she heard a sound just on the other side of the door.

Pierre was returning as promised.

Wendy snatched up her stake and raced to the top of the stairs. She flattened herself against the wall and waited. She'd only get one shot at this and she had to make it count. If she couldn't stake Pierre now she was signing her own death warrant.

The door began to open and she held her breath. He took a step forward and she struck, driving the stake into his chest, right over the heart as hard as she could.

There was a gasp and she looked up and found herself staring into David's eyes.

"Wendy," he whispered before collapsing on the floor.

CHAPTER FOURTEEN

Then Jesus beholding him loved him, and said unto him, One thing thou lackest: go thy way, sell whatsoever thou hast, and give to the poor, and thou shalt have treasure in heaven: and come, take up the cross, and follow me.

—Mark 10:21

Wendy screamed and fell on top of David, straining to yank out the stake that she had shoved into his chest. A moment later strong hands pushed her away and she realized it was Gabriel.

She fought against him, reaching for David, trying to bring him back to her. She could hear him wheezing and there was blood everywhere. She kicked and punched at Gabriel, sobbing.

"Let me go! I have to help him!" she shrieked.

"Be still!" Gabriel's voice boomed like thunder, echoing against the walls.

She ceased her struggles and looked at him. Gabriel pulled out the stake and dropped it to the floor. She noticed that it hadn't gone in as far as she would have thought.

Gabriel lowered his head toward David's chest and for one terrible moment she thought he was going to drink his blood. Instead he spat into the wound. Slowly he sat back up, nodding his head as though satisfied.

"What...what did you do that for?" Wendy asked, stunned at what she had just seen.

"Vampire saliva is a natural coagulant. It helps keep our victims alive for multiple feedings."

Wendy felt like she was going to throw up. Tears streamed freely down her face and she did nothing to stop them. She stared intently at David's face, struggling to see if he was alive.

"He will live," Gabriel said, as though reading her thoughts. "But we do not have time to tarry. We must go now."

"Is it safe to move him?"

"Safe enough. Luckily for him your angle was all wrong. You struck a rib, not his heart."

"Then why isn't he moving?"

"You hit one of his cracked ribs. Either he passed out from the pain or he hit his head on the step when he fell. I'm not certain, but I do know he will die if we don't leave now."

"Unfortunately, it is already too late."

Wendy spun with a gasp and saw Pierre standing in the middle of the basement. "How?" she breathed.

He smiled coldly as he stared past her at Gabriel. "When one spends enough time locked in a cage, one learns the usefulness of having two entrances and exits to every room."

"I searched this whole place," Wendy said.

"And you could have searched it until the end of your days and never found my escape route. I'm claustrophobic, not stupid."

He stared intently at Gabriel. "So, you've come to steal another prize from me," he said, his tone conversational.

"Nothing is stolen because nothing is yours," Gabriel said. He pushed past Wendy on the stairs, placing himself between her and David and the monster below them.

Wendy blinked in astonishment. Behind his back Gabriel was holding the stake she'd used on David. She wondered when he'd picked it up. She was certain that if she hadn't seen it happen, neither had Pierre. Gabriel walked slowly down the stairs.

"Please wake up, David," she whispered. If only he would then they could get out of there while Gabriel and Pierre fought.

"I saw the shrine in Vienna," Gabriel said.

Pierre stiffened. "You weren't meant to see that," he said, his voice sounding like that of a petulant child.

"Perhaps not, but I saw it anyway. It was wrong of you to collect so many things of hers like that. The paintings I understand and I can forgive. Heaven knows I've nearly commissioned paintings of her myself over the years. But the other things? Carissa would not have had you worship her, make her a false god like that."

"I'm not making her a false god," Pierre snapped. "I'm preserving her memory."

"Then be the kind of person she would have wanted you to be if you wish to preserve her memory. Hold her in here," Gabriel said, pointing at his heart.

"You ask too much of me," Pierre said.

"I ask only what I ask of myself."

Wendy could see Pierre shift his gaze from Gabriel to her. "I can't let her go," he said quietly.

"Yes, you can. You must. Carissa is dead. I know, I was there. That girl at the top of the stairs is not her. One person cannot be interchanged with another. She might have

Carissa's face, but she does not have her spirit, her soul. She doesn't even have her laugh."

"I only heard her laugh once," Pierre admitted. "And this one not at all."

Wendy stared at Gabriel, desperately wondering if that meant she should try and laugh. She wasn't sure she could force it, though. And what if she did and somehow by it being unlike her normal laugh it sounded more like Carissa's?

Stay silent.

The words echoed around in her head and even though she knew Gabriel couldn't see her she nodded anyway to indicate that she heard and understood.

"It was a beautiful thing," Gabriel said. "And now she is laughing in heaven every moment of every day."

"It's not fair," Pierre muttered, clenching his fists at his sides.

"Life isn't fair. It just is. It wasn't fair of you to falsely accuse her, have her thrown in that prison cell."

"Stop, please," Pierre said.

"She was trapped in that filthy, stinking cell, alone and afraid with only a monster to keep her company."

"Don't," Pierre said, his voice begging.

Wendy was stunned to see that Pierre had begun to cry.

"It wasn't fair that you condemned her to death."

"I can't listen to this."

Gabriel was only a few feet from Pierre now, moving steadily closer to him.

"It wasn't fair that she had to live a life of darkness and death instead of being surrounded by beauty and light."

"No, no!"

"It wasn't fair that she had to die the way she did," Gabriel said at the last.

"Stop, I beg you! No more!" Pierre wailed.

And then, quick as thought, Gabriel sunk the stake into his chest. Pierre glanced down at it for just a moment, as if he didn't even really see it. Then he crumbled into ash.

Gabriel turned, his face harder, fiercer, than Wendy had ever seen it. She shrunk away from him as he mounted the stairs.

"He was sick. There was something wrong with him," she said. "Maybe if he had stayed away or gotten some help." She was having a hard time reconciling the evil monster with the broken, sobbing man she had just seen.

Gabriel turned cold, dead eyes on her.

"There was no way he wasn't dying today."

She nodded. She knew deep down that it was right. It was for the best. He would have hunted her to the end of her days.

"Let's go," Gabriel said.

He scooped up David in his arms and ran up the stairs, Wendy on his heels. They made it out of the basement, turned toward the front of the building, and Gabriel froze.

The Baron stood in their way. Gabriel seemed to weigh his options. Wendy knew if the other vampire attacked he'd have only a microsecond to try to put David down without dropping him or immediately placing him in harm's way. He snarled. The advantage belonged completely to the Baron. Wendy could see no hostility in the Baron's eyes, though.

"I have no quarrel with you," Gabriel said. "You were a fellow prisoner, blackmailed into doing what you did. Let us pass and we will continue to have no quarrel."

"Pierre wasn't all bad. He had actually come quite a long way. He came to terms with what he'd done to Carissa a couple of centuries ago. If it had ended there, things would have worked out. His obsession with Carissa, though, only began to grow after that. I told him it would be his undoing, but he wouldn't listen."

"He was lucky to have a trusted friend tell him the things he didn't want to hear, regardless of whether or not he actually listened."

"Thank you."

The Baron's gaze slid from him to Wendy. "I know our world is strange to you. You have to understand, when friendships can last millennia, they are not easily broken over one whose lifespan is just a fleeting thought in comparison. I could not help you before. I will help you now."

Wendy didn't say anything and Gabriel didn't take his eyes off the Baron to look at her.

The Baron turned back to him. "I've heard rumors, nothing more, about what Richelieu has planned. I do know that whatever it is he's about to do, it will happen soon."

"Do you know where he's hiding?"

"No." There was truth in his eyes as he spoke.

"Your help would be deeply appreciated," Gabriel said.

The Baron nodded. "If I help destroy Richelieu...we would be even, yes?"

"Yes," Gabriel said.

The Baron nodded. "I have no quarrel with Richelieu. But I will consider it."

He stood to the side and Gabriel walked past. Wendy reached out to grip his upper arm, her terror still great.

He will not harm you, he told her silently.

Once outside she slid into the backseat of the car and he laid David down, his head resting on her lap. The bleeding had long since stopped, but he was still unconscious.

Gabriel got in the driver's seat, started the car, and

slammed the gas pedal to the floor. As Gabriel settled back in his seat and fixed his eyes on the road, Wendy kept stroking David's hair and staring down at his face. She tried not to replay the image of staking him over and over again in her mind but she was failing miserably. After a few minutes he began to stir.

"He's waking up!"

"Good," Gabriel said.

David opened his eyes and looked up at her.

"Are you okay?" she asked.

"Yes, I think so," he said, voice slightly hoarse. "I could use some painkillers, though."

"I don't have any. I'm sorry. I'm sorry for everything."

"You tried to kill me. Don't think we won't be telling that story to our kids someday," David said.

"Kids?" she asked, feeling breathless.

"You heard me," he said, eyes intent. "At least three of them. I figure as soon as we're married we should get started on that first one."

"Okay," she said, voice shaking.

"Glad that's settled. When we get back to Prague I'll get you a ring."

"Okay," she said again, her heart soaring.

"I'm going to sleep now, I think."

"You do that," she said, leaning down to kiss his forehead.

He smiled up at her then closed his eyes. A minute later his face relaxed and he was asleep.

"We're getting married," Wendy said, awestruck at the thought.

"Congratulations," Gabriel said from the front seat.

"Thank you."

She had come to Prague originally just to bury her

grandmother. She had ended up finding the love of her life and getting engaged. And, ironically, she owed it all to vampires.

She leaned her head back against the seat and closed her eyes. There was so much blood and chaos surrounding them and so much more yet to come. But for this moment she could be truly happy. She allowed herself to dream about their wedding. She saw herself in a white poofy dress standing in a sun-drenched field where no vampires could come. David was smiling at her in a way that melted her heart. The world was a beautiful place.

PRAGUE, PRESENT DAY

Susan's ankle was throbbing, but she was far too excited to care. She stared at the picture of her grandmother. She tried to pick it up, but she couldn't get the leverage she needed from her position on the couch.

"What is it you need?" Raphael asked.

"I need to see the back of it."

He turned it around for her. She kept her eyes fixed on his face, studying him for a moment.

"Thanks. I can't figure out why the frame is so heavy."

"It's gold," Raphael said with a shrug of his shoulders.

"Gold? As in, real gold?" she asked.

"As real as it gets," he said.

"Why on earth would someone make a picture frame out of real gold?"

"There could be a number of reasons. It can be a way to hide the wealth quickly and easily. It can also express the value of the painting either monetarily or emotionally."

"Pierre framed a portrait of my grandmother in gold," Susan marveled.

She looked down at the back of the picture. "There's something written on the back," she said, surprised.

Raphael had already moved toward the kitchen. "What does it say?" he asked.

"It's from the Bible. It says: 'Who can find a virtuous woman? for her price is far above rubies. The heart of her husband doth safely trust in her, so that he shall have no need of spoil. She will do him good and not evil all the days of her life.' Proverbs 31:10–12."

Susan looked up at Raphael, who was scowling. "Was this a reference to my grandmother?" She asked.

"Probably. Although it seems ironic given that he condemned Carissa, who was a virtuous woman herself."

Raphael returned with more ice for Susan's ankle, which he carefully wrapped around it. When he was finished he sat down in the chair next to her and studied the verse.

"I still don't understand why you had to risk your life to go and get this," he said.

He didn't sound angry, just truly curious.

Susan took a deep breath. "I can't explain it. It's like sometimes God tells me to do things and I don't know why. It's been getting stronger lately."

"Your grandmother had that."

"I wish I could have talked to her more about it. There's a lot of things I wish we could have talked about now that I know everything I know."

He smiled sadly. "That's often the way of things. So, God wanted you to retrieve this painting."

"I believe so."

"Well, then, there has to be a reason I would think. I bet Paul would have a theory."

"If only we could ask him," she whispered. Her grandmother, who had raised her after her parents had died, had recently passed. And upstairs Raphael's grandsire, who had raised him after his sire had disappeared, was dying. It was terrible and ironic how similar their situations were.

Raphael's phone rang. He answered it.

"That's great news. I'll tell her."

He hung up. "They rescued Wendy and the three of them are on their way back. She was being held in France, not that far from Bryas."

Susan sagged in relief and tears stung her eyes. "Thank You, God." She whispered the prayer out loud.

After a moment she looked at Raphael.

"Pierre?"

"Dead."

"Good," she said, shocked by the ferocity of her emotion. She was glad that he was dead. If he'd had a grave she would have wanted to dance on it for everything that he had done to Wendy and Carissa.

"Now, let's see if we can't figure out what's so important about this painting," Raphael said, returning to the matter at hand.

Susan nodded.

Raphael didn't know what she expected to find. Then again, if it really had been a prompting from God, then she was right: She herself had no idea what she expected to find.

"Let's try taking the back off. See if there's anything inside," he finally suggested.

"Okay," she agreed.

She was looking haggard. He knew she hadn't been sleeping and now that she knew Wendy was okay the adrenaline was clearly wearing off. He gave her ten minutes before she fell asleep.

He set down the picture gently and carefully took off the frame. "Found something," he said. He pulled a thick envelope wedged between the painting and the backing free and handed it to Susan. His fingers tingled slightly where they met hers.

She opened the envelope and pulled out a few papers with handwriting on them and about two dozen photographs. She set down the papers, looked through the photographs, and then handed them wordlessly to him.

Raphael flipped through them. "Your grandmother," he said, recognizing her instantly.

"All of them. It looks like pictures taken of her at different stages of her life. None of them are real pictures, though. It's like—"

"She didn't know she was being photographed."

"Exactly," Susan said.

"He didn't take them himself; too many of them are during the day. He probably hired a private investigator to follow her around."

"That is so creepy," Susan whispered. She yawned. Her eyelids were getting heavy. She was definitely heading for a crash.

"Obsession can be an ugly thing for humans, let alone vampires," Raphael said.

He put the pictures down on the coffee table next to the papers.

Silence.

He glanced up.

Susan was finally asleep.

He watched her for a few minutes, waiting to see if she would wake back up. He considered moving her to the bedroom upstairs where she could be more comfortable. As she slid deeper and deeper into sleep, though, he decided it was best just to leave her where she was.

He got up and went to check on Paul. The older vampire looked slightly worse to him, but he wasn't sure if it was real or just a trick of the mind. He lingered near him for several minutes, wishing things were different in so many ways.

Finally he left the house. He didn't like leaving Susan alone but he was confident that the house was well hidden enough no one would find her while he was gone. Besides, it had been far too long since he had gone out seeking word of Richelieu.

Sooner or later Richelieu would have to make his move. The frustrating part was that they had no idea what he was planning. They had managed to keep the relic in Prague away from him, but Raphael still wasn't convinced that the other vampire hadn't managed to steal some holy relics from other parts of Europe.

If he had the blood of Christ and found a way to safely ingest it, Raphael feared that the monster he had created would become truly unstoppable.

How did everything get so off track? he wondered as he paced streets teeming with nightlife. He slipped from shadow to shadow, unseen by all, noticed only as an odd feeling people had of being watched. It was best this way. Contact, interaction, that's what had kept him from dogging Richelieu's footsteps every waking moment.

But the time he was spending with Susan, helping her uncover her past, even rescuing her from the Raiders, had to mean something. He had felt he needed her by his side during this war that first night he had seen her in the cathedral. Had God been speaking to him then? His life felt upside down, out of control.

It had felt that way ever since he had laid eyes on her.

Maybe this was how love felt. His sire certainly believed that Raphael loved Susan. He was beginning to believe it himself. There was no other word that could possibly describe the deep aching he felt inside every time he thought of her. It would also explain how irrational he had become of late. He wasn't usually this distracted.

Maybe I'm the one who's become obsessed. That couldn't be good. Vampires who grew into an obsession instead of out of one always met a bad end.

He just knew that when he had been racing toward Pierre's office earlier he had told God that he would gladly trade his life for hers if it came down to it.

He didn't know if God had been listening, but he was intensely grateful that it hadn't come down to that. He couldn't die, not yet.

It was just as he thought this that something grabbed him by the back of the neck and threw him to the ground, face-first into a small puddle that reeked of garlic.

CHAPTER FIFTEEN

Let Christ the King of Israel descend now
from the cross, that we may see and believe.
And they that were crucified with him reviled
him.

—Mark 15:32

S usan!"

Susan woke groggily to the sound of someone shrieking her name. She pulled herself up to a sitting position and saw Wendy flying toward her. Her heart leaped as she hugged her cousin.

"I never thought I'd see you again," Wendy was saying, half sobbing, half laughing.

"Same here!"

After a minute Wendy sat down, wiping at her eyes. "You'll never believe the things I've seen, the things I've learned. I found some papers belonging to Carissa's father. Unfortunately, I wasn't able to bring them with me."

"Time enough to retrieve them," Gabriel said, looming suddenly over them. He was supporting David, who nodded grimly at her. There was blood coating the front of his shirt.

"What happened?" Susan asked.

"I tried to stake him," Wendy said, flushing red.

"What!"

"I thought he was Pierre coming back. Fortunately, my aim sucked," Wendy said with a smile. "But that's not the most exciting thing that happened."

Susan eyed her cousin warily. "I'm afraid to ask."

Wendy began to giggle uncontrollably, just like she had when they were girls. She kept going, laughing harder and harder and finally Susan looked up at David and Gabriel, hoping one of them could offer an explanation.

"I asked Wendy to marry me and she said yes," David said with a weak smile.

Susan was stunned. She stared from one to the other and words completely escaped her. She would never have believed that Wendy would be engaged and ready to settle down at this point. But she had seen the chemistry between her cousin and David, and the two of them together made a lot of sense.

"Well?" Wendy stopped giggling long enough to ask.

"C-congratulations," Susan said, beginning to smile and laugh herself.

"You're surprised, admit it!" Wendy crowed.

"Okay, a little bit, but I'm so very happy for you both," Susan said.

Wendy bent down to hug her. David looked like he wanted to, but he was in such obvious pain that Susan quickly said, "I'll hug you when we can both stand under our own power."

"You have yourself a deal," he said, visibly wincing.

"Where's Raphael?" Wendy asked suddenly, looking around.

Susan turned her head left, then right. "He was here when I fell asleep. Maybe he's upstairs?"

"He's out hunting down more clues as to the whereabouts of Richelieu," Gabriel said swiftly.

Susan nodded. That made perfect sense. Now that they had rescued Wendy they were going to need to focus all their attention on finding and stopping Richelieu.

"I'm going to check in on Paul," Gabriel said. "David should rest."

Susan watched him pick up David and carry him toward the stairs. David protested loudly, but she could hear the relief in his voice. He was clearly in a lot of pain. She watched them disappear up the stairs.

"I can't believe it," she said at last, turning back to Wendy.

Wendy gave her a shy smile. "I know, who would have thought it? Certainly not me. A week ago getting married was the furthest thing from my mind."

But not mine, Susan thought suddenly, her thoughts flying to Raphael. That way lay madness, though. She couldn't think about him, not in that context.

"Is Pierre really dead?" she finally asked Wendy, changing the subject.

Wendy nodded. "Yes. I've never seen anything like it either. Gabriel was...terrifying. And Pierre was completely out of his mind. He kept thinking I was Carissa."

Susan stared at her in shock. "Did he try to hurt you?"

"No. It was like he had this really obsessive thing for her."

Susan glanced at the back of the painting.

"What is that?"

"A portrait of Grandmother that Pierre had hanging in his office. I went and got it and we found Bible verses about the virtuous woman written on the back. Weirder yet, the frame is made of gold."

"That is too strange."

Susan leaned toward the coffee table and grabbed the pictures. She handed them to Wendy. "He was stalking Grandmother for years."

Wendy blanched. "I found a photo like these in the basement where he was keeping me." Wendy finished sorting through the photos and put them back on the coffee table. "What are these papers?"

"Oh! I can't believe I forgot," Susan said, surprised. "I heard you were safe and the next thing I knew I was falling asleep."

"We were only in the car for about half an hour before I passed out," Wendy said. "Even with all the excitement of David asking me to marry him, that was all I had in me."

Wendy picked up the papers and glanced at the top one. Her eyes suddenly began to bulge out.

"What is it?" Susan said, struggling to sit up more. She tested her ankle and found it felt much better.

"It's a love letter."

"To whom?"

"Grandmother. And it's from Pierre."

Gabriel was worried. David was a wreck. Wendy hadn't killed him but she had managed to do more damage to his injured ribs. Fortunately David was asleep as soon as he laid down on the bed. Paul was worse than he had been when Gabriel had left. There was a distinct odor of decay that was now filling the room.

And Raphael was missing. He hadn't wanted to alarm Susan. She'd already been through enough and she deserved at least a modicum of peace, especially if something had actually happened to Raphael.

Gabriel tried calling him but it just rang and rang before finally going to voice mail. He knew that Raphael had gone hunting Richelieu. He didn't need to be told that. What worried him was that he wasn't back yet.

Gabriel would have to go looking for him.

He headed back downstairs. Wendy and Susan were intently reading some old letters.

"Find anything useful?" he asked.

They looked up at him with great, round eyes. "Pierre was in love with our grandmother," Susan said at last. "She knew what he was and she rejected him, told him that while she valued his friendship she could never be with him."

"Because of what he was?" Gabriel asked, frowning.

"I don't think so," Wendy said. "The fact that he's a vampire doesn't seem to disturb her as much as the fact that he loves her but she doesn't love him."

"I just wish we knew if he loved her for herself or because she was related to Carissa," Susan mused.

"He never loved Carissa," Gabriel said, more sharply than he meant to. "Over the years he became obsessed with her. If not for her he would not have been cursed. And by the time he was free, she was gone and there was nothing he could do about it. What he felt was anything but love, trust me."

It was insulting to hear Pierre's rabid, pathetic attempts at connecting with someone described as love. It was nothing compared to the love he had had for Carissa, the love he still had and would carry with him until the day he went to meet his maker. The only reason he had spoken words of comfort to Pierre earlier was to get close enough to kill him without risking a fight that could see either David or Wendy injured.

Both women nodded slowly.

"There's more," Susan said, clearing her throat. "It seems our grandmother had a vision about the coming war. She knew we'd be here. She asked Pierre to look out for us."

Gabriel blinked. "Your grandmother was an amazingly insightful woman. How could she have trusted him that far?"

"Apparently he'd been the family lawyer for generations and he found the missing cross necklace for her. Because of that and his feelings for her, she thought she could trust him."

Gabriel bared his teeth. "He was the one who stole it once from your family. No doubt he did so again to make it part of his collection of artifacts. When your grandmother wanted it he probably gifted it to her and conveniently told her he had found it."

Susan and Wendy both nodded. "That would make sense," Wendy said.

"Was there anything else about her vision in these letters?" Gabriel asked.

"Yes, she said that she saw Richelieu swallow something that gave him the power to walk in the sunlight without burning."

"The relics he's been searching for with the blood of Christ," Gabriel muttered. "It would make him truly immortal."

"We stopped him from getting one of them, but who knows if he found something else," Susan said.

When they had realized that Richelieu intended to try to find a relic that had the blood of Christ on it so he could ingest it, thinking it would give him more godlike powers,

Gabriel had had his doubts whether it would work. But he knew from experience that the blood of every one of his victims was a part of him and the Bible was clear in its prohibitions against drinking blood. Taking the blood of a creature into yourself made that creature's spirit a part of you and even changed you in some ways. If the vision Susan's grandmother had had was true, if sunlight could no longer harm Richelieu, it was likely nothing would. There would be no way to kill him.

And if he could walk abroad during the day without burning, there was no limit to what he could do.

"We have to stop him," Gabriel said.

Wendy was pale but looked resolute. "We think he's going to do it during the eclipse. So now we know what and when, but not where. How will we stop him?"

"By finding Richelieu before the eclipse. I'm going out to help Raphael look for him. I'll be back before dawn," Gabriel said. He turned and left the house as fast as he could.

Susan stared after Gabriel. Clearly, they'd struck a nerve with him. She turned slowly back to Wendy. The two had been catching each other up on what they had learned while they were apart. And the letters between their grandmother and Pierre that they had just read had been extraordinary.

"Clearly she did consider him a friend or she would not have entrusted the deed and the key she meant me to have to him," Susan said at last.

"There is nothing veiled in these letters. She seems to be perfectly open and honest," Wendy added.

"Do you think that being unable to have her just made

his obsession with Carissa, and with her, that much more powerful?" Susan asked.

"It stands to reason," Wendy said with a shrug. "I'm surprised he didn't go completely postal on me when I made it clear he couldn't have me either."

Susan shuddered.

Wendy got up and retrieved the diary that Carissa and Fleur had shared. "So, where should we pick up? I'm way too wired to try to sleep now."

"Raphael and I found another of those loose-leaf parchments that Carissa wrote on that was tucked into the pages." Wendy found the place and read Carissa's account of what Raphael had done and how Gabriel had saved her from the burning cross. She glanced up at Susan, a question in her eyes.

"It was a long time ago. Raphael has changed," Susan said.

Wendy only nodded vaguely and continued to read Carissa's account of the journey to Bryas and how they managed to get into the castle. When Wendy stopped reading at the end of Carissa's pages, Susan glanced down at the handwriting in the journal. "Looks like we're back with Fleur now."

"You realize when this is all over we're going to have to make diaries so that hundreds of years from now our descendants can read about us?" Wendy asked.

Susan rolled her eyes. "I'd mock you, but the truth is I keep feeling the same way."

"I know, right? Even with these meticulous diarists, look how much of our own family history we've lost."

"It's terrifying when you think about it," Susan admitted.

"Are you ready?" Wendy asked.

Susan nodded.

" 'I rode with Paul toward Bryas, but my heart was troubled. I could not shake the fear that we would arrive too late. I prayed Carissa was safely at Avignon and that I might soon have word of her from Étienne, who I missed terribly.' "

FRANCE, 1198 AD

"Do you know where we are going?" Fleur asked Paul.

He rode beside her on the trail, his robes covering his body. She couldn't see his face but from the sound of his voice she could imagine him rolling his eyes at her question.

"I've traveled all of the roads of France before."

"So, is that a yes or no, then?" She bit her lip. It was an impertinent question, one she should never have asked a monk, let alone a vampire.

"Does that boy know what he is getting himself into falling in love with you?" Paul asked, sarcasm heavy in his voice.

"I have never been other than myself with him so I am sure he knows."

Suddenly, Paul swore. He hit the ground, grabbed her horse's reins, and pulled both animals off the road and into the trees. He held a finger up to his lips and put a hand on each horse. After five minutes Fleur finally heard a horse galloping on the road. She felt like she should hold her breath. She stayed as still as she could, marveling that neither of the horses moved or made any noise.

The rider came nearer until it sounded like he was

nearly on top of them. For a moment she thought she heard the animal start to slow. Her heart began pounding louder and louder. She saw Paul grimace at her and knew that he could hear it, too. She bit her lower lip and closed her eyes, praying that whoever it was would just keep riding. She tried desperately to calm herself, to slow the beating of her heart, to quiet her breathing, which sounded like thunder in her ears.

The rider kept going and slowly the sounds began to fade until she could hear them no more. Still she sat tense, waiting. She opened her eyes and watched Paul. When the tension in his face eased and he shifted his weight, she sighed.

"It is safe now, but we will wait and rest here awhile before taking again to the road," he said, moving to help her dismount.

"Who was it?" she asked.

"I do not know, but his thoughts were of a woman he must kill. A woman, and a vampire."

"Not us?" Fleur queried, heart beginning to pound even harder.

"No."

"Carissa!"

"I fear so."

"Then she is not in Avignon?"

"No, something tells me she's headed the same place we are," Paul said.

"What! Why?" Fleur asked. "Has she taken leave of her senses?"

"It is entirely possible," Paul said with a grimace. "Hatred has destroyed stronger minds than hers. A long time ago it tore me apart and turned me into a monster."

"You mean, when you became a vampire."

He shook his head. "No, before I became a vampire." He turned and looked at her and his eyes burned with a zeal that frightened her. She sucked in her breath. He bowed his head and a moment later when he looked back at her his slightly amused look, which seemed his natural one, was set on his features.

"Make no mistake, Fleur. There is not a vampire alive who was not a monster long before he became a creature of the night. And no matter how civilized any of us may now seem, the monster still lurks. We have just learned to control it."

She nodded and then took a seat on the ground. She fussed with her skirts to avoid looking at him. The more she knew about vampires the more she found to fear. It made no sense given that Paul had done nothing to harm her. He was right, though; underneath his calm exterior there was a monster lurking. She instinctively felt that it was only by the grace of God that he controlled it.

She found herself praying that Étienne would find her soon. They had left word for him at the monastery where they were going. She wondered if he had returned there when he had not found Carissa or if even now he was following her cousin. She prayed for his safety and her own. When she tried to pray for Carissa and the others, though, she struggled. Dark thoughts crowded her mind and she tried to deny them entrance. What was it the gypsy had told her when she and Carissa had first left Bryas and been traveling to the palace to meet her future husband?

Within the month you will know sorrow, but it will be brief and your joy magnified after. Your days will be spent with the sun shining upon your face and love surrounding you.

She should have asked the woman what kind of sorrow. She had known sorrow when she could not find Carissa. Was that the sorrow the gypsy spoke of, or was it something much darker? She feared for Carissa's life and there was none who could provide comfort about that.

I wish I did not feel so helpless. I wish I was traveling again with Étienne instead of a vampire who might turn on me.

She glanced at Paul uneasily, remembering that he could read her thoughts. He appeared to be asleep and she breathed a little easier. Nothing in her life had prepared her for this moment in time and she felt at a loss as to what to do or even how to act. She often used humor as a shield, but she could tell that Paul saw through that.

"The sun is nearly up. We will rest here and continue on when it sets. You might want to sleep," he said suddenly, though he didn't open his eyes or otherwise move.

"I would like that very much," she said. It would be preferable to dealing with the whirlwind in her mind.

"Go to sleep."

She noticed sleepily that his voice suddenly sounded much deeper, and then, she was asleep.

Hours later she rose with the setting sun and soon they were on their way again. They had only been traveling for two hours when Fleur began to shake and she felt like she was going to be sick.

"What is wrong?" Paul asked, as though he sensed the change that had come over her.

"I am not sure, but I think we're going to reach Bryas too late," she said.

"We are not far now," Paul said grimly. "As soon as Étienne catches up we give these horses the run of their lives."

"Étienne? Is he near?" Fleur asked, heart in her throat.

"Very near," Paul said.

A few minutes later Fleur heard a rider coming. She twisted in her saddle and strained her eyes, trying to make out the man's features. Finally she could see him clearly.

"Étienne!"

A moment later he was beside her and she reached out and grabbed his hand. She brought it to her lips and kissed it even as she cried with relief to see him.

"Glad you could join us," Paul said.

Étienne shook his head. "I did not realize that you would be willing to leave the monastery."

"It takes a very compelling reason," Paul said. "You still surprise me. I have a hard time understanding how you are so calmly accepting of the situation you find yourself in."

"I have a relative who believes in studying the world in order to better understand it. He would say something like, *If vampires exist, why? What makes them different? Is it supernatural or is it physical? What does this say about the rest of the world?*—things like that."

"You studied under this relative, did you?" Paul asked.

Étienne nodded.

"That is a dangerous thing to admit to."

Étienne shrugged. "I figured my secret was safe since you are a vampire, even if you are a man of God."

"Learning and worship go hand in hand," Paul said quietly. "Someday perhaps people will figure that out. Until then, your family's secrets are safe with me."

Fleur turned from one to the other of them. "We need to reach the castle."

"Then that is what we will do," Étienne said, kicking his horse into a run.

Fleur's horse leaped after and it was all she could do to hold on. *If Carissa could see me now she wouldn't believe it*, she thought. *I only hope she gets a chance to.*

PRAGUE, PRESENT DAY

"Why did you stop?" Susan asked as Wendy turned the page and looked up.

Wendy smirked. "Because the handwriting in the book just changed again. I think Carissa got the diary back."

"That must mean she and Fleur met up at Bryas!" Susan said, amazed at how excited the thought made her.

"Exactly what I was thinking," Wendy said with a grin. "You know, I have to admit, I feel like such a girl right now."

Susan studied Wendy. "How so?"

"Here we are on the verge of an apocalypse, we have two men down, two men out prowling around potentially getting into trouble, and we're freaking out over a love story that happened a millennia ago."

Susan smiled. "You're right. Carissa's story is a love story. I guess the classics never go out of style."

"I'm just hoping she gets a nice happy ending instead of something terribly tragic," Wendy said, wrinkling her nose.

"Me, too," Susan said. "I'd like to think that happiness is waiting out there." Once again her thoughts turned to Raphael.

Wendy picked up the book.

"'It was wonderful to be home, even if it was under such terrible circumstances. There were a thousand things I wanted to show Gabriel about my home, but I knew they would all have to wait.'"

BRYAS, 1198 AD

Carissa and Gabriel glided through the castle silently. When footsteps echoed down the hall, they ducked into an open room, sticking to the shadows.

Carissa could just see out and she watched the steward walking by carrying a tray with some parchments on it. When he had passed she leaned close to Gabriel and whispered, "It looks like he was coming from the study. I believe we will find Pierre there." Gabriel nodded and then followed her into the hallway.

Carissa's blood boiled at the thought of Pierre using her father's study and sitting at his desk. She led Gabriel down the family staircase. They bypassed the great hall and headed to a room toward the back of the castle. She took a deep breath and then opened the door and slipped inside. Gabriel followed, closing the door, which creaked on its hinges.

"I asked not to be disturbed," Pierre said in an irritable voice, not looking up from the desk at which he was seated.

At the sight of him hatred shot through her and she began to quiver with rage. She walked forward slowly, willing him to look at her.

"I apologize, I did not get that message."

He looked up suddenly, a look of shock spreading across his features.

"Carissa," Pierre whispered.

"Hello, husband," she answered, venom dripping from her voice. She moved to stand in front of the desk. Gabriel stayed where he was.

"I had heard that you were still alive."

"I know, your butchers have been out scouring the countryside for me."

"Yes, well, I could hardly let a witch roam free."

She slammed her hand down on the writing desk that used to belong to her father. "That is a lie and you know it."

He sneered at her and then looked past her to Gabriel. "And are you her lover?" Pierre demanded.

Carissa wanted to slap him. She was so furious she couldn't find the words to answer him.

"No. I am the monster you locked her up with."

CHAPTER SIXTEEN

And they compel one Simon a Cyrenian, who passed by, coming out of the country, the father of Alexander and Rufus, to bear his cross.

—Mark 15:21

Pierre turned white. "Get away from me, foul creature."

"It is you who is the foul creature."

Pierre stood up, knocking over his chair. He fumbled for a moment in his pocket and then pulled out the cross that he had taken from Carissa on that fateful night. He brandished it before him like a weapon.

Carissa cried out and lunged forward, intent on snatching it from his grasp. He jerked away from her, though, and put some distance between them.

"In the name of God, you shall not come near me," he hissed.

In the blink of an eye, Gabriel moved so he was standing before Pierre. Gabriel reached forward and wrapped his hand around the cross.

"Actually, God and I are on good terms," he purred, and grabbed the dangling chain, pulling the cross from Pierre's fingers.

The cross dangled from the chain. Gabriel looked at it.

Something changed in his face, but she couldn't tell what he was thinking.

"I recognize this cross," he said. He then held it out toward Carissa. "I believe it belongs to you."

She stepped forward and took it from him gratefully. The chain was broken where Pierre had ripped it from her neck. Tears began to fall from her eyes, dripping onto the metal. So much pain and death over something meant to bring peace and life. Warmth seemed to pass from it into her.

She looked at Pierre. He would never understand mercy; it wasn't in his nature. He couldn't comprehend the gift of forgiveness. In his passion for the law, in his blindness, how many innocents had he killed? He could have made such a fine man had he only learned restraint.

"Shall I kill him now?" Gabrielle asked, with a growl.

She gazed down at the cross, tracing her thumb over it. "No," she said slowly. "I have a better idea."

She looked up and locked eyes with Gabriel. He was watching her quizzically. She smiled. "I think he needs time to truly understand his crimes."

Understanding flashed across his face and he began to laugh. "Dearest Carissa, you are both wise and wicked."

"I shall claim the former, at least."

"What are you two talking about?" Pierre shrieked.

"Your future," Gabriel said.

Carissa watched as Gabriel breathed, his chest rising and falling with each lungful. He began to growl deep in his throat and a shiver danced up her spine.

"Stay away from me," Pierre said, moving backward.

Gabriel growled, grabbing Pierre by his shoulders. He sunk his teeth into Pierre's neck. Pierre cried out and tried to struggle, but Gabriel was far too strong. At last Pierre's body grew limp, held up only by Gabriel. Carissa moved closer to watch in fascination.

When it was finished Gabriel lowered Pierre onto the ground.

"You are now a widow," Gabriel told Carissa. He wiped the blood from his mouth and then kissed her. A moment later he pulled away and then knelt above Pierre and bit his own wrist. He pressed his bleeding wrist to Pierre's lips. Suddenly Pierre's eyes flew open and he grabbed Gabriel's wrist, sucking the blood from the wound.

After a moment Gabriel pulled his wrist away and Pierre's eyes closed. Standing, Gabriel crossed to Carissa.

"He should regain consciousness tomorrow night."

"So you are not going to kill him then?"

Carissa jumped and turned to see the man who had joined them without either hearing him. She recognized him at once as the German who had attacked them on the road.

Gabriel roared and leaped forward. He had nearly reached the man when Carissa heard the sound of a door closing and saw a dark blur slam into Gabriel.

Gabriel jumped to his feet, his eyes sweeping from Raphael to the Baron and back, debating which one to attack first. If he went after Raphael, the Baron might be able to kill Carissa. If he took out the Baron he had no doubt that Raphael would kill Carissa anyway, just to spite him.

"Baron, listen. The man with whom you made your deal is dead. I killed him and turned him into a vampire. We have a plan. Whatever he had hanging over your head you no longer have to worry about. Leave this place now and I will consider there to be no quarrel between us."

"I have a better idea," Raphael said. "Help me kill Gabriel here and I shall give you whatever you want. If you refuse, I will hunt you down and kill you."

Gabriel could see the indecision in the Baron's eyes as the three of them circled one another.

"For mercy's sake, help Gabriel," Carissa pleaded.

There was a sound in the hall, likely servants alarmed by the noise. Gabriel twisted, but the door remained closed. Before he could turn back Raphael was on him. The younger vampire slammed him to the ground and sunk his teeth into his shoulder.

Gabriel clawed at Raphael's eyes with his fingernails. He could hear Carissa shouting but couldn't see her. He rolled across the floor and pinned Raphael up against the wall. He managed to pull free of his grip and stagger to his feet.

The Baron was just a few feet away, a wooden stake in his hand, undecided.

"Get out!" Gabriel told him.

Behind him Gabriel could hear Raphael get to his feet and he jumped to the side just as Raphael flashed past him. Gabriel reached out and grabbed him by the hair and yanked hard, slamming the other vampire's head down to the ground. "We don't have to fight," Gabriel said.

Raphael threw himself to the side and was back on his feet in the blink of an eye. "Yes, we do."

Gabriel circled, trying to put his body between Carissa and the other two.

"You turned me into a vampire."

"You deserved it."

"You abandoned me."

"Not of my own free will," Gabriel said. Out of the corner of his eye he could see Carissa edging for the door. "I was abducted, imprisoned. I have spent the last half century chained in a cell, forced to kill and feed off other prisoners."

Uncertainty flickered in Raphael's eyes.

"I would think you were glad to have me gone. You tried to escape enough times. I would think you would be glad for your freedom. So why have you spent the last half century angry because you thought I abandoned you?" Gabriel asked. Carissa was almost to the door.

Raphael lunged and Gabriel turned back to him, but the other vampire stopped short and continued to circle. On his left the Baron shifted the stake nervously from hand to hand.

"Do you have any idea what happened to me after you left?" Raphael hissed.

"No. But I can imagine," Gabriel said quietly.

"I killed everything I ever loved."

"I am sorry," Gabriel said. Carissa was quietly opening the door behind Raphael.

"Now I will do the same to you."

Gabriel shook his head. "You're a few hundred years too late. I killed my entire family a long time ago."

"I can still kill her," Raphael said, whipping around and grabbing Carissa by the throat. He spun her around and pinned her so that Gabriel could see the fear in her eyes. "And I will make you watch," Raphael said.

Before Gabriel could move toward them, a necklace of garlic was flung through the open doorway, landing around Raphael's head.

Raphael dropped to the floor and Carissa staggered away. Marcelle stared grimly at Gabriel. "I helped save her once. I'd be hanged before I let the likes of him kill her after all that."

Gabriel gave the warden a brief nod before turning his eyes on the Baron. The man stood, several emotions vying for control, thumb stroking the stake he held.

"What will you do, Baron?"

"I suspect what he plans to do depends quite a lot on what you are going to do," Paul said, walking in from behind Marcelle, a girl hovering behind him. "By the looks of things you have made a mess again." He glanced around, taking in Marcelle, Carissa, the body of Pierre, and the retching Raphael.

"Are you here to help or to critique?" Gabriel asked.

"To help," Paul said with a smile. Gabriel noticed a young nobleman standing just outside the room, which had grown crowded rather quickly.

The girl behind Paul edged her way into the room. Carissa turned, saw her, and then the two were embracing.

"I take it this is the cousin?" Gabriel asked.

"Yes," Paul answered.

"What shall we do with him?" Paul asked, indicating Raphael.

"Nothing, just leave him," Gabriel said. "The lad and I need to have a talk and I want him good and sick when we have it."

PRAGUE, PRESENT DAY

Susan realized that she was crying as Wendy stopped reading. "Carissa and Fleur found each other."

"Just like us," Wendy said, a tear rolling down her own cheek even though she was smiling.

A moment later they were hugging each other.

"I keep feeling like everything that's happening now has happened before," Susan muttered.

Wendy pulled back slightly, wiping at her eyes. "You know what they say: Those who don't remember history are doomed to repeat it."

"I know, I just never dreamed it would be so literal," Susan said, forcing herself to laugh. She touched the cross necklace, once more safely around her throat.

"So, that's how Pierre got cursed. I wonder when it happened to the Baron?" Wendy mused.

"Hopefully, we'll find out."

"I just feel bad David is missing all the excitement."

David was fast asleep upstairs still. Susan winced, knowing that the cracked ribs must be hurting him. She wasn't sure how he was managing to do as much as he was given the shape he was in.

Unless one of the vampires has mesmerized him, convinced him to ignore the pain and the injuries or at least fight through them. She shuddered. It seemed cruel, dangerous. Surely that couldn't be what had happened. If so, wouldn't they realize that ignoring that pain could get him killed?

She bit her lip, refusing to believe that the vampires were being that careless with his life. *Or with ours*, she thought.

"Should I wake him?" Wendy asked softly.

Susan shook her head. "He needs the sleep worse than we do. We can fill him in later."

Wendy picked up the diary. "Ready?"

Susan nodded.

"'I felt like my heart was going to burst when I saw Fleur. I had feared that I would never see my beloved cousin again. And when I did I realized just how much I had underestimated her, and myself.'"

BRYAS, 1198 AD

Carissa cried and clung to Fleur, afraid that her cousin would somehow disappear. Finally, she had to let go. The men were talking but she had no idea what they were saying. She stared hard at the man in the hall. He looked vaguely familiar, but she couldn't place him.

"Who is that?" she finally asked Fleur.

"Étienne," Fleur said with a smile. "He has helped me search France for you."

From the way her cousin's eyes sparkled Carissa could tell that she loved him. She was so happy she hugged her again.

"And no need to introduce Gabriel," Fleur said roguishly, after a moment.

Carissa laughed. "His reputation precedes him."

"One could say that," Fleur said.

Carissa turned to the warden and offered him her hand. "Thank you, sir. You have saved us all, again. If there is anything I can do to be of assistance, please tell me."

The warden began to smile. "As it happens I have a problem of my own that needs solving, and I'm thinking I've fallen in with just the right group to help me with it."

An hour later Carissa found herself sitting down to

dinner in the main hall, her hall. Unlike her room, nothing in it had changed much. Even the servants were familiar.

With a few well-placed words to the steward, Paul and Gabriel seemed to have convinced the man, and everyone else, that there was nothing out of the ordinary happening. They believed Pierre to be in his chambers resting. No sooner had Raphael and the Baron been secured and locked up in the dungeon than they seemed to forget the vampire and the German existed.

The food appeared and was set before them. There was mutton, venison, and pheasant. A huge plate filled with fruit vied for attention. With her stomach rumbling Carissa fell upon the food with abandon.

"It is delicious!" she exclaimed. She remembered when she had eaten the like nearly every day but it seemed so long past that she could barely remember other meals. Gabriel smiled, clearly appreciating her enthusiasm.

"May I get milords something different?" the steward asked Paul and Gabriel, the only two at the table who weren't eating. Gabriel spoke so low she couldn't hear him. The other man's face took on a dazed, vacant expression. Without a word he left and then returned with two goblets filled with a dark liquid.

He then turned and left the room, shaking himself slightly as he did so.

"What did you do to him?" Carissa asked Gabriel.

"Mesmerized him," Gabriel said, looking suddenly uncomfortable.

"You can do that?"

"I can only mesmerize those over whom passion holds sway," he said. "When someone is experiencing strong emotions, they are less likely to think clearly, easier to manipulate."

"Like me that night I woke up after fainting," she realized.

"Yes," he confessed. "You were terrified and you needed rest."

Marcelle was listening with keen interest. "Why did you not do that to me so you could escape?"

Gabriel shook his head. "The wardens are picked for their ability to keep a level head. When I was strong enough to actually mesmerize someone, you were never in a state where I could control you."

Marcelle looked satisfied and returned his attention to his meal. Fleur leaned forward eagerly. "Paul can also read minds," she said.

"I knew it!" Carissa said, remembering their first meeting. She turned and studied Gabriel.

He threw up his hands and smiled. "Not me, only some of us can do that, and I am certainly not one of them."

If he was, he would have known a long time ago how you feel about him. It was Paul's voice, but it was inside her head. She blushed furiously.

"What did he say to you?" Fleur asked.

"It is not important," Carissa said. "So, while I am enjoying dinner, what happens next?"

Paul smiled. Fleur smirked and Étienne glanced at her briefly.

PRAGUE, PRESENT DAY

Gabriel stood just outside the front door, having returned empty-handed from searching for Raphael and Richelieu.

He remained still, silent, and unseen, listening as Wendy translated the writings of his beloved Carissa. He felt torn. Her diary had been private and he had never once violated that privacy. But hearing her description of dinner that night he couldn't help but remember what had happened afterward. He closed his eyes as the memories washed over him, as clear and sharp as if the events had only just happened.

BRYAS, 1198 AD

After dinner the humans went to sleep. Paul took himself off without explaining what he was planning to do. That left Gabriel alone with his thoughts. He wandered through the castle and made his way outside. Once there he found his way to the graveyard.

He found Jean's grave with ease and crouched down beside it. "Jean, it's been a long time. I have a problem and you are the only one I can talk to about it. I am in love with your daughter."

He stayed for a while, paying his respects to a brave man he had known once upon a time, a man who just happened to be Carissa's father. When he was finished he walked around, looking at some of the other gravestones. He found Carissa's mother and her aunt and uncle.

He was older than most of the crumbling markers that had been meant to pay tribute to the dead beneath them for eternity. Eternity wasn't what they thought it was. He was dead and yet he walked, doomed to live while all those around him died. Dust to dust and ashes to ashes for all but him.

He had thought about taking his own life more times

than he could count. By fire or the heat of the sun he could end his own wretched existence and join the fortunate dead at his feet. Those dark thoughts had reared their head less and less of late, though.

Punching through the clouds, the moon appeared. He looked up and marveled as he always did. It shone down upon his face and he stood motionless, soaking it in. This was his sun, his guiding light, and he had not seen it for far too long. He could feel his dead flesh stirring, responding. They said the ocean's tides were governed by the mother moon and he believed it. Even as the seas so his blood, the blood that he had taken, pulsed within him.

He had tasted death so many times. He had died himself to become that which he was. Yet it was still a mystery to him, something vast and unexplainable. He closed his eyes and remembered the souls whose lives he had taken. He remembered the first person who he had killed as a vampire, a young woman. He could feel her life as it slipped away, felt her heart slow and stop. He knew the moment that something left her. He called it a soul for he knew of no other word that could describe it. He would never forget that moment, the sure knowledge of the passing and how the body in his arms had grown inexplicably lighter.

He had cried for hours afterward, overwhelmed by the beauty and the horror of that moment. The heavens had cried with him, pouring out their tears to water the ground upon which her body lay. And somewhere all through the night he had heard a gentle sound, like the flapping of wings on a distant wind.

Carissa reminded him of that young woman in some strange way that he could not name. It was not her innocence, for the woman who had died so many years ago had been anything but. They bore no physical resemblance to each other. Maybe they truly had nothing in common, maybe it was something inside him that was similar.

The young woman had been his first intimate kill, the first life he had tasted. Carissa was a first as well, the first life he had saved. There was something else, though. She meant something to him. For the first time in his life someone had touched his heart. He didn't know what it meant, but he found it just as beautiful and just as terrible as the passing of his first victim's soul.

He had meant it when he said he would marry her. He wanted that more than anything. But standing among the dead he knew that a life shared with him was no life at all.

He threw back his head and shouted to the sky. Nearby a wolf caught his cry and echoed it in eerie counterpoint. He soaked it in, two beasts howling at the same moon.

"Gabriel?"

He spun, amazed that anyone could have snuck up on him. Carissa stood there, the moonlight shining down upon her skin and hair, infusing them with an unnatural glow. She was beautiful and something deep inside him began to ache. He wanted to reach for her, to fold her in his arms and never let her go. She was so alive and he was not.

Her eyes were wide and lips slightly parted. He knew she wanted to ask him something, but she seemed to be transfixed just as he was.

He didn't know who moved first but suddenly she was in his arms. He sobbed as he held her and she kissed him. He knew then that she could teach him something about living that he had never learned in five hundred years.

He let his lips trail from her mouth across her cheek and onto her neck. As he sunk his teeth into her throat they sank slowly to their knees. He took her blood there with only the dead to watch.

With her it had nothing to do with feeding, nothing to do with death, but everything to do with connecting, with wanting to be closer, to make her a part of himself.

At last he pulled his fangs from her and laid her back gently upon the ground. Her hair spilled out around her, shining silver. He lowered himself down beside her and gently stroked her arm.

Gazing into Gabriel's eyes, Carissa found herself over-whelmed with awe. Why could it not have been this way with Pierre? From there her mind took another leap. Why could it not have been Gabriel to whom she was married?

She rolled onto her side so that she could face him. She lifted her hand to touch his cheek. A delicious warm lan-guor crept over her, a feeling of well-being that she had come to associate with him.

She opened her arms and he moved closer, embracing her lightly, their bodies barely touching. She lifted her head and kissed him. His lips were warm, her blood was coursing through him.

She moved her lips to his neck and kissed it. The skin felt soft to her touch. A longing filled her to be closer to him, to understand him. Before she could think and stop herself, she bit his neck.

She heard him breathe quick and hard. As blood filled her mouth his arms tightened about her. She swallowed, though the coppery taste nearly overpowered her. For a moment horror filled her, but then she reasoned she was only taking back that which she had given him.

"No, you mustn't," he whispered.

She closed her eyes and drank.

"Stop," he begged, his breathing ragged.

She ignored him.

"Stop, before I do something I don't want to do," he said, his voice dropping to a growl.

Something in his voice broke through to her and she let go of him, sitting up quickly. She wiped her mouth against the back of her hand and then stared in frightened fascination at the blood.

He grabbed her hand and licked the blood off, his breathing ragged.

"You shouldn't have done that," he said very quietly.

"Am I a vampire now?" she asked, feeling suddenly sick.

"No, thank God."

"But I saw you feed Pierre your blood."

"He was dead. I would have to kill you first, drain all of your blood until you died. Then I would have to spill my blood into your mouth."

"Do you have to be the one to drain the blood? Can you turn someone who was killed by something or someone else?"

"No, a vampire can only curse one they have killed by draining their blood. I'm not entirely sure why, but I suspect it's more mystical than anything else."

She nodded, still tasting the copper of the blood in her mouth. "So, since I was still alive when I drank your blood, I am not a vampire."

"That's right."

"Then why did you stop me?"

"Humans are not meant to drink the blood of another. Besides, I was starting to lose control. For a moment I wanted to kill you, to bring you across."

"Would that have been so terrible?" she whispered, hardly believing that she had spoken.

"Yes. I would not curse you to this life that I lead. And, if I had lost my head that much, I might have done it wrong and not been able to bring you back. I have only ever turned three people."

Raphael, Pierre, and one other. She longed to know who that was. Instead she asked, "Would you again?"

"If I found someone who deserved it, perhaps."

"Is that what happened to you? Someone thought you deserved it?"

She didn't think he was going to answer. He just sat for a long time, quiet and looking off into the darkness.

"Yes."

"Why?"

"I was not a nice person."

"Tell me," she urged, needing to know.

"I killed people. A lot of people."

She sat very still, not sure what to say or what question to ask next. It turned out, she didn't have to.

"I was a great hunter. I hunted everything I could. When I turned twenty, I traveled to a far-off land where the people run wild with the animals. I killed a lot of wild creatures, and soon there was no sport left in it, so I started to kill the people."

He glanced at her briefly, as though gauging her reaction. She remained still, waiting for him to continue and trying not to let the dismay show on her face.

"I told myself that they were just savages, scarcely more than animals themselves. They even killed one another, sacrifices to their gods."

He stopped and turned his head up to the sky. She shivered, sick inside. She knew that the thirst had driven him to kill, but she had never dreamed that it had always been a part of his nature, even when he was human. She licked her dry lips.

"What happened next?"

He turned to her, a grim smile twisting his lips. "I met Paul. He was there learning to curb his own passions."

"Did you know what he was?"

"I had no idea. I did not know until after I woke up a vampire myself."

She shivered. "That must have been terrible for you."

"It was," he said, gazing at her with a look almost of surprise.

He stood abruptly and offered her his hand. He was right. They both needed to rest. There would be time enough to talk if they survived the next twenty-four hours.

CHAPTER SEVENTEEN

Save thyself, and come down from the cross.

—Mark 15:30

W̶ow," Wendy said as she stopped reading.

"Yeah, I know," Susan muttered, her own thoughts of Raphael burning inside her. She glanced toward the door. It was getting close to dawn and he should be returning soon.

As if in answer to her thoughts the door swung open. She started up from the couch then sank back down on it when Gabriel came in alone and shut the door behind him. His face was somber and she felt a shiver of fear trace its way up her spine.

"What's wrong?" she asked.

"Nothing," he said shortly.

"Where's Raphael?"

He flicked his eyes up to meet hers, just for a moment,

and then looked away. "I didn't find him. I have no idea where he is."

Raphael had no idea how long the fight had been going on. Of course, it couldn't be called much of a fight. It was more like having the life beaten out of him one inch at a time. He had managed to crawl away from the liquid garlic at some point, but his injuries were too extensive to allow him to fight back as blow after blow rained down upon him.

They couldn't continue this way indefinitely. The sun would be rising shortly, that much he was sure of. Before it did his assailant would finish him off or leave him, too weak to move, to burn to death in its harsh light. The only surprise was that he hadn't been staked or set on fire already.

Think! he commanded himself. Paul or Gabriel would have thought their way out of this by now even if they had been unable to fight.

"I have—," he managed to whisper before a steel-tipped boot broke the ribs on his left side *again*.

"Something—," he gasped, just as a fist hit him hard in the back of the head, driving his skull down into the pavement with a terrible crunching noise. He felt bone giving way and he struggled not to vomit.

"Ri-Rich-Richelieu...," he said, struggling to remember the name, let alone say it.

There was a merciful pause at the mention of the name. "Wants," he breathed at last.

"The only thing you have that my master wants is the girl," a voice growled. "So, unless you're prepared to tell me where she is, I think we'll continue."

"Something...he...wants...more," Raphael ground out.

It was true. There was something that Richelieu wanted more than Susan, or at least would, if he knew to want it. What was it, though?

His head was making sounds it shouldn't. He should be dead from the damage to his brain alone. But vampires didn't work that way. Even now, with just a moment's respite he could feel things healing, blood congealing, matter knitting itself back together. The nerve endings seemed to all be firing at once inside his brain and he wanted to howl with the pain.

At some point he'd lost the ability to see and smell anything, but he could still hear and now there was a roaring sound in his ears. He didn't know what it was, but he was sure it wasn't good.

"What could he possibly want more?" he heard the voice ask, barely audible above the roaring noise.

"Artwork."

No, that wasn't the right word. What was it he was thinking of? Words seemed to slip through his mind like so much sand through an hourglass. "Art-artifact."

That seemed better, closer. But something told him it still wasn't the right word.

"What are you talking about?"

"Wood," he managed to say, even as he could feel his ribs healing.

"What wood?"

He couldn't think, the roaring had turned into a buzzing and his head was throbbing, pulsing. What was wood? Trees. What was made of wood? Table. No. House. No. Frame. No. Random images seemed to flash through what was left of his mind.

"Stake."

There was a hollow laugh. "A stake is what he wanted me to give you, but I knew that was too quick, too *good* a death for you."

"No, not stake," he managed to slur. "Splinter."

"You're making no sense," the voice growled. "I guess I beat it all out of you. Lucky for you, sun's coming up. Time to put this to an end."

Raphael saw a slight blur, his vision coming back slowly. And he realized that the roaring sound he had heard had been water and not his brain mending as he had imagined. It was the river. They were on top of one of the bridges.

He knew what he had to do. He kicked out with what little strength he had. He got lucky, connecting with the other vampire's kneecap. He heard him fall just as he managed to roll over twice and plummet into the icy water below.

Wendy was worried for Susan. Her cousin looked stricken when Gabriel had announced that he had been unable to find Raphael. She prayed for both their sakes that the vampire was alive and safe.

"Maybe he found something and he's holed up somewhere for the day. We'll hear from him as soon as night falls, you'll see," she said, hoping her words sounded more confident than she felt.

"I guess so," Susan muttered, but she looked pale and Wendy could see that her hands were shaking.

We've been through too much, both of us. The stress, the uncertainty, is wearing us down. Wendy took a deep breath. "Shall we get back to Carissa?" she asked, forcing her voice to sound cheerful.

Susan nodded woodenly.

Gabriel started up the stairs as Wendy picked up the diary and began to read. "'I can't believe our plan worked and that it's all over now.'" She stopped with a frown.

"What is it?"

"There's a section here that's too faded for me to read. I don't know if water spilled on it or something was wrong with the ink."

"What do you think happened?" Susan asked.

"I can tell you," Gabriel said from the stairs.

They both turned to look at him and he took a seat on one of the steps. "Étienne's uncle was a magistrate. We were able to send to him to come and bring a couple of the other magistrates he trusted with him. They saw Pierre as a vampire, condemned him, sentenced him to the same prison that he had sent Carissa to. Then they petitioned the king on her behalf and he restored to her everything that she had lost."

Wendy sagged, relieved and slightly disappointed at the abbreviated telling. "What of the Baron and Raphael?" she asked.

"Well, as you can see, I let Raphael live. The Baron, well, it was not my intention that he end up the way he did," Gabriel said.

BRYAS, 1198 AD

Gabriel felt nothing but relief. Paul was with Marcelle, making plans for Pierre's transportation back to the prison where he would be put into the same cell that Gabriel had spent so many years in.

It really was the safest place for him. As a new vampire he'd go through several years of insanity and uncontrollable passions. This way it would at least limit the number of people he hurt.

He had gotten Pierre from his room and dragged him down to the dungeon where he'd thrown him into one of the cells. The Baron was awake and glaring at him but not nearly as intently as Raphael was.

"Time you and I had a talk," Gabriel said to Raphael.

"Let me out, then."

"No, we'll talk first."

The younger vampire began to fidget after a moment of silence and then finally his shoulders slumped and the fight eased out of him.

That was when Gabriel showed him the small jeweled box Raphael had once been entrusted with. He had taken it from him during the fight.

Raphael's eyes narrowed.

"I was surprised you still carried this, and the relic, after all these years."

"Were you?"

"Why? Both would have fetched you a king's ransom if you had chosen to sell them."

Raphael turned his eyes away. "Before you found me I did not believe in demons. I did not believe in God even."

"And now?" Gabriel prompted.

Raphael looked down at himself. "Seeing is believing."

"And as Christ once told Thomas 'Blessed are they that have not seen and yet have believed.'"

"I still do not believe in God," Raphael said.

"Then why did you want the relic?"

Raphael was silent.

"I think you want to believe," Gabriel guessed.

"Even if that were true. I do not think God would understand or forgive."

Gabriel shook his head. "If God could not forgive a vampire then vampires would never reach that state of understanding and repentance."

"You believe that?"

"There is a legend. I do not know if it is true, but many believe it. They say that God Himself, and not the devil, created us. When Cain killed his brother Abel, God cursed him and put a mark upon him so that others would know him for who he was."

"Cain was the first vampire?"

Gabriel shrugged. "It is only a legend, I do not know if it is true. But when Cain brought his offering to the Lord it was rejected; he'd brought things he had grown in the soil whereas Abel had brought a lamb. Those who believe the legend claim that since vampires are made only after drinking the blood of another vampire that all of us have drunk the blood of Cain and we share a kind of memory of that event that haunts us to this day."

"How?"

Gabriel smiled. "According to the legend, Cain's offering was garlic."

Raphael threw back his head and laughed. "Of course it was! Because now everything makes perfect sense."

"I turned you because I thought, like me, you had an obsession with killing. I have come to believe that is not true. I think your problem is somewhat different."

"And just what do you think my sin is?" Raphael asked.

"Arrogance is as good a name as any. You seem to think of yourself as a god."

There was a long silence.

"I am not a god," Raphael admitted finally. "A god would be able to control himself when he chose to."

"One day you will," Gabriel said. "But only because you see yourself as you truly are."

Gabriel handed the box containing the relic back to Raphael. "You were charged with its safekeeping. I do not know why, but I believe God has a plan for you."

Raphael took the box gingerly, closing it in his hands and bowing his head briefly. "I do not believe that."

"Just keep it safe."

"I can do that."

"In exchange for giving this back, I have a favor to ask of you. It involves Pierre," Gabriel said.

"I am listening."

"Years from now, when they tear down the prison where he will be, collect him and teach him."

Raphael tilted his head to the side. "Because you are so good at abandoning your children?"

Gabriel didn't rise to the bait.

"I will," Raphael agreed finally.

Gabriel nodded. That was good enough. He turned his attention to Pierre, who had been howling and clawing at his own eyes throughout the entire conversation. "Time to feed him," Gabriel said grimly.

He threw open the door to the cell that held the Baron, grabbed the assassin by the scruff of his neck, and tossed him in the cell with Pierre.

The Baron screamed as Pierre descended upon him like some kind of wild animal. It would be at least another day before Pierre began to speak and think again. Until then he was no better than an animal. He lunged at the Baron, knocked him to the ground, and pinned him down with an arm across his throat. Pierre sunk his tiny fangs into the man's throat and began to drink.

The Baron screamed and thrashed, but Pierre was fast and soon the man was barely moving. He was all but dead.

And then the Baron bit the arm that was pinning him down.

Gabriel shouted and lunged forward, but it was too late. The Baron had tasted Pierre's blood.

Pierre shrieked and tore his arm away, retreating to a corner of his cell.

The Baron was wheezing out his last few breaths, but there was blood on his lips. In another moment he'd be dead. And then he'd be cursed.

"How did you know to do that?" Gabriel demanded.

"Legends," the Baron hacked out before his eyes closed.

"Well, that's a fine mess," Raphael said, sarcasm dripping from his voice.

"Another word and I *will* kill you," Gabriel said, turning to pin him with a stare. "Or leave you in here to rot with them."

Raphael opened his mouth in a silent snarl, but the fear in his eyes was genuine.

Gabriel double-checked that all the cells were locked and then swept out of the dungeon, ignoring Raphael's shouts. He was going to have to talk to Paul about the Baron. His first instinct was to just kill him, but Paul might have different ideas.

PRAGUE, PRESENT DAY

Gabriel reflected on the past. Vampires tended to curse those they thought were like themselves. He had thought Raphael a murderer when he first met him and only later had he realized the younger man thought of himself as a god. It made sense then that Raphael had cursed Richelieu. Richelieu had once been a man of God who had grabbed for more and more control, more power, and started thinking of himself as a god as well.

But, unlike Raphael, the years had not mellowed Richelieu. He still thought of himself as godlike in his powers and abilities.

And now he wants to make himself even more so by taking the blood of Christ. It was a chilling thought and Gabriel knew they had to stop him before he could do it.

"And now you know how it all ended," Gabriel said. He stood abruptly and headed upstairs.

Susan turned to Wendy after the vampire was out of sight. "Not nearly," she muttered.

Wendy nodded. "Fortunately, once we get past the illegible section, there's a little bit more left in the diary."

"What are you waiting for?" Susan urged.

Wendy began to read. " 'I never understood freedom until I lost it. I cannot believe it has been restored to me.' "

BRYAS, 1198 AD

Carissa sat in her own room and savored the taste of freedom. She looked around and breathed in deeply. For the first time in months she felt herself begin to relax. Even if it was greatly changed it was still her room. She smiled up at Gabriel.

"Thank you. I could not have survived all this without you."

He smiled. "I think God must have smiled on you tonight." There was a tightness around his mouth, though. She knew something had upset him earlier and she guessed it had to do with their prisoners. She knew he would talk about it if and when he was ready.

"God smiled on *us*," she corrected.

"Yes."

She put her cross necklace on the table next to the bed. "Gabriel, how did you recognize the cross?"

"I knew your father...during the Crusades. That cross was a gift from your mother and he put something very special inside it."

"Inside it? What?"

Gabriel knelt down in front of her. "A piece of the true cross."

CHAPTER EIGHTEEN

*And saying, Thou that destroyest the temple,
and buildest it in three days, save thyself. If
thou be the Son of God, come down from the
cross.*

—Matthew 27:40

PRAGUE, PRESENT DAY

Susan gasped and Wendy stuttered to a halt, the diary slipping from her hands onto her lap.

They looked at each other and then slowly looked at the cross necklace. "That must be the secret Grandma was talking about in her letter," Susan said in hushed tones. "And all this time Gabriel knew and never said anything."

Wendy reached out and touched the cross, her eyes enormous. "We haven't tried using your key chain to open it yet," she said.

"No. Do you think we should?" Susan asked.

"I want to see it," Wendy said, pale but resolute.

Susan got up and raced into the other room. She grabbed the key ring and came back. They put both the cross and the key ring on the table and studied them.

"Look at the notches in the key ring," Wendy pointed out. "What if you pressed it down on top of the cross? Maybe it will let you then twist it open?"

"I'll give it a try," Susan said, picking up the two objects. She realized her hand was shaking as she fitted the silver key ring so that the indented part was over the top of the cross. She pressed down and tried to turn but nothing happened.

"Maybe you have to press harder?" Wendy suggested.

"I don't want to hurt it."

Wendy raised an eyebrow. "This thing has seen more than eight hundred years of history and been through at least one war. I think hurting it is the least of our worries."

Susan pressed down harder. She tried twisting it slightly. It wiggled a little and then depressed more with an audible click. She glanced at Wendy, who was staring wide-eyed. Then she twisted and the top of the cross came off.

Slowly, she lifted up the top portion of the cross and the key ring and placed them both back on the table. Holding her breath, she tilted the rest of the cross upside down over her palm and gave it a little shake.

A tiny splinter of wood fell out into her palm and the moment it touched her skin she felt heat flash through her entire body and shivers danced up her spine.

"I can't believe it," she whispered. Yet it was true. She knew it, could *feel* it.

Slowly she held it out to Wendy. Her cousin reached out a finger and touched it but did not take it.

"Even I can feel that," Wendy muttered. "It's real. It has to be."

After a few more moments Susan carefully replaced it in the cross and sealed it back inside.

"That explains why this cross can kill a vampire. Even

touching the chain burned Raphael," she murmured, blushing as she remembered the kiss that had led up to that incident. She held out the cross to Wendy. "You should wear it."

"But it's yours," Wendy protested.

"I know, but I'd feel better if you wore it." She didn't want to explain about how she was thinking about Raphael, that if he was alive she wanted to hold him, embrace him.

Wendy took the necklace and put it on. "How do you think Carissa felt when she found out what her father found in the Crusades?" she asked.

"I imagine something like what we're feeling now. Let's see if she says."

Wendy picked up the book and began to read again.

"'I was stunned, my head so full of strange and wondrous thoughts, but it all seemed to come together.'"

BRYAS, 1198 AD

Carissa gasped. It was unimaginable, and yet, suddenly so many things made sense. "The actual cross?"

He nodded. "I was there when he found it."

"Tell me," she begged.

He told her and she closed her eyes and pictured it all. "Thank you," she said when he had finished.

"You are very welcome." He turned to go and paused at the door. "I will be just down the hall, on the left, if you need me. Good night."

Her heart began to pound wildly and she heard panic creeping into her voice. "Gabriel, wait!"

He turned at the door. The candle he held cast eerie shadows over his angelic face, making him look like a demon. She shivered, wishing she hadn't asked him to stop.

"Yes?" he asked.

Her eyes dropped to the ground as she struggled with herself. Finally she whispered, "Would you stay in here tonight?"

He was so quiet that for a moment she thought he hadn't heard her. Just as she was debating whether to repeat her request or let him go, he set down the candle and blew it out. In a moment he was at her side.

He folded her into his arms. She stiffened, afraid and grateful all at the same time. He held her close and she leaned into him. After a moment the tears came and she sobbed brokenly.

"It's all right," he said reassuringly, his hand rubbing up and down her back. After a couple of minutes the storm passed and she pulled back. "I'm sorry."

"Don't be," he answered. "Do you still want me to stay?"

"Yes," she whispered. "I do not want to be alone."

She crawled onto her bed, too tired to even think of changing. She heard a slight rustling as Gabriel laid down on the floor. She closed her eyes and started to drift.

"Carissa?" Gabriel whispered.

"Yes?" she asked.

"Just so we are clear. After Paul marries us, I'm sleeping in the bed."

Her heart skipped a beat.

"That is quite distracting, you know," he said.

PRAGUE, PRESENT DAY

"Okay, even I feel like I need a cold shower and Gabriel really creeps me out," Wendy said, putting down the book.

"Hmmm?" Susan asked, temporarily lost in her own thoughts of Raphael.

"I'm starting to wonder what Carissa has written about in the diary going forward. There are some things I'm pretty sure I don't want to read about," Wendy said.

Susan suppressed a grin at the embarrassed look on Wendy's face. "I guess we could always stop...."

"What, and not find out how it all ends? Never!"

They both broke into laughter. Susan glanced at the clock on the far wall. "We probably should at least stop for a little while and get some sleep."

Wendy looked at her in surprise. "I'm surprised you said that knowing that Raphael is still out there somewhere."

"If he's alive then he's about to sleep now. It makes sense for us to rest as well." She tried to keep her voice calm and practical sounding even though the thought of Raphael being in danger terrified her.

"I'll grab some pillows and blankets from upstairs. You can have the couch and I'll sleep on the floor," Wendy said, already heading for the stairs.

Susan was too tired to argue with her.

Wendy returned a minute later. "David was groaning in his sleep. Do you think I should wake him?" she asked as she positioned the pillows and blankets on the floor next to the couch.

Susan shook her head. "He's got pain medicine up there and water. If he gets bad enough he'll wake up and take it. Until then sleep's the best thing he can do."

"Okay," Wendy said, sounding unconvinced as she lay down.

Susan twisted around on the sofa until she was reclining. She closed her eyes and moments later she was asleep.

Raphael was in the water and it burned. The wounds all over his body were beginning to heal, but slowly. The sun was rising and he needed to be somewhere else, somewhere safe. He drifted underneath another bridge and something splashed into the water near him. He looked and saw a body sinking but one look at the corpse and he knew it had been completely drained of blood.

Raphael strained and managed to hear two sets of footsteps retreating along the bridge. "Serves him right if you ask me," he heard a man say. "Never question the master. It's bad for your health."

The master. They were talking about Richelieu, he was sure of it. He had to follow them. He turned his head slowly and saw the shore. He moved his arms, each feeling like a leaden weight, and struggled to swim to it even as broken bones and torn muscles tried to fix themselves.

He reached out and grabbed hold of a fistful of rocks that cascaded down the embankment. He wanted to scream in frustration but dared not lest he attract the attention of the two men he wished to follow. The first rays of the sun hit the bank and touched his hand, sending liquid fire through him.

The pain was more than it normally was, probably due

to his weakened condition. That meant he couldn't rely on having as much time as he normally would before burning to death.

He pressed on, gritting his teeth and slicing open his own lips with his fangs. He didn't know how, but he made it onto the embankment. He crawled up it, still too injured to stand. When he finally reached the top he could see the two men walking away from the bridge. Their pace was leisurely and the sun was bathing their backs in light.

Not vampires.

With a groan he heaved himself to his feet. His left knee buckled but he forced himself to stay upright even as the sinews healed. If he could follow them, maybe they would lead him to Richelieu. He couldn't be far, or they wouldn't have walked here, carrying the body.

He limped forward, hoping that neither turned around or listened too closely. He didn't have the strength to move swiftly and silently. The pull of the sun was making him want to sleep and he knew he had ten minutes or less before sleep came whether he wanted it to or not. Hopefully he could accomplish a lot in those ten minutes.

Wendy lay awake listening to Susan's gentle breathing. She kept a tight hold on the cross necklace as she prayed for healing for David, safety for all of them, and the ability to find and stop Richelieu. After that she stared at the ceiling, wishing that sleep would come.

After about a half hour she got up and went quietly over to the computer. Apparently she wasn't going to be getting any sleep for a while. The least she could do was spend her sleepless moments productively.

First she went online to half a dozen medical websites to try to see if there was anything more they could do for David. Unfortunately the best people seemed to be able to recommend for broken ribs was resting and taking it easy.

"Like we have an option," she muttered to herself.

Then she began looking up and reading everything she could about Richelieu. She wanted to know as much as she could about the enemy they were all facing. You never knew what bit of information might come in handy.

She read until the words blurred on the screen. Then she finally got up and went to lie down. She prayed once more for all of them before she drifted off to sleep.

David woke up and for a moment had no idea where he was. Slowly it came back to him and he remembered that he was in the house in Prague. Wendy should be downstairs. The thought made him smile with relief as he slowly sat up. He resisted the urge to touch his chest where his ribs felt like they were on fire.

There was weak light still streaming in from the window, which meant night had not yet fallen. He made it into the bathroom, removed the bandage, and examined the puncture wound where Wendy had stabbed him with the stake. He poured more peroxide on it and then bandaged it with liberally applied antiseptic.

Finally he walked down the hall slowly. He glanced into Paul's room. The vampire looked the same to him. Gabriel was sitting up in a chair, though, and the sight startled David.

"Glad to see you up," Gabriel said.

"Surprised to see you up," David responded.

Gabriel's eyes flicked to Paul.

"How is he?" David asked.

"Worse."

"How do you know?" David asked, alarm filling him as he stepped into the room to take a closer look.

"I can feel it. I don't think he has much longer."

David prayed out loud then and there for Paul, begging God to spare him.

"Thank you," Gabriel said when David had finished. "I hope He pays more heed to your prayers than He has to mine."

David nodded mutely and left. Downstairs he found Susan awake on the couch, blinking up at him. Wendy was still asleep, curled up on the floor, and she looked like some kind of angel to him. He fought the urge to stoop down and wake her with a kiss.

He glanced at the clock. The sun would be setting shortly and it gave him a sense of foreboding.

Susan got up and went about making them something to eat as David woke Wendy. Her ankle felt much better for the rest she'd given it. She kept glancing outside, counting the minutes to sunset.

Gabriel joined them downstairs moments after the sun dipped below the horizon, looking even more grim than usual. As he grabbed a packet of blood out of the refrigerator Susan couldn't help asking him the question that had been burning in her mind.

"You knew the cross our grandmother gave us was her cross, Carissa's cross, the one with the shard, didn't you?"

He nodded.

"Why didn't you tell me?"

He pinned her with an unfathomable stare. "The fewer people who knew the true power of that necklace the better."

Another thought struck her. "If you knew the secret, does that make you the vampire who saved Jean's life?"

"I saved him from Raphael," Gabriel said with a slight smile. "I had no idea at that point that saving his life would one day save mine."

"Are you talking about Carissa helping you to escape from the prison?" she asked.

"Among other things."

"What happened to her?"

It was as though a veil passed over his face and all she could see were his eyes, burning with some indefinable emotion. "The same thing that happens to all God's creatures. She died."

He turned, clearly putting an end to the conversation.

Just then the front door burst open and Raphael staggered inside. He looked terrible. His clothes were hanging off him in tatters and he was covered in blood and grime. Susan didn't care. She was so relieved he was alive. She ran forward and threw her arms around his neck, grateful that she had given Wendy the cross to wear so she didn't have to worry about hurting him more.

"Thank God you're alive," she whispered.

"What happened to you?" Gabriel asked.

"Got in a fight."

"With who?" Susan asked, still hugging him. And he was hugging her back as if his life depended on it.

Raphael shook his head. "I never saw his face but if I had to guess I'd say it was with our final Raider."

"The four of them make the younger you look perfectly civilized," Gabriel said with a disapproving growl.

"At least there's only one of them left. I got away, but I didn't kill him," Raphael explained.

Susan shuddered. Knowing their mission, she wouldn't breathe entirely easy until the last Raider was dead.

"I did manage to follow a couple of Richelieu's human servants," Raphael said. "I didn't find him, but I've got an idea that he's sticking close to his old haunt."

"So the historical center of town clearly holds some draw for him," Gabriel mused.

She stepped away from Raphael. "You should get cleaned up," she said, hoping her voice wasn't shaking.

He nodded. A minute later he and Gabriel went upstairs.

"So, what did I miss?" David asked.

Wendy burst into hysterical laughter.

"What?" David asked.

Susan smiled at him. "We discovered the secret of the cross necklace."

"Without me?" he said, sounding disappointed. "Well, what is it?"

Wendy cleared her throat and her hand flew up to touch the cross where it rested at her throat. "It holds a piece of the true cross that Christ was crucified on."

David's eyes bugged out of his head. "Are you kidding me?" he asked in awe.

"No," Susan said. "That's the big secret. Jean found it during the crusade and Gabriel knew all along that was what was concealed inside the necklace."

David walked over and touched the cross around Wendy's neck carefully, reverently. "Who would have guessed?" he whispered.

Susan walked into the kitchen and wiped some of the grime off her shirt from where she'd hugged Raphael. She was so relieved he was okay. When she returned to the living room, Wendy was sitting on the couch, the diary in her hand, looking at her expectantly.

"Where's David?"

"He needed to rest some more."

Susan settled down next to Wendy. "Time to find out how it all ends for Carissa?"

"I hope so," Wendy said fervently. "I don't think my nerves can take any more surprises."

"You're preaching to the choir."

Wendy picked up the book and began to read. "'The next day Marcelle left with Pierre. It was such a relief to see them off. Tomorrow Paul is going to take the Baron with him. Somehow the Baron was also changed into a vampire. Gabriel seems upset by it, but Paul is calm, as always. Everyone is departing and as much as I love being back home, I know the time is coming when I, too, must leave.'"

BRYAS, 1198 AD

Carissa knew Gabriel planned to return to Avignon and reclaim his home. She would be going with him. She gazed outside her window where she could barely make out the shapes of two men walking in the graveyard beneath the moon. She believed them to be Gabriel and Paul, but as she strained her eyes she finally realized that the second man must be Étienne.

She turned away and went to Fleur's room. Her cousin was wide awake as well.

"It seems we are both creatures of the night now," Fleur said with a smile.

"Do not joke about that," Carissa rebuked her gently.

"I am sorry. I am just so glad that things have been set right. Everything will be wonderful again, you will see."

Carissa could tell that Fleur had already guessed she was going to be leaving even though neither of them wanted to bring it up yet.

"Étienne is a good man," Carissa said at last.

Fleur nodded. "He has helped me this entire time, asking nothing for himself."

"That should be remedied," Carissa said, smiling at her cousin.

Fleur flushed and Carissa laughed. For just a moment all that had happened seemed to melt away and they were girls again, giggling over a suitor.

"Are you sure you can't stay?" Fleur asked. "We could both be married at the same time."

Carissa shook her head. "My last wedding was public; this one will be private. Paul has agreed to marry Gabriel and me."

"Will I ever see you again?" Fleur asked, tears beginning to stream down her cheeks.

"I hope so," Carissa said before throwing her arms around her cousin. Fleur returned the embrace and they began to weep.

"Where will you go?" Fleur asked at last when Carissa pulled away.

Carissa wiped her eyes and then smiled. "Whithersoever he goest."

"His people will be your people, his God, your God," Fleur suggested.

Carissa shook her head. "There is one God and we both know Him."

Carissa slipped the cross over her head and stared at it for a long minute. Then she held the cross out to Fleur.

"I cannot take it," Fleur protested. Carissa had told her what it contained.

"You must. This cross has been entrusted to us to safeguard. I do not know yet where I am going. You and Étienne have each other and you have Bryas. I want you to have this as well."

Fleur took it with a trembling hand. "I wish I could have heard the story from Uncle Jean of how he found it," she said.

"Me, too," Carissa admitted. "But at least I heard it from someone."

"Bryas is yours, the king said so."

"I know, and I'm giving it to you. Think of it as a wedding present."

"What can I possibly give you?" Fleur asked.

Carissa smiled as she thought of Gabriel. "I already have the only thing I want."

When Gabriel and Étienne returned to the castle an hour later Carissa found them downstairs in her father's study.

"I thought you were asleep," Gabriel said with a smile.

Étienne bowed and left the room, closing the door behind him.

"I want to marry you."

His smile broadened, revealing his fangs. "I believe that is the plan."

"Not tomorrow or next week, but now, tonight."

He blinked at her in surprise and then suddenly he was standing in front of her, his eyes fixed on hers. "Are you sure?" he asked, his voice rumbling in his chest.

"Never have I been more sure of anything," she said.

"Then I will get Paul," he said.

Her mind blurred with happiness as Gabriel returned with Paul. The king had agreed that given Pierre's condition the marriage between him and Carissa could not have existed. A woman could not be married to a demon. And for her part Carissa knew that when Pierre had died whatever bonds had chained her to him in the eyes of God and the church had been broken as well.

Paul performed the ceremony with great solemnity but had a twinkle in his eye the entire time. When it was finished, the kiss that Gabriel gave her held a promise of endless nights together, loving each other. It made her shiver in the best way possible.

Three weeks later Carissa gaped in awe at the castle in Avignon.

"Do you like it?" Gabriel asked as he helped her down from the carriage.

"It is wonderful. I want to live here with you forever."

He turned his eyes on her. "Are you sure?" he asked. "Forever is a very long time."

She smiled back at him. "In this life and the one to come after. I am yours and always will be."

The moon soared high above the castle, drenching it in silver. "You saved me, you know," she whispered.

He shook his head. "You saved me."

He touched the gold cross necklace on her throat that he had given her as a wedding present and smiled when it didn't burn at all.

PRAGUE, PRESENT DAY

A shout from overhead caused Wendy and Susan both to gasp. Susan leaped up from her seat on the couch and raced toward the stairs with Wendy steps behind her.

When they burst into the room where Paul lay, Gabriel, David, and Raphael were already there.

"What is it?" Susan gasped.

"He's fading," Gabriel said, horror in his voice.

Susan's eyes dropped to Paul's body and she clutched her chest even as she heard Wendy scream. Paul was completely ash gray now and the ash itself seemed to be moving, transparent, as though it were being blown away by a wind. Right before her eyes Paul was disintegrating.

CHAPTER NINETEEN

And, having made peace through the blood of
his cross, by him to reconcile all things unto
himself; by him, I say, whether they be things
in earth, or things in heaven.

—Colossians 1:20

No!" Susan shouted. "You can't die, not like this!"
She dropped to her knees next to the bed. She
could feel hands pulling at her.

"You shouldn't see this," Raphael said roughly. She
glanced up and saw the bloody tears streaming down his
cheeks.

"Not like this. Not now," she said, feeling dazed.

"There's nothing we can do about it. God's calling him
home," Gabriel said quietly.

God. God could stop this.

"Wendy, the cross!" Susan said.

Wendy grabbed for the necklace, yanked it off, and handed it to Susan. Susan turned back to Paul.

"I don't want to kill him," she sobbed.

"Come away," Raphael said, gripping her tighter.

"No!"

He jumped back, clearly afraid of the cross in her
hands.

"Gabriel, in Carissa's diary, the more you believed, trusted in God, the less crosses burned you. Is that true?"

"Yes," he said, eyes quickening with thought.

"You'll kill him," Raphael said.

"Or save him," David replied, clearly catching on to what she was planning to do.

Either way it was now or never. She looked frantically for a piece of him that did not look like it would collapse under the lightest of touches. Only his hands seemed to still hold any mass to them. Slowly, carefully, she lowered the cross down toward them.

"Please, God, save him," she sobbed.

The cross touched the skin of Paul's right hand and then sunk through it into the bones beneath. She gasped and started to jerk her hand away but Gabriel grabbed her elbow and pinned her arm in place.

A moment passed and she could hear David and Wendy both praying out loud behind her. She fixed her eyes on Paul's face, willing it to look normal again.

And then she thought she saw the merest flicker of movement.

"What was that?" she gasped.

"What? Where?" Raphael asked.

"His mouth. I swear it started to move."

The room went silent as they all stared intently, waiting, hoping, praying for a miracle.

Was it her imagination or did he look slightly less gray? Susan blinked several times. No, she wasn't imagining it, he definitely looked more bone white than ash gray. And he seemed more solid, too.

She felt Gabriel tugging on her elbow. He lifted it and she turned and saw that the bones and tissue around the cross were beginning to solidify. Together she and Gabriel lifted the cross clear until it was just touching Paul's skin.

As the gray retreated there was no black or red from the fire damage visible anymore, just the white of his natural skin tone. Then, at last, he looked exactly like he should.

Susan stared around at the others and saw the same wonder in their eyes that she was feeling in her heart.

She saw Paul's mouth move again.

"He's trying to say something."

They all leaned in closer.

"It's about time."

Susan blinked in surprise and then looked up at David. He had been crying openly but a smile began to appear on his face and then he laughed. The others joined in.

Susan watched Paul in awe. She could see the different muscles in his face begin to twitch and finally he opened his eyes and looked up at all of them.

"Enjoying a good laugh at my expense?" he whispered.

Raphael disappeared and reappeared moments later with a packet of blood from the refrigerator downstairs. He helped Paul drink it and Susan didn't look away.

"To think, all this time that was all we had to do," Wendy marveled.

"I was so afraid," Susan murmured. "I've seen this cross incinerate a vampire."

"Then what made you think to use it on Paul?" David asked.

"Something Carissa had recorded that Paul said came back to me. That the touch of God only harms those who struggle against it. It was something like that."

Gabriel smiled. "He has said that to me often."

"And to me," Raphael added.

"And suddenly I thought that if the cross had the power to kill then maybe it also had the power to heal. At any rate, he was going to die if we didn't try something."

"So, the cross…it really is something special?" Raphael asked.

"You don't know?" Susan asked him.

Gabriel smiled. "I know Raphael has long suspected but has not been sure. In the Holy Land Jean discovered two shards of the true cross. He gave one to the king and hid the other. The one he gave to the king is now in the possession of Richelieu. The one he hid has been safely tucked away inside that cross for eight-and-a-half centuries."

"The true cross," Susan said, staring down at the necklace that was still dangling from her fingers. Any lingering doubts she might have had had vanished with the healing of Paul.

"I was the only other one who knew that he found two pieces of the cross that day. When I saved his life, I felt the power in the cross necklace he was wearing and I knew what he'd done with the second piece."

"I just realized that's why Pierre was ranting about the cross, about letting it slip through his fingers," Wendy broke in. "He has letters from Jean about how he found the shards, though he never risked writing down what they were."

"Pierre got the cross back at some point," Susan said. "It was lost for many years. But he must not have known the secret when he gave it to Grandma."

"No," Wendy agreed. "He'd have only learned that when he stole the letter from Jean to Carissa from you."

"Pierre's tragic flaw was always not recognizing the

value in the things in his possession until it was much too late," Gabriel said.

Paul interrupted. "Now that all of you have been caught up would someone please catch me up? Have we killed Richelieu yet?"

"No," Gabriel said.

"That's disappointing. Has anyone gotten married yet?"

"No," David said.

"Also disappointing," Paul said, with a gleam in his eye that Susan had thought she'd never see again.

"So, what have you all been doing while I've been incapacitated?"

"I'll bring you up to speed," Raphael said. "But first, I've been thinking about the few things I overheard this morning when I trailed Richelieu's two minions. I'm pretty sure whatever he's planning, he has dozens of vampires and minions in place around the world waiting for it. I'm also sure he's somewhere near the center of the old town still. I just wish I knew how to find him."

"You know him best: What would he do before something big?" Gabriel asked.

"Relax, enjoy himself," Raphael said. "The question is how?"

"I might be able to help with that," Wendy said, her voice sheepish.

"How?" Susan asked.

"I, um, have been doing some research. Richelieu was well known for his politics, but there were...are...many facets to the man. He collected an amazing library and bequeathed it to his nephew along with money to maintain the collection and instructions that it be made available to scholars. He was a great patron of the arts. And in a day when it was not respectable and was seen as being of questionable morality, he was an avid theatergoer."

Susan blinked. "Impressive research, but how does that help us?"

Wendy smiled. "There's a new play opening tonight in the city by a famous playwright."

"And?"

"And I think it's time we took in some culture," her cousin said with a mischievous grin.

"Brilliant," David said, kissing Wendy. "You are brilliant."

"It would make sense," Raphael said slowly.

"Then it's agreed. Let's get dressed and head for the theater," Paul said.

"I don't think you should go," Raphael said.

"Are you kidding? I've missed far too much already. And you won't believe what a new man I feel like."

Several hours later Susan was standing in a theater wearing her long, black velvet dress, convinced that she had lost her mind. She was a fool to be hunting vampires in a dress and heels at night when they were awake. A part of her, though, was convinced that she really had nothing to worry about. Given that Richelieu wanted to take over the world it seemed silly to think he would be interested in attending a theater performance.

Still, she attempted to look casual as she talked with Wendy in the lobby and simultaneously tried to view everyone who entered. She glanced at her watch. There were just a few minutes left until the performance began and fewer people were coming in the door. The people who had been waiting and mingling in the lobby had begun moving into the theater itself.

Paul and David were watching the theater from outside, while Raphael had taken Gabriel to the place where he had earlier lost track of Richelieu's minions in hopes they could find his lair. She wished they were all together, but at this late stage in the game, divide and conquer was their best hope. Besides, the theater seemed like such a long shot and, as it was nearly time for the curtain to go up, she began to think about their next move.

She could feel herself starting to relax slightly. Wendy had been wrong. They would not have to face Richelieu that night. She glanced toward the theater and then back to the front door just as it opened.

It was Richelieu. She ducked her head, praying he didn't see her. His dark hair was slicked back and slightly longer than that of most of the other men present. He moved with a kind of fluid grace that she had often noted in Raphael. He didn't glance their way but continued to walk toward the door leading into the theater.

When he drew opposite her, though, his step slowed and he tilted his head to the side before coming to a sudden stop and swinging around to look right at Wendy beside her.

Wendy gasped, and Susan felt like she had just been dowsed in ice water as his eyes raked over them both. They came to rest on the cross around Wendy's neck and he took a step forward.

The lights in the lobby flashed, an indication that the performance was about to begin and he hesitated. Two other men drew up beside him and he whispered something to one of them. They both nodded and left and he turned back and continued into the theater.

Susan grabbed Wendy's hand and began to pull her toward the exit. With her other hand she was pulling out her phone to call David.

Two steps from the door, in the space it took her to blink, one of Richelieu's men stepped in front of them.

With a gasp Susan spun around, accidentally knocking Wendy off balance. A second man towered behind them. She turned back to the first, her hand slipping into her clutch and wrapping around the stake inside.

"Our employer would like to invite you ladies to watch the play from his box."

"That's very kind, but I'm afraid we couldn't," Susan said, trying hard not to let panic creep into her voice.

"He insists," the man behind them said.

"But we were just leaving. We realized that we forgot—"

"Our instructions were to escort you ladies to the box. It is a great honor. Surely you won't make this...difficult...on yourselves."

And suddenly a powerful hand grabbed Susan's arm just above the elbow and squeezed tightly enough that she lost her grip on the stake. She turned and saw that the other one had hold of Wendy.

"Screaming would change nothing," the one next to her said conversationally.

She glanced around. Where there had been theater patrons and ushers a few moments before now the lobby was empty, the doors into the theater closed. Still, surely someone would hear and come to help if she screamed.

And then they'll just get killed.

She took a deep breath, grabbed Wendy's hand, and allowed herself to be marched forward.

They were halfway up the stairs when Susan stomped

down on the instep of the man holding her. She turned and began to bolt down the stairs. Wendy ripped the cross from her neck and thrust it into the face of the man who held her.

He laughed and grabbed it away from her before shoving it in his pocket.

"I'm not a vampire," he said as he tripped Susan.

She fell heavily on the stairs, landing hard on her knee. Her captor leaned down and picked her up.

"Try that again and you won't make it to see the master," he said menacingly.

Standing outside a side exit of the theater David waited for a signal from Wendy or Susan that they'd spotted Richelieu. Paul was standing beside him, his eyes searching the area for the man. Fear prickled at David's scalp, and he began to feel the overwhelming urge to act quickly. Finally he turned to Paul. "I think we should go inside now."

"It's not time," Paul said.

David turned back to look at the theater. "It's past time," he whispered.

Paul touched his shoulder and looked deeply into his eyes. Then he nodded. "Okay, let's go."

They walked through the front door and approached an usher.

"We're late," Paul said, his voice rumbling.

"Do you need help finding your seats?" the man asked, face going slightly slack.

"No."

They walked inside the theater and the man closed the door behind them. David glanced around and wondered where among the few hundred present they would find

Richelieu. He turned back to Paul. His eyes were probing the darkness, seeing far more than David could in the dim light.

"Do you see him?" David asked.

"I do," Paul said, his voice hushed.

"What's wrong?"

"He has Susan and Wendy with him."

David turned his eyes upward as one in a dream and he saw Wendy standing in one of the boxes, body rigid, as a man held her by the arm.

He lunged forward, but quick as thought Paul clamped a hand on his shoulder and jerked him to a standstill.

"I have to save her!"

"Then let's think before we move. We won't get but one chance to do this right."

"Well, well, well. What have we here?" Richelieu asked, eyes glowing in the darkened box.

Wendy lifted her chin defiantly. She was standing beside the chair Susan had been forced to sit in, struggling to hide the fact that she was trembling like a leaf.

"Where's that exquisite cross you were wearing earlier?" Richelieu asked, leaning forward.

She did her best not to flinch. The man who had brought her upstairs fished it out of his pocket. She snatched at it, but he was quicker and moved it easily.

"She tried to burn me with it." The man chuckled, extending it slightly so Richelieu could look at it.

The vampire pulled a glove out of his jacket and slid it on his hand. Wendy held her breath as she watched him reach for it. Could it be this easy? Would his own curiosity kill him?

His gloved hand came within an inch of the cross and then he withdrew it so quickly that she could not see the movement.

"Fascinating," he whispered.

She lunged forward again, trying to grab at the cross or to at least knock it toward him. One touch, that was all it would take.

The thug who had it knocked her onto the floor with a blow across her cheekbone. She gasped in pain.

"Do not touch her," Richelieu roared.

"On that we can agree," a new voice said.

Wendy blinked past the pain and saw two men just inside the doorway. David and Paul.

Paul seized the man who had struck her and slammed his head into the wall. She could hear a startled cry from someone in the adjoining box. The second thug lunged forward and was dispatched in the same way.

David grabbed Susan and shoved her out of the room. Wendy moved quickly across the floor to the fallen men. She rolled the one over and scrambled, searching for the necklace.

"Great-grandfather," she heard Richelieu say.

She found the necklace and, spinning around, brandished it in front of her.

"You have been a very bad boy," Paul said, advancing toward Richelieu.

Wendy used the chair to help pull herself upright. She staggered forward, still thrusting the cross before her. Richelieu turned his eyes from Paul to her. He smiled. "I hope to see you soon," he said before leaping off the balcony.

Screams of fear and pain erupted from below and

Wendy fought the temptation to rush to the edge to see. Paul turned and raced from the room. Her leg buckled beneath her and David caught her.

He supported her weight as he half carried her out of the box and into the hallway outside. Susan was standing there and together the three of them moved toward the stairs. They ran down as fast as they could, then across the lobby, before plunging outside into the cool night air.

They raced around the building but could see no sign of any vampires, either friendly or hostile. Finally they stopped to catch their breath, leaning against one of the walls.

"What just happened?" Wendy asked.

"Where did Paul go?" Susan echoed.

"I think he chased after him," David said, panting. "He called Gabriel and Raphael. Hopefully one of them will be able to run him down."

"If not we're in serious trouble," Susan said. "The eclipse is tomorrow. We have officially run out of time."

"Time, that's what it's all about," Wendy said, beginning to pace.

"What do you mean?" Susan asked.

"Time. As in the right time, as in symbolic. Richelieu wants to take over the world, right?"

"That's my understanding," David grunted. "And we already know he plans to do it during the eclipse tomorrow. We just don't know exactly what he's planning."

"Well, if he wants to take over the world, I imagine whatever he's about to do will be public. He does have a passion for theater."

"So then people can see him first in darkness and then in sunlight. That is as long as his plan to swallow a relic with the blood of Christ really works," Susan said.

"We know he's got a shard of the cross, but given how he reacted to the necklace I'm pretty sure even he knows not to touch that."

"But we should still assume he managed to get something, one of the thorns, or a piece of cloth, something," David said.

"So, he's going to be looking to make a big scene. If you were a vampire in Prague looking to show power and reveal yourself to mankind, where would you choose to do so?" Susan asked.

Wendy grinned. "I'd do it in front of the Astronomical Clock where scientists from around the world plan to gather."

A figure rounded the corner and they all tensed until they realized it was Paul. "I agree. That's where it's got to be," he said, clearly having overheard them.

"What happened to you?" David asked.

Paul shook his head. "I tried to track him back to his lair. I wasn't successful, but I am fairly certain he's holed up somewhere near the castle complex."

"Of course he is," Wendy said. "Because that's what the symbolism is about, that's what he thinks of himself as: a leader, a monarch."

"So, if we can't find his lair tomorrow morning before the eclipse then we've lost," David said.

"It's worse than that," Paul said. "Richelieu won't be in his lair tonight. He'll be somewhere very close to where he wants to be for the demonstration. The eclipse will only completely cover the sun for less than five minutes. That means he's got that amount of time to wake up, get to where he needs to be, ingest the blood, and get people's attention."

"That's assuming he hasn't already tried to swallow whatever relic he has," David said.

"That would mean he might already be walking in daylight, which means he could be anywhere tomorrow morning," Wendy said.

"I don't think so," Paul chimed in. "I think he's going to do it while the eclipse is happening, a public display, setting himself up as having a connection to God and the Messiah."

"If that's true and he's going to do whatever it is he's going to do in front of the Astronomical Clock, then he will have to be sleeping somewhere close to it. Maybe we do have a prayer of finding and staking him in the morning," Susan said.

"He'll have a bevy of human guards both sane and insane," David said. "Those two tonight would just be the tip of the iceberg."

"It's important that we find and kill him before the eclipse is complete," Paul said. "We need to start searching now, but carefully. We can immobilize any of the human guards we come across. Unfortunately, once the sun rises, I will no longer be able to help you. You will be completely on your own."

A couple of minutes later Gabriel and Raphael arrived.

"Did you find him?" Wendy asked hopefully.

Raphael shook his head. He walked up and put his hands possessively on Susan's shoulders. "Are you all right?" he asked.

"Better now," she said.

"We're pretty sure he plans on making his move tomorrow at the Astronomical Clock where all the astronomers and tourists are going to be gathered," Wendy said.

"She was right about him showing up here tonight, I think she's right about this," Paul noted.

"I suggest we split up our efforts," Gabriel said. "Raphael, Paul, and I will hunt while we can tonight and then find the safest place to sleep near the Astronomical Clock. The three of you go get some rest and start the search in the morning. If all else fails, be ready to be at the clock before the eclipse starts and hopefully we can stop him there if we haven't already."

Once they arrived back at the house, David made sure that Susan had some painkillers and plenty of ice packs for her bruised and swollen knee and elbow. She fell asleep as soon as she crawled into bed. Wendy was sharing with her while David was supposed to be sleeping on the couch.

Only he wasn't. He felt trapped, restless. The end was coming and it didn't feel right to sleep somehow, no matter what tricks he tried or what arguments he gave himself. After about a half hour the door to the bedroom cracked open and Wendy slipped out.

"Can't sleep either?" she asked as she joined him.

He shook his head. Her blond hair was tousled, her eyes bright. "You looked beautiful tonight. That dress suited you," he noted.

"Thanks. Not sure I'm going to want to wear it again after tonight, though," she said.

You'd look beautiful wearing anything, he thought. She was beautiful wearing her baggy sweats.

"I'm worried, freaked about what's going to happen tomorrow," she admitted.

"All you can really worry about is the present, how you will do things now."

"And tomorrow?"

"The Bible says that sufficient unto the day is the evil thereof. The evil of tomorrow is overwhelming, but it doesn't have to cripple us tonight."

"If that's true then why are you awake?" she asked.

"Because not stressing out about what's going to happen is a lot easier said than done. I guess that makes me a hypocrite."

"I don't think you're a hypocrite," she said.

He smiled down at her. "Really? What do you think I am?"

"Cute."

She reached up and put her hands on his shoulders and then kissed him. It took only a moment for him to wrap his arms around her and kiss her back.

She clung to him, kissing him like there was no tomorrow, which in their case could easily be true. After a few minutes he picked her up and carried her back to the couch where he sat, still holding her in his arms.

He didn't know how long they kissed, but at long last they broke away. She moved to sit on the couch next to him. She leaned her head on his shoulder, laced her fingers through his, and within moments was asleep.

He tilted his head so it was leaning against hers and yawned. Moments later he, too, was asleep.

CHAPTER TWENTY

And being found in fashion as a man, he humbled himself, and became obedient unto death, even the death of the cross.

—Philippians 2:8

Raphael was uneasy as he slipped from shadow to shadow, trying to see without being seen. Gabriel was so much better at this than he was. He was more of a go-in-swinging sort of guy.

I'm a warrior, not a hunter.

He, Gabriel, and Paul had split up, each taking an area near the Astronomical Clock. He had been thinking about it for two hours and the only thing that even made sense about Richelieu's plan was that he intended to go public, reveal the existence of vampires and himself to the world.

It was madness and he needed to be stopped.

Raphael thought he heard a stealthy step behind him and he spun around but there was no one there except a drunk couple heading home. Was he just being jittery or was someone following him?

He turned back around. He was nearly done checking the buildings in his section. He remembered all the eclipses in the past that he had lived through. There had always been a sudden, bone-wrenching waking that felt unnatural because his body knew that it was not yet nighttime. It was never enough time to really do anything, just a few minutes to wait it out until sleep was once again forced upon him.

This time would be different, though. It had to be.

There, behind him, was another step, he was sure of it.

He spun around, his eyes easily piercing the dark alley. It was empty. When he turned back around, though, the street in front of him was not.

The final Raider. It had to be. The man was huge and devilish looking.

"What, no puddles of garlic to knock me into this time?" Raphael said, stepping carefully.

"Change of plan. Richelieu wants you alive now."

"How nice. Why don't you tell me where he is and I'll go pay him a visit."

The Raider smirked and then he flashed into action.

Raphael was taken aback by the suddenness of the attack, but he was still able to sidestep the monster. He grabbed a stake from the back of his waistband and sunk it into the other vampire's back. A moment later the last Raider was dust.

Raphael blinked. There was something wrong about that. The two he had fought had been so hard to kill. Could he have really gotten that lucky? Something wasn't right. He took two quick steps backward. It felt like a trap.

And as he turned and faced a street full of vampires he realized it was.

An hour later, reeking of garlic, Raphael was kneeling

in front of Richelieu in the basement of the last building he was supposed to be checking.

"Father, so good of you to join me," Richelieu said, a broad smile on his face.

"You keep capturing me. I keep escaping," Raphael said. "Why don't we try and work out some sort of new arrangement? Say you give up trying to take over the world and I'll get you that puppy you always wanted."

"I've always enjoyed our chats," Richelieu said, "so it's a pity that they're going to have to end."

"And why is that?" Raphael asked, counting the number of vampires in the room. He could never fight his way through so many.

"At the start of anything great and new—a government, a religion—there has to be sacrifice. God asked Abraham to sacrifice his son, Isaac, whom he had been promised he would father a nation through. That was the birth of Judaism. Christ, the son of God, is crucified and resurrected and we have the birth of Christianity. The rise and fall of every great nation on earth has been drenched in bloodshed and sacrifice."

"I should point out that Abraham didn't actually sacrifice Isaac. God was just testing him and provided an animal to sacrifice instead."

"True, but the sentiment was important nonetheless, and thousands of years later God sacrificed His only son and not an animal."

"Okay, I get it. You want me to sacrifice you," Raphael said, still trying to figure a way out. "To be honest I'd hoped for a fuller life for you, but, hey, who am I to stand in the way of history?"

"Who indeed?" Richelieu said with a smirk. "And trust

me, history will be made tomorrow. I will lead the vampire race out of the darkness and into the light. It's a role I was born to play."

"For all of five minutes before they burn to ash," Raphael countered.

"Not when I feed them my blood after I myself have fed on the blood of Christ."

Raphael could only stare at him. Was such a thing even possible? Could Richelieu even consume the blood without it destroying him in some way? Crosses burned vampires, but what would the blood of Christ actually do? And even if it granted Richelieu all the power he thought it would, could he possibly pass that on to his followers?

"How are you going to do that, you don't have the sudarium," Raphael said.

"A pity really, given how much blood is on it. But ultimately, a little drop should do and I've had a thorn in my keeping for quite a while for just such a purpose. I keep it in here with my other relic."

Richelieu produced the familiar box. The one that held the shard of the cross that Raphael had been entrusted with. It still grated on him that Richelieu had stolen it from him. He didn't deserve to be the keeper of a holy relic.

If it truly is a holy relic.

As much as Raphael had always wanted to believe, he'd had his doubts as well. The same could be said about God. But there was no denying the sense of power that emanated from the shard inside the bejeweled box.

"All these years and soon I will unleash the power of this shard," he said.

"And how do you think you can wield it when you can't even touch it?" Raphael asked through clenched teeth.

Richelieu gave him an unsettling smile. "Tomorrow during the eclipse you will see exactly how I intend to wield it."

Susan awoke, suddenly, and it took a moment for her to remember where she was. She glanced toward the window and saw that it was still dark outside but that the sky in the east was lightening. She heard low voices talking downstairs and she went down to join them.

She saw Wendy, David, and Paul standing in the kitchen, heads close together, staring at a map that was spread out over the counter.

Wendy glanced up and saw her. Her cousin's face was determined and she quickly moved to give Susan a hug. She was wearing black leggings, tennis shoes, and a black turtleneck. The cross hung on a new, long chain around her neck.

"What's the deal?" she asked.

"I managed to incapacitate twenty guards, including the ones from the theater," Paul said. "Gabriel and Raphael must be still sweeping the buildings. It looks like they are, indeed, planning on using the area in front of the Astronomical Clock. Unfortunately, there are more than half a dozen locations close enough to that where he could hide during the morning. All of them show some traces of vampire presence, so while there might be vampires sleeping in all of them come dawn, I have no idea which one holds the vampire we're looking for."

David passed a hand over his face. "Then we're going to have to split up. I'll check three of them, Wendy and Susan together check three of them."

"No! We shouldn't split up," Susan said.

David shook his head. "In a perfect world, we wouldn't, but this is far from perfect in so many ways. We'll check in by cell phone every twenty minutes and alert each other when we move to a new location."

"I don't think—"

Wendy laid a hand on Susan's arm, interrupting her. "David's right, we have to be able to cover ground faster." She slipped the chain from around her neck and put it around Susan's. She felt the comforting, familiar weight of the cross. "Wendy, I—"

"You should wear it. Grandmother gave it to you for a reason. Besides, we both know you're more skilled when it comes to fighting vampires."

Susan wanted to object; Wendy needed the protection more. But her cousin seemed calmer somehow than she had before. The other girl glanced at David and there was a light in her eyes that made Susan feel the warmth between them, despite all the death and chaos.

Love finds a way, she thought, shaking her head.

Raphael. A pang cut through her as she thought of her vampire. She remembered every moment they had spent together. She tried to tell herself that it was the danger, the idea that she was attracted to and not the man, but she knew that wasn't true. She just prayed they both made it through this alive.

"Which places are we searching first?" she asked.

Paul pointed to a spot on the map. "You and Wendy will check this building first. It has an extensive basement system and it connects up to the sewers."

Susan shuddered, remembering her first foray into the city's sewers. Paul noticed and misinterpreted.

"Don't worry, you won't have to go into the sewers.

Anywhere they lead would put Richelieu farther than he'd want to be from his staging area. Okay?"

She nodded.

"David, you'll start with the building two down from this one. With any luck one of these two will have Richelieu and we can get this done quickly."

"Where are you going to be?" Wendy asked.

Paul hesitated. "Nearby."

He doesn't want anyone to be able to force the truth out of us, Susan realized. She looked him over. *If we fail, we won't be able to reveal where he and the others are.* There were so many questions she'd love to ask him. Hopefully there would be plenty of time for the asking and the answering after their task was complete and Richelieu was stopped.

They each got a map and made sure everyone's cell phones were fully charged. Paul led them in a prayer for victory, and they said good-bye to him, possibly for the last time.

It was the moment of truth. As the first rays of dawn arced across the sky, Susan, Wendy, and David stood in front of the building the two women were going to search. Susan pretended not to look while Wendy and David kissed good-bye. Finally, he turned and walked down the street to stand in front of his building.

Susan didn't know how, but Paul had managed to get them keys to all the buildings. She glanced at David, who nodded, and they both stepped forward, unlocked the doors, and headed inside.

As soon as they closed the door behind them Wendy turned on the flashlight she had brought. It was pitch-dark in the house. There were blackout curtains in every room preventing light from penetrating. Their quarry could be in any room of the house, not just in a basement like the encounters David had described to her earlier.

"We should probably split up so we can search faster," Wendy said, voice quavering.

"No!"

Wendy didn't argue. Susan moved to the stairs and Wendy followed behind. Together they climbed upward, trying hard not to make any noise. The vampires should be asleep, but they had no way of knowing if Paul had actually gotten rid of all their human keepers who might hear and attack them.

They made it to the top floor and one by one entered each room. The first three were empty and they made their way to the last one. They crept inside and Susan's heart nearly stopped.

There, sprawled on the bed, were a man and a woman. Were they both vampires? Or was the woman in the man's control?

She moved silently to the side of the bed where he was sleeping. She glanced over at Wendy, who was holding the flashlight in her left hand and a stake in her right.

Susan took the cross and touched it briefly to the skin of the man's hand before jumping back, bumping into a dresser as she did so and knocking over a perfume bottle, which broke with a crash.

The man sat up and stared straight at her. "Who are you?" he demanded.

Stunned, Susan just blinked at him. Why hadn't he burned? Was he like Paul, immune to the touch of a cross? She yanked a stake out of the back of her waistband.

"What the— Are you crazy?" the guy asked, shouting.

And then it hit her. If he was a vampire he wouldn't have woken up. But if the woman beside him was human, she should have. "It's her!" she hissed to Wendy, leaping around the bed.

The man jumped after her, grabbing at her sweater. Susan pushed the cross down against the woman's bare foot and a moment later the woman caught on fire.

With another shout the man jumped backward and Susan and Wendy raced for the stairs.

"Are there any others?" Wendy gasped.

"I don't know, but we need to find out."

They hit the ground floor and ran from room to room, throwing open a few curtains for good measure to add light, but they saw no one. "Is there a basement?" Wendy asked.

"If there is I can't find one," Susan said as smoke alarms began to go off.

"We need to get out of here," Wendy screamed.

"We need to look one more time," Susan said. "Check the kitchen and I'll check the hall," she said, even as she could hear sirens in the distance.

Susan ran to the hallway looking for some kind of doorway. There was nothing. She turned to go, but something tugged at the corners of her mind and she turned back. There, behind a small decorative table with flowers was a very subtle line in the floral wallpaper.

She shoved the table to the side as she heard footsteps upstairs. It was only a matter of moments before the man came downstairs and the fire department arrived. The line was actually a hair crack. She hooked a fingernail in it and yanked hard.

Her nail snapped off as the hidden door opened a fraction. "Wendy!" she shouted.

Her cousin came running. "Nothing in the kitchen!"

"It's here, help me!"

Together they opened the door and stepped inside before slamming it shut behind them.

Wendy's flashlight played over stairs leading down into darkness that was complete and stank of evil.

"I can't go down there!" Wendy said, echoing Susan's thoughts. It was just like Pierre's office, but this time the stairs were darker, and she knew what was before them. But unlike then, this time she was not alone.

Susan could hear the pounding of many feet on the other side of the door. There was a deadbolt and she slammed it into place.

"Yes, you can. Going out the way we came will get us arrested for murder or arson or both."

They clung to each other as they took the ancient stone stairs. They kept descending far longer than they should have until Susan's imagination had them climbing down into the bowels of the earth.

At last they saw the end of the stairs and a stone floor. They exited into a room half filled with army cots that had been slept in until recently from the looks of them. Susan moved forward and touched one pillow. It was still warm. A human had been sleeping there. She touched the next pillow. It was cold. Vampire. She touched a few more and found an equal mix of warm and cold pillows.

"They must have heard us coming and moved their masters," she said at last.

"Where?"

"Shine your light on the walls, there has to be another door or a tunnel out of here."

The light played over slimy stone walls, reminding

Susan of the sewers and with a start she realized that was where they were. Something flashed out of the corner of her eye.

"Wait, go back."

Wendy reversed the movement of her light until it played over a low arch, no taller than three feet, in the far wall.

Susan felt the hair on the back of her neck prickle as she knelt and glanced into the tunnel beyond the arch. Slowly, every nerve poised, she stood up, throwing all faith upon that guiding voice that had never failed her. The stake in her left hand was pressed firmly against her chest and her right held the cross.

There was a rustle of cloth as Wendy came up beside her. She could feel her cousin's hand on hers.

"We have to follow," Wendy said.

"I know," Susan whispered.

They crouched down low and tried to shuffle through the tunnel. It only took a moment to realize they weren't going to go far or fast that way.

"We have to go on all fours," Wendy said, sticking the flashlight in her mouth and dropping down.

Susan flinched as her hands touched damp stone and the accumulated centuries of filth and mildew. *I can't do it*, she thought, panic ripping through her.

Ahead of her Wendy scrabbled forward, taking the light with her. In moments that light would disappear and Susan would be alone and trapped in the dark.

Whimpering, she put her hands down again and scuttled forward, trying to detach her mind from the horror of the situation. They traveled that way for more than a minute when she saw Wendy climb out of the tunnel and stand up.

Susan joined her. The tunnel had widened and was double the height, enough for them both to stand.

"Are you okay?" Wendy asked her.

"No, how come you are?"

"I'm not claustrophobic."

"I'm not—" Susan turned to look at the tunnel they had just exited and she thought she might throw up. "You're right, I'm claustrophobic," she said. "And germaphobic."

As Wendy played her light along the walls, it was swallowed by the darkness of a tunnel ahead. Susan slipped the chain from around her neck to hold the cross in her hand, so she'd be able to wield it more easily.

They began walking, moving much faster.

"How much of a head start do you think they had?" Wendy asked.

"Enough," a man's voice said out of the darkness.

As she squinted to see the speaker in the dark tunnel, something brushed Susan's head and then a rope dropped around her and tightened, pinning her arms to her sides and knocking her down. Wendy hit the ground beside her a moment later and the flashlight rolled away, illuminating a pair of expensive shoes that were just inches from her head.

A hand reached down and ripped the stake from her hands. Other hands reached out, grabbing her. She managed to shove the cross necklace in her pocket, praying they didn't find it and take it from her.

Wendy's eyes were wide, terrified. Someone knocked away the flashlight so that she couldn't see her cousin. Wendy screamed and the sound was choked off.

Susan kicked for all she was worth, striking someone who fell with a roar. She struggled to a kneeling position, shimmying her shoulders to try and loosen the rope and get it back up and over her.

"Fight, Wendy!" she shrieked.

Something hit her in the back of the head and she fell back down, unconscious.

When David exited the first building it was with feelings of frustration. There had been half a dozen vampires there, but none of them had been Richelieu. Fortunately, thanks to Paul, there hadn't been any humans either. He stood on the porch, the pain in his ribs pushing against the painkillers he had taken. As he pulled out his cell to call Susan, he registered the sound of sirens. He looked up the street as an emergency vehicle rocketed around the corner. He turned and looked back toward the building Susan and Wendy had gone into and saw flames jutting out of the upstairs windows.

He ran forward but was stopped by a fireman. Short of knocking him out cold there was no way past the man. As three more vehicles pulled up David realized there was nothing he could do to get inside the building.

He dialed Wendy on his phone and it rang four endless times before going to voice mail. "I'm staring at a burning building," he said. "Tell me you're not in it," he said, turning slightly away from the firemen.

He hung up and looked for someone in charge. Firefighters were bringing a man out of the house who was coughing and staggering. David grabbed the attention of a guy who seemed to be barking orders. "I think there're two young women in there as well," David said.

The man turned, not really looking at him, and nodded. He sent more firefighters in, presumably to search. David backed away slowly, glancing up at the sky. He didn't have time to wait if he was going to continue to try and find Richelieu.

He gritted his teeth, fear for Wendy and her cousin ripping through him. *There's nothing you can do here, but you still have a chance to finish your mission*, he told himself sternly. *If Wendy's alive you will see her later. If she's dead then you owe it to her to kill every last vampire you can get your hands on.*

With grief gnawing at him he forced himself to turn away and walk quickly out of sight before breaking into a run as he headed for his next target building.

He raced through the next two buildings, killing a dozen vampires and knocking two minions senseless in the process. Finished, he checked his messages for the third time but there was nothing. He tried calling both Wendy's and Susan's cells but still got voice mail.

Richelieu hadn't been in any of his target buildings. He pulled out his map and marked the location of the third building Wendy and Susan were supposed to inspect. He took off, hoping to find Richelieu before it was too late and praying that he would find Wendy and Susan there safe and sound.

It took fifteen minutes to get there and he glanced worriedly upward at the sun. They were fast running out of time. He wasn't sure he could clean out this house and make it to the next before the eclipse started. He didn't have a key to the front door, but as it turned out he didn't need one.

He twisted the doorknob and it opened easily. A man who had been drowsing just inside the door leaped to his feet. "Can I help you?"

"I'm looking for my master."

"Please come in," the doorman said.

David closed the door, took two steps past him, then slammed the man in the back of the neck with the butt of a stake like Paul had shown him. The man dropped to the ground and lay unmoving. David took half a dozen steps across the foyer and entered the main room where he stopped, his stomach lurching.

The building wasn't just a safe house for a few vampires. It was a dormitory for hundreds.

CHAPTER TWENTY-ONE

*And that he might reconcile both unto God in
one body by the cross.*

—Ephesians 2:16

David stared in horror at the dozens of vampires he could see from where he was standing. Richelieu's army, it had to be. He was standing in a makeshift barracks. How many more like this were there? How was he controlling all of them? Surely this many vampires in one place would draw attention.

Unless, like the astronomers, they're just here for this one event, he realized.

He couldn't possibly stake them all. He ran to the back of the room and threw open the heavy curtains, hoping to let in the light. His jaw dropped as he realized they had blacked out all the windows. He kicked at one of the windows and nothing happened. *Shatter resistant? Bulletproof?* He picked up a heavy antique lamp and slammed it against the glass.

A fine spiderweb of cracks appeared. He swung the lamp again and the cracks widened. Once more and the glass broke, falling out of the casing and letting the light of day inside.

David stepped back and the three vampires who were close enough to the window to be touched by the light were incinerated.

Three? Only three? He turned back to look at the window and realized that the sky was growing darker. The eclipse was coming and he was out of time.

He ran upstairs and made it to the room farthest from the stairs. He had to kill them all before the eclipse started. He yanked his lighter out of his pocket and set fire to the clothes of the vampire in the center of the room. He ran to the next room and repeated his actions. As he finished his work on that floor and made it back to the stairs, smoke detectors were clanging and he could smell burning flesh.

He ran from room to room on the ground floor trying to light vampires who were touching others so that the fire could spread from one to another. For good measure he lit curtains on fire as he ran past them. If the eclipse came before they had all caught fire the house itself might be enough to trap them.

As he skidded into the kitchen, the final room in the house, he saw the stairs leading to the basement. Fire was already raging behind him, the curtains had gone up like paper and vampires were turning to burning piles of ash everywhere.

He grabbed the garbage can, filled with junk from the minions by the looks of it, and lit it on fire. He waited until the flames took hold, until he couldn't stand it anymore. Then he hurled the entire thing down the stairs into the darkness and slammed the door shut.

With smoke choking the air he raced back toward the front door. He grabbed the jacket of the doorman, pulled him out the front door with him, and dumped him on the sidewalk before making his way coughing and choking to the next target.

As he breathed in fresh air he glanced up at the sky. The moon was touching the sun. It was almost time. *Wendy and Susan, where are you?*

Gabriel was uneasy. He had forced himself awake a half hour before. He'd managed to enter two buildings and stake a couple of dozen sleeping vampires in that time. But still there was no sign of Richelieu and neither he nor Paul had had word from Raphael before the sun rose that morning.

He had moved himself into position with a good view of the Astronomical Clock moments before the eclipse began. As soon as it did he was out in the square, moving through the crowds of normal people who were huddled there to observe the phenomenon.

Susan awoke, her cheek pressed to cold stone. She opened her eyes and saw Wendy, her eyelids flickering. Susan sat up and a moment later Wendy did the same. Wendy reached out and ripped the rope off Susan. Then she retrieved the flashlight that was still lying on the ground.

"What happened, where did they go?" Wendy panted.

"The eclipse," Susan said, lurching to her feet as panic filled her.

Something rushed by her, then another, and another, until it was like wind was buffeting her about.

"What is it?" she gasped.

"Vampires," Wendy said, her voice shaking. "I think they're headed to the clock."

If they were awake, then they were too late. But they had to try anyway. "Quick, follow them," Susan said.

She grabbed Wendy's hand and together they raced down a passageway. Light began to stream into it after a few seconds and then they could see vampires and human servants racing ahead of them while others passed them.

We must be too late since they don't even care that we're here, she realized in despair. Then she saw a ladder that the others were climbing, up and to the surface.

Susan leaped at the ladder, hoping Wendy was behind her. Seconds later they burst into the middle of the square where the Astronomical Clock was.

And above her the moon was covering the sun. It was a jarring sight. How ancient man had seen such an event and been terrified made even more sense to her now. Ancient man probably realized it freed vampires to walk abroad before nightfall.

Around them were hundreds of scientists and an equal number of tourists.

And then a booming voice filled the square. "Welcome, ladies and gentlemen, to my coronation!"

Murmurs went up from the crowd and heads turned to see Richelieu, standing on a dais, with an altar in front of him. Six vampires strapped a man in chains down onto it and then yanked off his hood.

"Raphael!" Susan wailed as she recognized him. She lunged forward, trying to push people out of her way.

"I am a vampire and today, today I am liberating the world from the den of vipers who have abused, misled, and corrupted this world and you! For I am not just any vampire, I am one apart from the rest. I shall walk in the daylight and protect you from those who slink in the darkness."

His voice was powerful, hypnotic, and people pushed

toward him, their interest in the solar phenomenon eclipsed by something even rarer, the chance to see an actual vampire. Because they believed him. *He was hypnotizing all of them*, she realized.

The press of bodies became overwhelming and no matter how hard she pushed they did not want to give way before her as she tried to get to the stage.

All Susan could do was watch, helpless, as Richelieu strutted around the altar where Raphael was tied. She glanced frantically around, looking for the others, but couldn't see any of them. Even Wendy had been swallowed up by the crowd.

She groaned and continued to try to fight her way forward. Bodies gave way inch by inch and she kept pushing. She didn't apologize to those who glared at her as she jostled them and stepped on toes. Nothing mattered more to her than saving Raphael.

The moment Richelieu appeared Gabriel had lunged forward, only to be surrounded by a wall of the undead, flashing fangs at him. He staked two simultaneously as he battled his way toward the stage.

Raphael blinked in the brightness all around him. The eclipse had plunged the day into darkness, but it was still so much brighter than the night he had called home for eight centuries. He thrashed against his bonds, but he was making very little progress, weakened by the garlic.

He glanced up at Richelieu. The man was showing his fangs, clearly savoring the moment. "My people have been in positions of power for years, waiting for this moment, for the sign, and now it has come. As God the Father sacrificed

His son to save the world, so shall I, the son, sacrifice my father so that I might be a god and save the world."

Raphael strained against his shackles, terror filling him. Richelieu was insane and they were all going to pay the price. Starting with him. *It doesn't end here! It can't!*

And then he saw David leap onto the stage, a stake in his hand. "You're doing it wrong!" the human roared.

Richelieu turned to look at him, rage twisting his features. "How dare you challenge me?"

"Because you are doing it wrong. The father should always sacrifice the son, not the other way around."

Raphael worked against his bonds, so grateful for David giving him extra moments that could maybe save them both.

"Unfortunately, I have no son to sacrifice," Richelieu said and even Raphael could hear the note of regret in his voice.

"No, but you have a great-great-great grandson," David said.

"That's impossible," Richelieu whispered.

"It's not. Raphael lied to you about your daughter and grandson dying in order to protect them. Had you ever reached the point where you were capable of knowing the truth he would have reintroduced you to your family."

"No, that can't be true."

"Oh, but it is. I am your last living descendant, and by rights, if you're going to sacrifice anyone, it should be me."

Raphael's bonds broke and he leaped to his feet with a roar.

Richelieu spun and pulled a knife out of his coat and the swell of power was overwhelming. Horrified, Raphael saw the shard of wood that was inserted into the tip of the knife. *The shard from the cross!*

He was going to die.

He saw the knife descending toward him and knew there was nothing he could do to stop it. *God, help me!* he pleaded as it plunged toward him.

The shard pierced his skin and he felt like it was on fire. He squeezed his eyes tight, but a moment later opened them when he realized he wasn't engulfed in flames.

The knife was buried in his stomach and he could feel the presence of the shard. It suffused him with warmth, real warmth like he had not felt since he was human. But it went beyond the flesh and warmed his mind and his heart. *I have a soul*, he marveled as he could feel it, too, responding. He looked up and could see his enemy's eyes, wide with fear and wonder.

Raphael reached up and pulled the shard from his flesh. He could feel power coursing through it to him. This then was what he had sworn to protect so many centuries before.

He looked up at Richelieu. The other's eyes had grown wide and he took a step back. "You can't stop me," Richelieu said. "I have agents everywhere, every government, every organization of power. They will act and there will be a new world order, uniting everyone under a single monarch as it was meant to be."

"Perhaps, but that monarch won't be you," Raphael said.

"How could you have kept my family from me?" Richelieu demanded, his eyes darting toward David.

"Simple. I wanted them to live. You, not so much."

And out of the corner of his eye he saw a man next to the stage fall and a second later Susan raced onto it, brandishing her cross. Richelieu, who had his eyes fixed on Raphael, didn't see her.

When she touched the cross to his skin there was a single moment where Raphael thought it hadn't worked. Then the former cardinal dropped his eyes, saw the cross touching his hand, and with a scream burst into flames.

Paul rushed onto the stage, a look of triumph on his face. "Burn in hell!" he spat as he kept moving, diving off the other end to battle the vampires posted there.

Raphael plucked the bejeweled box out of the ashes—miraculously it had been spared—and shoved it into his pocket.

"What are we going to do?" David shouted. "People have seen, they'll know!"

And then a dark figure, cloaked in black, took the stage. Raphael recognized Gabriel's face, but his sire's demeanor was even more foreboding than he had ever seen it.

"People!" the voice boomed. "Finish enjoying the rest of the eclipse. And thank you for supporting live theater and the pranks of this afternoon. Give a round of applause to our actors as they take a bow and take their leave of you."

Surely, not even he would think this could work. There were too many to mesmerize. Raphael looked out over the sea of faces and that was when he realized, most were too far away to have seen with any certainty what had happened. All the vampire had to do was convince those who had been closest, who had seen.

And what they had seen their minds already wanted to forget.

"We have to go, now!" Paul shouted.

Raphael took Susan's hand and raced for the safety of

a nearby building. He didn't know where the others were, but he hoped they were safe.

God, make them safe. His second prayer.

Wendy and David had given up trying to fight the remaining vampires and instead were running to get out of the way as the legions of the undead stampeded for cover. Their master was ash and the sun was beginning to emerge from behind the moon.

But then two stopped, turning toward Wendy.

"That's one of the women he was constantly going on about. Something about 'great power,'" one said, as he moved to grab Wendy.

David lunged forward, a stake in his hand but quick as thought the first vampire tripped him and as he sprawled toward the ground the second one hit him hard in the back of the head.

He didn't move after that.

Wendy screamed even as she pulled a stake out of her boot and waved it at both of them. *Aim upward, aim upward*, she coached herself, but in her heart she knew she was going to fail.

And then suddenly both vampires turned to ash in front of her. She blinked. Standing behind them, a stake in each hand, was the Baron.

She blinked at him in shock.

"Tell Gabriel I came and things are square between us," he said.

Vampires began to converge on them, drawn no doubt by what the other two had said. "You take him and get out of here."

"They'll kill you," Wendy whispered.

He nodded. "It's about time, too. I've been hunting the women of Bryas long enough."

She grabbed hold of David, who, to her relief, was beginning to stir, and helped him to his feet. She threw his arm around her shoulder and with strength she didn't know she had half dragged, half carried him away from the fighting.

When they were a safe distance away she turned just in time to see the sun finally burst forth from behind the moon. One by one vampires burned into nothing. And the Baron turned and gave her one last smile before the fire took him as well.

Susan and Raphael made it inside a restaurant that was only open for dinner, and Raphael dragged Susan down into the cellar where he found them a place to hide. His movements were slower and slower as he descended.

"Are you okay?" Susan asked, once they were seated on the floor.

"Yes," he said, putting his head against her shoulder. "Must sleep."

Susan watched with pounding heart as Raphael slipped into a deep sleep. She marveled at it, and everything that had happened as she stared at him. She fingered the cross that was once more around her neck. Had she really killed Richelieu? Had that been her?

Although from what he'd said there was much, much more to do before his evil influence could be purged from the world. Who knew how many vampires in Prague and beyond had sworn allegiance to him and were as broken as he had been?

She leaned her head back against the wall and pulled

her cell phone out of her pocket. She tried calling Wendy but couldn't get any signal. She prayed she was all right and that David was with her.

Despite the whirring of Susan's thoughts her body began to slump more and more as the adrenaline left it. Finally, she, too, fell asleep.

When she awoke again she could hear people bustling about in the kitchen upstairs. A few minutes later Raphael woke as well and together they snuck out of the restaurant and back onto the streets.

"We'll head for the house," he said, leading the way. "If the others are alive, they'll probably be there."

"I'm sure they're fine," she said around the lump in her throat.

"That would be a miracle."

"That's okay, because, after all, it wouldn't be the only miracle that happened today."

"You saw that, huh?" Raphael asked, his voice strange.

"Yes, what does it mean?"

"I think, as Paul would say, I'm now a believer."

She squeezed his hand, unable to express the joy she was feeling. "And now, what does that mean?"

"I don't know. I know I'm not going to turn to ash and go straight to heaven. I'm still a vampire and haven't turned human. I guess I get to try and continue to live as I have, but with one major difference: Now I know God."

When they reached the house the rest were already there. Susan gasped in relief as she hugged first David, then Wendy. Paul was standing quietly talking with Gabriel.

"Did the mesmerism work?" Susan asked.

"It seems to have. Everyone's talking about the prank a

theater group pulled during the eclipse. No one seems to think it was real. If they do, they're not talking about it," David said.

"So, what next?" Susan asked.

David shook his head. "We've managed to piece a few things together from what Richelieu said and what some of his goons were willing to say after he was dead. He was planning a worldwide takeover with today's event as the call-to-arms. We have no idea how many people he had in different governments who were stopped from revealing themselves. These could be vampires or humans whom he mesmerized. Either way there will be a threat as long as they are still in whatever positions they are in whatever conditions they are."

"That fits with what he told me and with what I over-heard," Raphael said with a weary sigh.

"What are you going to do about it?" Paul asked, glancing at each of them in turn.

Raphael shook his head. "I don't know. But I don't think we can afford to let them continue working in the dark. The time for hiding and fading into shadows has passed."

David laced his fingers through Wendy's and the two shared a look. "We will find them," David said, clearing his throat.

"And I will help you," Raphael said.

David shook his head. "You've earned a rest." He turned and looked at Susan. "You both have. We've got this from here on out."

Susan felt like she should protest, but the wave of relief that surged over her was too great. She turned and locked eyes with Raphael and could see the same relief in his eyes. He had hunted Richelieu for a century. He was tired, frustrated, and in need of a rest just as David had said.

For a moment everyone just stood in silence. It was a turning point, Susan could feel it. Someone's stomach growled, breaking the silence.

"Anyone up for breakfast?" Wendy asked. "Or dinner? I hate to say it, but I've worked up quite an appetite."

"Right with you," David said, grinning.

"I have to begin the journey home. I'll take this opportunity to say good-bye," Paul said.

They all moved to shake his hand. Raphael was last and Susan watched as something powerful and unspoken passed between them. "I have something for you," Raphael said. Out of his jacket he pulled the small bejeweled box that Richelieu had carried. "The shard is back inside, where it should be," Raphael said. "You're right, I've carried it far too long. I'm passing the burden on to you."

To Susan's surprise Paul hugged Raphael tight. "Bless you, my son, my grandson," he whispered, before stepping back. He slipped the box inside his robes.

"I know," Raphael said, clearly choosing his words carefully, "that you have always lamented that you weren't there...at the cross. After all these centuries it's only right that you should be its keeper at the last."

Tears shimmered in Paul's eyes as he bowed and then turned to go.

Gabriel looked thoughtfully at Raphael. "I did not choose poorly in cursing you."

"Thanks," Raphael said, voice thick with sarcasm.

Then Gabriel turned to look at Susan and she felt something dark move inside her, responding to his gaze. He seemed to search her very soul. In his eyes she imagined that she could see places and people from far away and long before. "Your cousin might look like her, but you...You're so much like her," he murmured, reaching out to brush a strand of hair away from her face. His touch alone was electrifying, hypnotizing without needing the aid of his voice or eyes.

Raphael's hand settled on her shoulder and she jumped slightly, shrinking back from Gabriel into the protective circle of Raphael's arms.

"You think you are the only one who can fall in love with a lady of Bryas?" Raphael asked.

"I thought I was the only one smart enough to," Gabriel said with a wry smile. He continued to stare at Susan. "Protect that cross well. The women who have worn it have always been...exceptional."

Susan cleared her throat. "Actually, I have decided that since she and David are going to continue the fight that I'm going to give it to Wendy."

She heard Wendy gasp, but she kept her eyes riveted on Gabriel.

"I'm not surprised," he said.

Not at all.

She blinked. Was that his voice that she had heard in her head? He just smiled at her. She remembered the voice inside her head at the cathedral that first day in the city, the one that had told her she was bleeding. It had been Gabriel there, watching, waiting. But why?

This was his fight and it could not be won without you.

She pressed her hand to her heart as she felt his presence slip from her mind.

Gabriel looked up at Raphael. The two men nodded at each other. She blinked and Gabriel was gone.

Susan shivered and turned around to press her face into Raphael's chest.

"Are you okay?" he asked, stroking her hair.

"He scares me," she admitted.

"You know, after all this time, I think he scares me even more than he used to."

"What did happen to Carissa?" Wendy asked quietly.

"Yes, please tell us," Susan said. She needed to know, now more than ever.

"He killed her."

Susan stiffened and her heart stuttered. She heard Wendy give a muffled gasp.

"He killed her?"

"Yes."

"Why?"

"She was very old, sick. She was in a great deal of pain. And in the end, she asked him to. He has carried that horror with him ever since."

"I would never ask that of you," she whispered.

"Thank you," Raphael said, kissing the crown of her head. Then he tilted her chin up so that she was looking into his eyes. "Do I scare you?" he asked.

"No."

"Why?"

"I love you," she whispered.

"For everything that I am?"

"And for everything you're not."

"Susan of Bryas, I love you and I will devote myself to your happiness. I can tell you this won't be easy."

"I know," she whispered.

He hesitated then brought a hand up and touched the cross around her neck. A look of awe passed over his face as he did so without harm.

"But at least we don't have to do this alone," he said.

She shook her head. "We'll never be alone again."

He bent down to kiss her and she surrendered herself to it and all that it promised for their future.

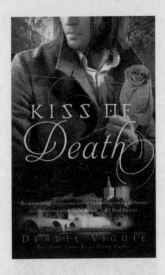

In the wake of a failed attempt to defeat the vampire Richelieu, Susan and her friends are weakened and divided. Raphael must set aside his animosity and join with his enigmatic sire, Gabriel, to discover a powerful weapon before Richelieu claims it. Meanwhile, Susan and her cousin Wendy translate a twelfth-century diary belonging to their ancestor Carissa to learn the origin of their family's connection with vampires.

Available from FaithWords wherever books are sold.